For my grandchildren

SPECIAL MESSAGE TO READERS

THE ULVERSCROFT FOUNDATION
(registered UK charity number 264873)
was established in 1972 to provide funds for research, diagnosis and treatment of eye diseases. Examples of major projects funded by the Ulverscroft Foundation are:-

- The Children's Eye Unit at Moorfields Eye Hospital, London
- The Ulverscroft Children's Eye Unit at Great Ormond Street Hospital for Sick Children
- Funding research into eye diseases and treatment at the Department of Ophthalmology, University of Leicester
- The Ulverscroft Vision Research Group, Institute of Child Health
- Twin operating theatres at the Western Ophthalmic Hospital, London
- The Chair of Ophthalmology at the Royal Australian College of Ophthalmologists

You can help further the work of the Foundation by making a donation or leaving a legacy. Every contribution is gratefully received. If you would like to help support the Foundation or require further information, please contact:

THE ULVERSCROFT FOUNDATION
The Green, Bradgate Road, Anstey
Leicester LE7 7FU, England
Tel: (0116) 236 4325

website: www.ulverscroft-foundation.org.uk

THE HOUSE ON ROSEBANK LANE

Leith, 1953: The war is over, a young queen has been crowned and eighteen-year-old Kirsten Mowat is glad to be out and about with her handsome, dark-haired sweetheart Duncan Armstrong. But there's a secret in her heart that needs to be told — and when Duncan insists on a shotgun wedding it sets Kirsten's life along a downward path. Married life brings tragedy, and Kirsten's husband and grudging mother-in-law harden their hearts against the young bride. Beset by grief, Kirsten finds herself alone with her two daughters and vulnerable baby Dixie to care for. She must seek out a haven for her children among the most unlikely of people, until the kindness of strangers and her own strength of will create bonds that will draw this family together in new and unexpected ways.

MILLIE GRAY

THE HOUSE ON ROSEBANK LANE

Complete and Unabridged

MAGNA
Leicester

First published in Great Britain in 2019 by
Black & White Publishing Ltd
Edinburgh

First Ulverscroft Edition
published 2020
by arrangement with
Black & White Publishing Ltd
Edinburgh

A catalogue record for this book is available
from the British Library.

ISBN 978–0–7505–4813–7

Published by
Ulverscroft Limited
Anstey, Leicestershire

Set by Words & Graphics Ltd.
Anstey, Leicestershire
Printed and bound in Great Britain by
T. J. International Ltd., Padstow, Cornwall

This book is printed on acid-free paper

1

1953

It was a time of great joy, but also unrest in Scotland, and indeed all over the United Kingdom.

Hogmanay of that year saw Kirsten Mowat meandering her way along Edinburgh's Fountainbridge. The brown-haired, turquoise-eyed lassie was walking arm-in-arm with her sweetheart, Duncan Armstrong. She breathed in with deep satisfaction as she thought how exciting the year had been. Most importantly to her, in the year she'd turned eighteen, Duncan Armstrong had fallen as madly in love with her as she was with him.

Kirsten hunched her shoulders and gave a quick sniff as she conceded that the year had also seen other great things happen. Firstly, the beautiful young princess Elizabeth had been crowned as Queen, then there was the launching of the Royal Yacht *Britannia*, followed by Edmund Hillary conquering Mount Everest. She allowed a soft grin to adorn her face as she recalled how she and Duncan had cheered and cheered with all the other dancers in the Palais de Dance when the mountaineer's triumph was announced.

She tucked her arm more firmly through Duncan's as they continued to stroll down Lothian Road. It was at this point that she acknowledged there had been other less glorious happenings, too. Some she was not so sure about; like the hanging of Derek Bentley. He had not actually committed murder — unlike John Christie, who was also eventually hanged, but rightly so. To Kirsten, Christie was the epitome of evil. The demon had lied about Timothy Evans being responsible for his wife and child's murders. Those lies resulted in Evans being found guilty of the crimes and hanged. Kirsten shivered as she thought how Evans's mother might now be awarded a full pardon for her son, but that would not bring him back from the dead. Kirsten's thoughts now turned to the Cold War. She loved all the intrigues and complexities of politics! Russia was dangerous; she just knew it. The country had tested its own hydrogen bomb, after all. Oh yes, the threat of war seemed to be looming again. But as they dawdled their way on to Princes Street, it was not this pending conflict that was really on Kirsten's mind. Something else required her urgent attention.

Inhaling deeply, she drew herself up straight. Time, she acknowledged, to stop reflecting on the world's concerns. They were out of her control. It was time to think about the anguish and strife that would engulf her and all she held dear when she released her own explosion of atomic proportions.

She shuddered: there was nothing else for it now but to get on with what she had to do. Duncan, the darling of her heart, would be the first to be acquainted with her confession. This was only right because he was the one, like she, who would be most affected.

'Duncan, darling,' she ventured. 'I have something I need to tell you . . . '

Her face fired. She trembled. She could not go on.

'Like what?' he said, as he began to dance around her affectionately.

'Know how . . . well . . . ' She paused to swallow some air. 'We did what we should not have done until we were churched?'

'Yeah, I liked that. Hope you're saying you fancy doing it again tonight.'

'I certainly am *not!*'

'And why not?' He was nudging her playfully. 'Admit it, you liked it too, because I was good at it . . . very good.'

'You're right there. Too good by half, you were.' She sniffed. 'But, there's always a price to pay for sinning — and in our case . . . ' She stopped and turned towards him. 'Duncan, I'm pregnant!'

'You're what?' Duncan blustered. His feet stopped dancing and his jaw dropped.

'You heard. You've put me up the Swanee!'

'Eh! Oh no. Gosh!' He grimaced, then added, 'What am I going to tell my mum?'

'Tell *your* mum!' Kirsten gasped as she started blubbing like a child. 'Don't you think that what we say to *my* mum is what will take some doing?'

'There, there, sweetheart,' Duncan soothed, taking her into his arms. 'You know I want to marry you, so now it will be sooner rather than later.' He stopped to take a deep breath before adding, 'So what? Stop bawling and I'll tell you what we'll do.'

'Run away?'

'No, there's no need for that. You see, we just won't tell anyone about the baby coming until we are married.'

'But who would marry us? I mean, where will we go to get churched?'

'No church, darling. I'm afraid it'll be the registry office for us.'

'But you know how my mum is with her Island ways: if I don't marry in the church, well . . . she'll go stark raving bonkers. We'd never hear the end of it — *what will they say back home in Shetland*, on and on she'd go — '

'Maybe so, but you having an illegitimate bairn would be even worse for her to thole!'

Kirsten cringed when she heard Duncan utter that word: *illegitimate*. Surely she hadn't been so irresponsible as to have her child labelled a bastard!

But as they walked on, they both agreed that their wedding day should be arranged as a matter of urgency. Without either of them telling another soul.

2

On the morning of their special day Kirsten managed to secrete her handbag and purple Tammy hat, along with her loose three-quarter-length new tweed coat in a lovely soft shade of lilac, into a shopping bag. Discretely leaving the bag behind the outside door, she then waltzed into the kitchen of her mother's home on Largo Place.

'Mum,' she began gaily, 'I'm meeting up with Harriet at the baths. After we've had a swim we'll be going to the pictures, so don't worry if I'm home late.'

Her mother, Aileen Mowat, was a dumpy, canny woman. This being so, Kirsten was not surprised when she replied, 'That's just fine, my dear. But wait a wee bit and I'll make you and Harriet up a shivery bite.'

'No thanks, Mum,' Kirsten replied as she tucked her wrapped-up towel even tighter under her arm.

'But, lassie, it'll be a long day for you, and you won't be wishing to embarrass yourself by fainting with the hunger.'

'I won't be peckish because we're having a chippie before going on to the Palace Picture House to see that Laurel and Hardy film,' Kirsten answered before going forward and kissing her mum on the cheek.

Truth was, Kirsten was swamped with guilt.

5

Lying to her mum didn't come easy. That was because her mum was so very truthful in her dealings with people. Added to that was the important fact that Kirsten was the youngest of Aileen's three children. She was also her only daughter. Kirsten's heart sank as she remembered that her mum was putting a little bit by every week so her 'baby' could have a wonderful white wedding.

Aileen was about to respond further, but before she could start the outside door had clicked shut, leaving her with nothing but the fading echo of Kirsten's high heels as they raced from Largo Place.

Before going into the registry office Kirsten nipped into Leith Victoria Swimming Baths so she could don her finery in a damp little changing cubicle. Finally, as she fitted on her hat, the guilt that had swamped her all morning disappeared to be replaced by a surge of utter elation. Within an hour she would be Duncan's legal wife. Her treasured dream would come true. She was not simply in love with him, but was completely besotted.

As she emerged from the swimming baths, she caught a glimpse of Duncan waiting for her at the registry office door. Today, if it was possible, he looked even more handsome and desirable, with his dark hair shining in the sun. Kirsten pushed aside the thought that she had been keeping a secret from him for two days: it was the right thing to do. To be his wife was all that mattered to her.

Before entering the wedding booth to pledge

6

themselves to each other, they had to ask two passing strangers if they would assist them by being their necessary witnesses.

And then it was done. With none of the finery of Kirsten's dreams, but her heart swelled at the sight and feel of the pale gold band on her finger.

Then, after a celebratory cup of tea and slice of shortbread in the café on the corner, the newlyweds decided to face the music. Duncan rightly insisted that his mother should be the first to be told that they were now husband and wife.

It would take some doing to tell Jessie Armstrong that her precious son, Duncan, was now a married man. Big and buxom, Jessie had been the stair-heid bully of 35 Admiralty Street before she had been rehoused a year or two back in Edinburgh Corporation's new Granton Housing Scheme.

It wasn't just that Duncan would be leaving the family home that was the problem. Oh no. What mattered was that his earnings would now be going to support Kirsten and not Jessie. This being the case, Kirsten decided that this was the moment, before they boarded the number 16 bus on Great Junction Street, to tell Duncan the secret she had been keeping. She prayed he would welcome it and see that it could soften the blow for Jessie when Duncan told her of their marriage.

She sidled up close to him. 'Duncan, darling,' Kirsten began, coyly. 'Know how I said that I was expecting, and believe me I probably will be soon, but as from the day before yesterday, well . . . I'm just not!'

Wrenching himself free from Kirsten, Duncan stared at her with incredulity before hissing, 'You're *not?* Don't flipping tell me that you knew there was no need for us to rush into a shotgun wedding and you still let us go ahead with it!' He tore at his hair. 'Kirsten, are you saying that you're *not?*'

Tearfully, she nodded.

'No, no,' he stammered. 'I can't believe you allowed me to go into that registry office when there was no need! Are you mad?'

Taken aback, Kirsten desperately felt for the wall. Driving herself hard against the rough brick, she mumbled, 'But, but, we are in love. So it's only right that we became husband and wife. Duncan, our marrying means that we can do anything we please. So what's the problem . . . darling?'

'The problem, *sweetheart*, is that you trapped me. And now I have to face my mum and tell her I got married, and not because I had to do the decent thing by you. Kirsten, she would have accepted that.' He paused. 'Och, can you no' see that your mum and mine would have been able to cope with us having made a mistake, but now it will look as if we're sticking two fingers up at them.'

But if Kirsten thought that Duncan's reaction was fearsome it was nothing to what she experienced when they told Jessie.

★ ★ ★

It wasn't just Jessie's flexing of her upper arms, which resembled the swinging hams that the

8

Danish Bacon Company supplied to the Leith Provident store, that terrified Kirsten. No — utter terror engulfed her when Jessie folded these muscular arms across her capable, heaving bosom and spat, 'You're nothing but a little shit, Kirsten Mowat. Don't you realise that I need his wage packet coming in here. Need it especially now his dad is dead and gone. True, my lassies work — naw, slave — like I did, right enough. No' in the Roperie but in Crawford's Biscuit Factory. But the two of their wages, even with two bags of broken biscuits thrown in, doesnae make up what a man brings in. So how the hell can I, without any forewarning, hope to get ends to meet? And aw because a wanton lassie couldnae keep her knickers on.'

Jessie then sank down on one of the kitchen chairs and, having shoved a pile of crumpled banknotes off its bleached white surface, began to gently bang her forehead off the kitchen table.

'Mammy,' Duncan pleaded, while he tried in vain to restrain her, 'please stop hurting yer puir heid. Mammy, I never meant to hurt you, but Kirsten said she had a bun in the oven and all I was trying to do was do the right thing by her.'

As the words registered Jessie stopped hammering her head off the table. Very slowly she lifted her head to face Kirsten. Her eyes were now jigging in time to her twitching mouth. She got to her feet and began to advance towards the girl. Duncan, realising what his mum was about, jumped towards her, hollering, 'Quick, Kirsten, get yerself out of here before she kills you!'

Kirsten leapt to put distance between Jessie

and herself, but as she crossed the doorstep Jessie caught her by the hair and dragged her backwards.

'Dinnae fash yourself . . . True, I should gie you a right good pasting, but ken something, scum like you is no' worth daeing time for.'

By now Kirsten's head was pulled so far back she felt Jessie's spittle on her face as she spoke.

'But listen, and listen good, because I'm putting my curse on you now. Someday you will remember what you did to me and my laddie this day. Oh aye, you'll get your comeuppance. Paid back seven times worse than what you've done to me, you'll be. And when it happens you'll hear me thanking my good God for getting even with you. Oh aye, Miss Hoity-Toity, you'll ken then what it feels like to have the feet kicked from under you.'

Uncurling her fingers from Kirsten's hair, Jessie gave her a violent push. Terrified, Kirsten, who up until then had never experienced so much as a raised voice at home, found herself lying in a bedraggled heap on the floor.

She now had two compelling desires. One was to escape from her mother-in-law. The other was to physically retaliate — punch and slap Jessie. Retaliate she could have done, but she wasn't the street fighter Jessie was. This being so, she knew she would come off worse and it would be in her interests to scarper and live to take Jessie on another day. That would be a day when Jessie was weaker and she was stronger.

Getting herself up, she escaped by bolting out of the door and into the stairway. Daylight

10

streamed down on her when she finally stumbled out into Royston Mains Gardens. Thankful, but without allowing herself the luxury of catching her breath, she immediately headed north towards the bus stop. Here she would be able to board a bus that would take her home to Leith.

Leith, where sanity reigned, and where she would be safe.

Twenty-five minutes later, as Kirsten alighted from the bus, she felt pure relief. She then, and only then, let her tears cascade. As the moisture trickled down her cheeks she turned into Largo Place and headed for home.

3

The scene at Jessie's left Duncan with a dilemma: should he run after Kirsten, his lawfully wedded wife, or should he remain with his mum and try to salvage something of their relationship?

Before he could make a decision, Jessie hollered, 'Like your useless faither before you, so you are!'

Duncan flinched at the venom in her voice, but asked meekly, 'What do you mean, Mammy?'

'That you too have abandoned us! Callously left your sisters and me to fend for ourselves!'

Duncan's face was now a picture of perplexity. 'Mammy,' he began hesitantly, 'Dad didnae desert us . . . he died.'

'Aye, but he chose to gasp his last.'

'What do you mean?'

'Just that other folk trip up and hit their heid on the causeway but they dinnae leave their family in the lurch. Naw, naw, they get up and get back on with their job.'

Duncan shook his head. He knew it was useless to argue with his mother, whose warped reasoning always suited her 'all the apples fall on me' view of the world. Instead, he said quietly, 'Mammy, I ken Kirsten took me for a hurl but she's young and she loves me and all she wanted to do was make sure I never strayed from her.'

'That right? And what will happen now to our Nancy, who has nae chance of catching a man because of that damn birthmark that covers the whole of one side of her face?' Jessie stopped to purse her lips and sighed deeply before adding, 'And the blame for poor Nancy's affliction is again aw down to your useless faither.'

'How come, Mammy?'

'Just that: Nancy's affliction is his fault.'

Even more bewildered now, all Duncan could do was blow rhythmically out through his mouth.

'You can huff and puff all you like, my boy, but your faither's obsession with having beetroot with everything — even his beer — made his sperm the same damn colour as a beetroot! Then there's Jane stretching herself to six feet. I mean, where's she gonnae get a man to take her on? Even if she can change the electric light bulb without standing on a chair . . . '

Duncan knew it was pointless to challenge his mother. It was pointless to try to reason as to why his mother looked at things the way she did.

Truth be told, he already knew.

★ ★ ★

JESSIE'S STORY

Jessie's father had died when she was just twelve years old — and he was thirty-three. Her mother, Maggie, had then sarcastically proclaimed that his early demise was due to his unwillingness to get out of his bed and toil longer than fourteen hours a day in all weathers for a mere pittance. To be truthful, when he was well enough to work, the few bawbees he earned couldn't even purchase his family nourishing food and a warm, watertight shelter.

The foregoing being true, Maggie's erstwhile husband's demise meant that she had no choice but to become the family's breadwinner. In addition to providing for herself, she had to support her three young daughters. The thought of the entire burden landing on her shoulders was just too much for Maggie. She therefore petitioned the Leith School Board, asking them to release Jessie, her eldest, from school. In her application she stated that her reason for this request was that Jessie would be required to keep the house while Maggie herself went out to work to support the family. What actually happened was that Maggie immediately took Jessie along to the Roperie and got her a job. Maggie's contribution to the family's woes then became seeking comfort from Red Biddy, the poorer of Leith's preferred anaesthetics.

Tired and weary, young Jessie would come home at night to find her sisters, ten-year-old Agnes and nine-year-old Susie, waiting for her. She would rustle up something for them to eat, while their mother spent more and more time in the jug bar. Undeterred, Jessie grew determined that she and her sisters would pull through. By sheer guts and determination, she found the strength to survive in the harsh, cruel workplace to which her mother had sentenced her.

Time passed slowly, but eventually Agnes and

14

Susie came of working age. Her sisters were, in Jessie's opinion, too fine and delicate to work at the bleak and brutal Bath Street rope works; those rope works where you learned quickly or your life was intolerable. Indeed, holding on to her principles was the reason why Jessie had become such a feared virago. Yes, many a louse of a man learned to his physical detriment that he shouldn't try coaxing handsome Jessie, or any of her less-able pals, to have a dinner-time tumble in the hemp bales. This being the case, Agnes was found work in Duncan's of Edinburgh chocolate factory and Susie at Crawford's Biscuits.

As the years passed, Maggie steadily drank herself to death. Jessie then decided it was time to find a healthy man to marry. One of her requirements being that he would come home to her and hand over his wage packet unopened!

She wasn't really thinking of this solution to her problems as she trudged into work one particular day, but as she passed the dispatch bay two men hollered, 'Look out, missus.' Maggie turned to find a thick rolled-up rope mooring hawser bouncing off the loading platform.

Grabbing the arm of her young lassie companion, she hurtled herself and Nessie out of the path of the careering monster. Breathless and terrified, both of them landed in a thankful heap in the side-door entrance to the main offices. By that time the two men had scampered down from the platform and the taller of the two helped Nessie to her feet. The second man then tried to assist Jessie.

'You some sort of an idiot?' she screamed at the man.

'It wasnae my fault,' he protested.

'Suppose you will be saying Nessie and me shouldnae have come into work this morning,' she replied, roughly pushing the man's hands off her chest, where they had wandered.

Once upright she realised she towered five inches above the man — a man she knew, albeit from a distance, because he worked in the dispatch area rather than the actual factory unit where she worked.

'Look, I'm sorry,' the man continued, 'and to make it up to you, could I buy you a drink after work?'

'A drink? You want to buy me, a strict teetotaller, a drink? Huh. And what would your wife have to say about that?'

'I havnae got one. Naw, naw, I have to bide in the Lodging House because I am all alone.'

Dougal Armstrong was not alone for long after that. He was just what Jessie was looking for: a man she could mould into her way of thinking. The bonus for Dougal was he got a home, was fed and was allowed to father Jessie's three children.

And so life was easier for Jessie until Dougal tripped and fell, hitting his head on the pavement kerb. After his unfortunate demise Jessie was back to fending not for her sisters, now they had flown the coop, but for her three offspring as well as herself.

★   ★   ★

16

Duncan looked at his mother with sympathy. Jessie just shrugged and sighed. Today, yet again, she had been kicked in the teeth. The galling thing was this time it was her adored only son, Duncan, who had caused the hurt. Duncan who, by marrying that silly slip of a girl, had robbed her — robbed her of his own apprentice's wage packet (often boosted by overtime).

Oh yes, up until now she'd relied on Duncan to bring in more than the two girls could earn together. She'd have to think of something, and fast, to keep the wolf from the door. Now was the time to make more of that wee money lending venture of hers.

4

'Where in the name of heavens have you been?' Kirsten's normally soft-spoken mother shrieked, 'And what exactly have you been up to, my girl?'

'Mum, I . . . '

But all Kirsten could do was push the door to, throw herself down on a chair and weep.

Next, her mother surprised Kirsten by saying, 'Before you start, you'd just left today when Harriet arrived looking for you. And know what? She knew nothing about going for a swim or anything else. So sit up, dry your eyes and out with it.'

'Mum, please don't be angry.' She drew in a long breath before uttering, 'I got . . . I got . . . married to Duncan Armstrong today.'

This shocking confession took the wind right out of Aileen's sails. 'You what?' she yelled. She dropped herself down on the couch. Acid tears burned her eyes. 'Oh no, please don't say you are . . . '

'No, Mum, I'm not, but I thought I was. Then when — and it was only yesterday or maybe the day before — I found out I had made a mistake . . . '

'A mistake, you say. The mistake, missy, is what you did that had you thinking you were with child.' Aileen breathed in deeply. 'Don't you know that fornication is a sin in God's eyes? While we are at it, I'm not keen on it either.'

18

Before Aileen could go on, running footsteps stopped at her door. The door was then flung open and Duncan entered.

'And what, might I say, do you think you're doing coming into my house after the disgrace that you have brought down on us?' Aileen greeted Duncan with disdain.

'Look,' he started, on the defensive, 'Kirsten and me love each other. Okay, she did con me into doing, as I thought, the right thing by her.' He stopped to run his hands through his hair. 'But please, don't be too hard on her; it's just that as she loves me so much she just . . . '

'Loves you so much — do either of you know what love is all about? You can take it from me that you don't. Believe me, you have confused love with *lust*! Love is when you would do anything — even sin so hard that you forego your place in Heaven — just to help your loved ones!'

Her chest now heaving with wracking sobs Kirsten could only mumble, 'Mum, I am . . . I am so very sorry to have made such a mess for everybody. I never meant anybody to get . . . to get hurt. Mum, please try and understand that I just wanted to love Duncan — to be his wife.' Complete exhaustion had now overtaken her and her pleading cries were reduced to a pitiful whimper.

Instinctively Duncan moved to take Kirsten into his arms. 'There, there, love. Don't cry. I love you and we *will* get out of this hole we dug for ourselves and make a go of things.'

Looking at the two bits of bairns, as Aileen now saw them, she thought of her dream of

19

Kirsten floating down the aisle in a sea of virginal white tulle. She would have to find another dream now. Nonetheless, there was a bright side to everything perhaps. She looked again at the two lovers. Compassion and pity mingled in her heart for them.

'Come on now, Kirsten,' she urged, as she pressed a handkerchief into her hand. 'Dry your tears. Believe me, this time next year when you are cradling your baby in your arms we will all be smiling.'

'Mum, you haven't listened — I am *not* pregnant!'

'Not today, right enough, but in a few weeks you will be. So let's forget what's gone before and welcome the future.'

Kirsten should have been astounded. However, this was Aileen all over. Yes, she quickly accepted whatever problems the day brought and was not crushed by them. Tonight, she would put clean, fresh sheets on Kirsten's bed and then these two 'lovebirds' would climb into bed and start their lives as man and wife.

5

Aileen was right. Kirsten and Duncan blossomed just by being together. In a little more than a year Kirsten gave birth to a beautiful daughter, Bea, and the following year baby Jane — named for her aunt — arrived. Jane's arrival coincided with Duncan finishing his first year as a fully trained fitter engineer.

Kirsten and Duncan then sat down to work out what would be the best way for him to earn the most he could, now that he was experienced and certified in that role. Their plan was to save enough so they could get a home of their own. With some reluctance, they agreed that for them to become independent, Duncan signing up as a fifth engineering officer with one of the Leith shipping companies was the most sensible thing to do.

And so their first priority was to scrape together enough money to buy the uniform. Once it was purchased, and Duncan donned it, Kirsten almost swooned. Surely she was the luckiest woman alive to be married to such a handsome, dashing officer! However, when she discovered that his first trip was to be with the Ben Line shipping company her delight turned to misgivings and then to rising unease when she realised that the Ben Line, whose offices were based in town, up at North St David Street, dealt in long-haul tours of duty. Indeed, they could last up to two years.

As the realisation sank in, Kirsten was overtaken by a deep melancholy. She just could not cope with the thought of her and Duncan being parted for that length of time. She was so distraught, in fact, that she nearly got down on her knees to beg Duncan to seek employment with the Leith shipping companies that sailed weekly to and from the Continent.

When Kirsten tearfully pointed out that up to two years could pass before they were together again, Duncan gave the impression that he too was gutted. The truth was the romantic idea of being carefree again, while sailing the seven seas, had captured the young man's imagination. Leaving the home, which they still shared with Mr and Mrs Mowat, now had an overpowering appeal for him. This was partly because his two bairns, who were still in nappies, slept in a cot wedged up at the end of the bed. The room he and Kirsten were lucky to have was so small it was claustrophobic. To add to all this pressure, Kirsten was continually going on about how hard her life was. Daily she pointed out that she hated living in such cramped conditions. Her nagging made Duncan feel inadequate and these feelings of being a failure ran especially high when she moaned on and on about how short of money they were. As a result, marital bliss was blissful no more for Duncan. Oh yes, he couldn't wait to set out for a new life on the ocean waves.

★   ★   ★

In fact, Duncan's first trip did last nearly two years. During this time he was promoted to fourth engineering officer — quite an accomplishment. When he returned, Kirsten and he naturally started to enjoy something of a second honeymoon. But just one week into their renewed love affair, a telegram boy arrived at the door with an urgent message for Duncan.

Aileen was just about to pass the envelope to Duncan when Kirsten sprang forward and snatched it from her bewildered grasp.

Ripping open the envelope she dragged out the message and read the contents. 'Duncan,' she whimpered, her eyes wild, 'it says, it says, it says here that *as agreed* you have to rejoin your ship in three days' time.'

'Yeah,' he replied as he tried fruitlessly to encircle Kirsten into his arms, 'I was going to tell you but with all that has been going on I sort of . . . forgot.'

'Forgot! Do you expect me to believe that you forgot to tell me that in three days' time you are leaving me and the girls again!' Kirsten wailed as she turned towards her mother. 'Mum, what should I do?'

Her mother simply replied, 'Well, dear, it is a good drying day so between the two of us we can get all his clothes washed, dried and ironed.' Aileen then turned to look from the window. 'Look, isn't that just dandy our good God has sent us a bit of sunshine along with a breeze.'

Kirsten stared at her mother in disbelief. But then she should have known that, being born and bred in the Shetland Isles, she would think nothing of Duncan going back to sea so soon. Shetland people were mariners: the sea was not only in their blood; she also became their mistress.

Grasping the opportunity that Aileen had afforded him, Duncan sprang forward and this time he managed to wrestle Kirsten into his arms. 'Kirsten, darling,' he pleaded, 'try and understand that they are making me up to third engineer. Do you hear: third engineer? I was just so bowled over when the chief told me.'

'Bowled over,' she wept. 'You might have been, but I am gutted! Surely another three days is not all I am going to have of you. And Bea and Jane are just getting to know their daddy again.'

But her tears were for nothing — and their second honeymoon was washed away at the scrubbing board.

All Kirsten could do was grit her teeth as she and Aileen made Duncan's uniform immaculate again. For the rest of the week she seethed at her husband's ill-concealed delight at being seaward-bound again, and he left with things between them far from on an even keel.

★ ★ ★

Fortunately, Duncan's second trip lasted only fifteen months. And when he did get home, his pockets were full of money.

Immediately some of this money was used to sweeten a clerk in Michie's, the housing factor in Constitution Street, to let them jump the queue. This piece of bribery saw Kirsten, Duncan and their two children move into a ground-floor flat in Balfour Street.

The house they were allocated was on the left-hand side of the street when entering from Leith Walk. The houses on that side were, in Kirsten's opinion, much larger. That is if you could call a living room with a recess, two bedrooms, a cupboard for your cooker and a toilet spacious accommodation. All the same, it was a small mercy to be grateful for.

It was no surprise that having a bedroom all to themselves rekindled Duncan's ardour. And so Kirsten was pregnant again in no time at all.

Immediately she was sure that another baby was on the way she went over and sat on Duncan's knee. While idly running her fingers through his hair she wheedled, 'Darling, you do realise that when our new baby is born I will struggle to cope. What I mean is, I will need you at home to help me. Darling, I don't manage so well when you're not with me.' She felt Duncan's body grow tense. 'Nothing else for it, darling,' she continued, as she played the helpless woman, 'other than for you to put an end to your love affair with long-haul sea voyages.' He grimaced. 'Sweetheart,' she continued as she nibbled his ear, 'really, you now have to concentrate on little old me and our children.'

Downhearted, a reluctant Duncan accepted that his escape voyages were over. He shook his head as he conceded that his place must now be at home. There was no doubt that he loved Kirsten as much as he could love anyone — and he accepted that three children would be more than a handful for her. And the result of his capitulation was that he then took himself down to Granton, where the Newhaven-Granton fishing fleet was based. Luckily, although not a bowtow, a trawler skipper who could see that Duncan's engineering capabilities were of value to him took him on. Kirsten was delighted. After all, everybody knew that trawler men earned good money.

In Duncan's case, that money turned out to be very hard earned, but more than sufficient for their needs. Kirsten squirrelled away any surplus to modernise her home — her 'wee palace', as she saw it. She even had a bathroom installed in the walk-in windowed cupboard using the adjacent living-room recess. This grand modernisation, many thought, was a sign that Kirsten was getting above herself. Even her mother accused her of having delusions of grandeur. But Kirsten didn't care what anyone thought. She had a vision of how her home could be. And her feeling of 'to hang with the lot of you' was especially strong when she was soaking — actually purring — in the bath. Indeed, nothing relaxed her more than when the sensuous aroma of a Radox cube was wafting out of the open bathroom window.

Five months pregnant, Kirsten was soothing herself in the warm, scented water and allowing her thoughts to wander. She thought how when she had reached the end of her pregnancies with Bea and Jane she had become acutely aware that Duncan found her bulging figure off-putting. In fact, he was quite repulsed. Splashing the soft water on her swollen abdomen she came to the understanding that unlike some men he did not see her swollen tummy, feet and ankles as proof of his virility. No, Duncan preferred it when other men envied him because Kirsten was slim, attractive and vivacious.

To add to Kirsten's concerns, in the warmth of the bath, she acknowledged that her present confinement felt so different from her other two. This time she was troubled with very little of the violent morning sickness that had affected her before. However, by the time she was five months gone she was so swollen she resembled a stranded whale. A floundering mass that had to be helped in and out of the bath.

'Are you sure you are only having *one* baby?' Duncan asked when responding to Kirsten's plea for assistance.

Kirsten answered with a gulp. However, she knew it was crunch time. For a week now she had been afraid to tell Duncan what the nurses had suggested to her at the maternity clinic. Drawing in a deep breath she spoke quietly. 'Darling, to be truthful . . . the Sister at the Maternity has sort of . . . ' At which point, her courage began to desert her. Really, she was afraid to continue, but she had to, so she hung her head and whispered, 'That I should be prepared for more than one baby.'

'More than one!' Duncan exclaimed. 'Naw. Naw, Kirsten, we're no' haein that. You'll just hae to tell them we havnae the room for any more than one. Jesus!' he gasped. 'Look, I agreed to come ashore for one baby. I never signed up

to twins. Twins! God in Heaven help us . . .
please . . . no twins! I couldnae cope with twins.'

But then five weeks later Kirsten received the
news that she knew she could not confide to
Duncan unless she wished him to have a heart
attack. No way could she tell him that, instead of
twins, triplets were now on their way!

6

1960

Kirsten's labour started on the Thursday of the third week of the seventh month of her pregnancy. As luck would have it, this was the day before the Trawling Fleet docked after their week of fishing.

'Why, oh why,' she screamed as the first pains gripped her, 'do these bairns have to make an early entrance? Do they not know that tomorrow would be more convenient?'

Fortunately, Aileen had decided that she best stay with Kirsten at nights while Duncan was at sea. This meant she was on hand when Kirsten's first screams awakened her. She jumped out of bed and threw a coat over her. Without saying a word, she dashed from the house to summon a taxi from the phone box on Leith Walk. The cab arrived within ten minutes and whisked Kirsten away to the Elsie Inglis Maternity Hospital.

The babies were in such a hurry to get into the world that Kirsten had just got installed in the labour suite when child number one slipped from her. Before she could ask 'Boy or girl?' she was gripped with the labour pains of baby number two, who arrived a short ten minutes later. Infant number three, also in an immense hurry, made its entrance a quarter of an hour after that.

Giving birth to three children in under an hour left Kirsten on the brink of complete exhaustion. It was a struggle, but still she managed to sit up. 'Is there a boy among the three of them?' she gasped. 'My husband would like at least one of them to be a son.'

No one in the labour suite responded. All seemed to be busy with the triplets; the senior midwife was severing the umbilical cord of the last-born baby. Kirsten was about to ask again when she heard a doctor, either in her cubicle or nearby, whisper, 'With such a rushed and intense labour I fear she'll never have any more children.'

'No, no,' she almost protested, 'my three little darlings just slipped happily into the world.' She then stifled a giggle as she thought, 'Besides, I don't care about not having any more, because five is more than enough for Duncan, and for me!'

As she glanced about her, Kirsten became aware that two of her babies were now being placed in incubator-like contraptions before being wheeled out of the ward.

'Please, will someone speak to me,' she cried. 'Tell me if I have boys or girls. And, wait, why are they being wheeled away?'

By now the senior midwife's face was showing signs of alarm as she stared down at the third infant's face.

With her own alarm surging through her, Kirsten demanded that the midwife allow her to hold her baby.

Ignoring Kirsten, the midwife turned to her

30

colleague. 'Wrap him in a blanket,' she whispered, 'and take him immediately to the nursery. They will know how to attend to him there!'

'Take him to the nursery in a blanket?' the young nurse questioned. 'Why is he not being put in that incubator?'

With a swift wave of her hand the midwife indicated that the nurse must immediately carry out her instructions. At which point Kirsten threw open her arms.

'No! No, he is my baby. I've carried him for nearly eight months. And I *demand* that you let me hold him.' Tears brimming, she sobbed, 'And I wish to hold my other two babies. Kiss them. Tell them they are welcome. Tell them their home and their sisters are ready and waiting for them!'

Ignoring Kirsten's pleas once more, the midwife opened the door and signalled with another brisk wave of her hand for the nurse to leave.

Once the door closed the midwife's full attention was honed on Kirsten. 'Mrs Armstrong,' she began, as she reached out and grabbed Kirsten's fluttering hands, 'please calm yourself. You cannot hold your babies just yet. You see they all weigh less than three pounds and that means they have to be in the care of the special baby unit. Now, once your husband arrives, you and he will be allowed to go and see them.'

'Why can't I go now? I must see them now!'

Before the midwife could respond, the young

nurse re-entered and with a stern nod she indicated that she had something important to say. The midwife released Kirsten's hands down onto the bed before turning and following the nurse out into the corridor.

A few agonising minutes passed before the midwife returned. Lifting up Kirsten's hand again, the midwife sat down on the bed. 'Mrs Armstrong,' she began. She gently massaged Kirsten's hand as she spoke. 'You gave birth to three boys. Unfortunately one of the babies, the last one to be born, was very underweight and he was stillborn.'

Kirsten grabbed her hand away from the midwife. 'Are you saying one of my babies is dead? Dead and I never held him. Brushed my lips over his forehead. Let him know he had a mum who loved him and wanted him.' Hot salt tears were now coursing down Kirsten's face. But, with dignity, she demanded, 'What kind of people are you?'

This outburst unsettled the midwife. 'Look, my dear, I think what you need right now is rest. Sleep so that when your husband comes in you can go to the nursery and . . . ' The midwife's voice trailed off. 'Come on now,' she began again, pressing two tablets into Kirsten's right hand. 'Here is a glass of water. Now, just you swallow these pills down. Believe me, when you awaken you will feel more able to cope with . . . '

Kirsten groaned and fell back against the pillows. Terror welled within her. Why was the midwife being so officious and yet so vague? Why was she not being allowed to hold her babies?

Was there something wrong with all of them? And if there was, and she required help, what would she do? Her mother, her anchor in the storms of life, would soon be returning to her native Shetland — that blow had been delivered only yesterday.

Aileen, her voice full of enthusiasm, had exclaimed, 'Here, Kirsten, when you are back on your feet after your babies are born, Dad and I will leave Leith. Going back to Shetland, we are. Our hearts have always been there and now Dad has a job up there we are going to jump at the chance.'

Kirsten sighed. Mum and Dad's return to Shetland was yesterday's news. Today was today, and —

'Look,' she almost whispered, hoping the tight-lipped midwife did have a heart, 'please get my babies back. I just want, no, *need*, to hold them.'

But, as ever, Kirsten's entreaty was ignored. 'You are becoming overwrought, Mrs Armstrong. Now, be a good girl and take these pills. They will help you sleep.'

'I am not a girl, I am a mother. And I don't wish to sleep. Didn't you hear me? All I want is to hold my babies!'

The midwife simply pushed the glass of water towards Kirsten again.

'And as to these blooming pills, you can stick them where the monkey sticks its nuts. And in case you don't understand, that means swallow them your blooming self!'

'Look, Mrs Armstrong, I am only trying to

33

help you. It would be best for you to sleep until your husband arrives. And when he does he will take all necessary decisions about your sons.'

Kirsten, eyes blazing, mouth gaping, started to get herself out of bed. Immediately the midwife restrained her. 'Try and understand, my dear, your babies are very tiny and need to be in the hands of specialists . . . ' She blew out her lips before adding, 'Mrs Armstrong, they must be in isolation. Protected from germs. Given time to grow.'

'Be that as it may, I've had enough. So get me a wheelchair and take me to the nursery to see them.'

The midwife lowered her head. 'As I have explained it would be best to wait until your husband gets here. When did you say his trawler would dock?'

Kirsten's eyes flew to the clock. 'Not until three this afternoon and it is only just midday now.'

'Precisely. Now take the sleeping pills. You are in no state to make decisions, that's what your husband will do!'

'And what exactly do you mean by that?'

'At present a husband is the head of the household. His name is on the rent book and in law he makes all decisions regarding the family. That is what I mean, Mrs Armstrong.'

Any desire to argue further with the midwife ebbed from Kirsten. She knew what the woman had said was true. Men made all the decisions and women, in the eyes of the outside world anyway, obeyed. And hadn't she, when she

34

married Duncan, agreed to obey, but somehow never did?

Lifting her hand to her mouth Kirsten swallowed the pills, not out of defeat but because, somehow, she knew she would have to be strong when Duncan arrived. After all, if her precious babies did have any little problems she would be the one to fight for the best life they could have.

7

A gentle touch on her hand woke Kirsten from her troubled slumber.

'Duncan, it was three boys but one wee soul,' she mumbled, before she became aware that her husband was weeping. 'Oh Duncan, sweetheart, don't cry.' She struggled to sit up. 'And it is true that we have lost one but we still have two.'

Duncan sought for her hand before softly brushing his over it. 'Kirsten, dear, you and I have to be brave.'

At his words, she jolted herself upright and snatched her hand from his grip. Frustration and deep concern overwhelmed her. So much so that she forgot her mother's teaching that a lady never uttered profanities. 'What the bloody hell are you saying?' she snapped. Then, before she caught control of her tone, she added, 'First I am not allowed to hold my babies. Then I was drugged against my will. And now you, my *loving husband*, are saying I have to be brave . . . About exactly bloody what do I have to be bloody brave is what I want to know!'

A nurse quietly walked over and pulled the screens around Kirsten's bed. This action only added to Kirsten's terror. A lump in her throat started choking her and hot tears burned her eyes.

Duncan tenderly bent over her and began to brush away her tears. 'Kirsten, love, another of our babies didn't pull through. And the one who is left, he is so tiny and fragile that . . . '

'Duncan, oh Duncan, please tell me that at least one of our triplets is going to hold on?' However, more to herself, she thought that the remaining baby *was*, like his brothers, so seriously underweight that he too may . . . No, she could not think that. 'Duncan,' she whispered, 'he will make it. I just know he will, and we will be there every step of the road, willing him on.'

But Duncan knew the best thing to do was spell out to Kirsten exactly how difficult rearing the baby was going to be. Taking a sharp intake of breath he blurted, 'Kirsten, *if* he makes it, and I am praying he does, but it doesn't look good.'

Within seconds Kirsten was kneeling up in the bed. Her clenched fists pummelled into Duncan's chest as she cried, 'What in the name of Heaven are you saying? No, no, you can't mean he too will . . . Look, he will make it and I will be with him every step of the way.'

'My darling, the poor wee soul is fighting hard, but the odds are . . . '

Energy spent, Kirsten flopped. 'No, no, no. No, no, no,' she repeated over and over. 'Please tell me he is going to be okay!' she pleaded. A fierce determination she did not know she had, nor did she know where it came from, surged like a fire within her. 'But what kind of a mother would I be if I accepted that I would lose him too?'

Amazed at the energy in Kirsten, Duncan tried to restrain her. But she threw back the bedcovers and, before he could stop her, had leaped out of the bed. The special care baby unit was where she wished to be. So, before anyone could restrain her, she raced in that direction.

With Duncan and a nurse at her heels, Kirsten reached the unit entrance.

'Where is my baby?' she demanded. 'I must see my son and right now at that!'

The duty sister floated towards Kirsten. 'You must be Mrs Armstrong,' she said, her Irish voice melodic.

'I am, and I demand to see my child.'

'And you shall. Now come with me.'

The duty sister took time to draw herself erect before turning towards Duncan. 'I am sure,' she began sweetly but emphatically, 'that I am correct in assuming you are happy to allow your wife to see *her* baby?'

If Duncan thought he would like to contradict her, a withering, warning glare from Kirsten had him meekly nod *yes*.

Tucking Kirsten's arm firmly under her own, the Sister led Kirsten to the far end of the nursery, where three special cots were situated.

'This is where we keep the babies who are in need of a little more attention than is normal. See here in the last incubator is your baby . . . Do you have a name for him yet?'

Kirsten's breath was now coming in short pants. She'd been preparing herself to gaze down on an ugly child, but when she looked into the cot she felt nothing but an overpowering sense of love for her baby. To her he was so handsome, so adorable. A quiet gasp of joy escaped her lips as

38

she noticed two kiss curls, plastered to his forehead with sweat. Instinctively she bent forward and put her right index finger into his curled-up hand. What she didn't see, because she chose not to, was that he was no bigger than a bag of sugar.

'Sorry, Sister,' Kirsten almost sang as she gazed at her son. 'I was just so delighted to see my beautiful baby I forgot you'd asked the name we had chosen for him. Richard . . . but you know, now that I look at him I think that I will shorten it to Richie.' Kirsten looked towards Duncan. 'See, darling, our *son*. Isn't he just so adorable?'

Duncan was transfixed. He did not see a precious darling baby. His thoughts took him to the future. It was true he had been told that in all probability Richie would not make it . . . but if Kirsten could will her child to survive, then she would. Duncan slumped. He could picture their new life as a family. This tiny baby would require a lot of care. It would take him years to make up ground. For him to thrive Kirsten would not only have to sacrifice herself but also Duncan and their two girls.

As if in contrast to Duncan's thoughts, Kirsten began to softly croon a lullaby. With a shrug, Duncan realised that he would now always take second place in Kirsten's life.

He hunched his shoulders and turned his thoughts to what he would now need to do: arrange a funeral for two dead babies. He would prefer to leave something like that to Kirsten, but she couldn't be expected to deal with it. Pursing his lips, Duncan wondered whom he could get to help. Relief seeped into him at the thought of the other strong woman in his life. His mother.

★ ★ ★

'Please, please tell me that I am hearing wrong,' Jessie Armstrong cried when Duncan told her that two of the triplets had died and the other wee soul wasn't quite three pounds. 'No, no, surely your gormless, heartless wife has no' mucked up bringing the bairns into the world?' Duncan nodded, his eyes blank. 'And I hope you told her that we Armstrongs have full-term big bouncing babies! No weaklings in our clan. Yes, that wee underweight soul is a Shetlander for sure.'

'Mam,' Duncan whispered as he bent over and looked at the floor, 'there is something else.' He hesitated. 'Mam, could you help me out by — '

'Are you saying you are you needing a handout?'

'Naw. Wish it was just a shortage of money I had to think about right now. Oh Mam,' he sobbed. 'I have to get the bairns buried. Cannae face it myself, so I was hoping you would help me . . . to get it all over and done with.'

'Oh, I see,' Jessie haltingly replied. Her thoughts were now racing ahead of her.

'Wondering, I was,' Duncan continued, 'if we could have them buried in beside Dad?'

Jessie bit on her lip and the clock ticked the minutes by. Eventually she sniffed long and hard before saying, 'No. The wee souls cannae go in beside your dad. Knowing Kirsten as I do, burying the bairns would just provide a shrine for her to be always attending. Never get over losing them, she wouldn't.'

Bewildered, Duncan looked towards his mother. Always he had thought that she'd meant every word of the curse she'd spat at Kirsten when, enraged, she believed she had trapped her son into marriage. But here she was thinking what would be best for Kirsten. She could see that if the babies were buried Kirsten would tend their grave every week, her grief never-ending.

'Mam,' Duncan asked tentatively, 'are you saying we should have them cremated?'

'Just you and I will be there to see the wee lambs go,' Jessie confirmed. 'And their ashes should be scattered in the Garden of Rest.'

Duncan nodded his consent. Now that his mum was involved all would be taken care of.

He was about to leave when his mum said, 'Funny old thing, life is — all ups and downs. Here was me riding on the crest of a wave about . . . oh, Duncan, wait until I tell you some good news.' She stopped and rubbed her hands with glee. 'Our Nancy, your clever sister: one of the gaffers at Crawford's has proposed to her.'

A silence fell between mother and son. Eventually Duncan spoke. 'So, you're saying all that babysitting for the guy when his wife died last year has paid out for Nancy?'

'Mair than paid out.'

Duncan looked perplexed.

Jessie chuckled. 'Aye, you see, not only has my smart Nancy snaffled him but she also gets a couple of bonuses thrown in.'

'Bonuses?'

'Aye, like a detached house in Trinity along with a manager's pay packet. Cannae be bad, so that cannae.' Jessie patted her hair and straightened her jumper before musing, 'Oh aye, your snooty Kirsten might hae thought she had scuttled us when she ran off with you but she didnae. You see, my Nancy has gone one better than her . . . going to be a real lady, my Nancy is.'

Duncan bent his head as a wry smile crossed his face. This was his mum. One minute she was concerned for Kirsten and then, in case he thought she was going soft, she had to pretend that she was getting her revenge on Kirsten.

★ ★ ★

Richie was just a day old when Kirsten again visited the special baby unit. She wanted to be alone when she spoke to the Sister in charge of her son's care.

'Sister,' she began as she advanced towards the incubator, 'I was wondering about breastfeeding Richie. I can feel my milk coming in.'

The Sister's stern face relaxed for a moment. 'So you would like to breastfeed him? Good, but first you will have to express the milk and it will be fed to him through a nasal tube.'

'But why, when I am willing to be here when he needs fed?'

'Right now, my dear, he is too weak to suck,' the sister said kindly. 'But when he is strong enough you can come in and breastfeed him.'

'Do you think he will be at that stage when I have to leave here — in ten days' time?'

The Sister shook her head. 'No. If we are not too busy, they may allow you to stay on for a couple of days more, but after that you will have to come in every day to express your milk. On the bright side once this little one has put on sufficient weight and once he is out of the incubator you'll be able to breastfeed him yourself.'

Kirsten knew the Sister was being truthful, but still she felt downcast. What she wanted was to take Richie with her when she left the maternity unit. 'Sister, what weight does he have to reach before I can take him home?' she asked.

The Sister smiled before saying, 'Just five pounds!'

Kirsten gulped. Her son was only two pounds fourteen ounces right now. Her tortured mind imagined that it could take him months to reach the target weight. Best thing, she thought, was to check. Taking a deep breath, she quietly asked, 'And how long do you think it will take for him to reach five pounds?'

'Barring infections or slipbacks . . . ' She shrugged. 'Ten weeks, give or take. And when the great day comes you can take him home.'

Hearing the words 'take him home' brought tears to Kirsten's eyes. The Sister was giving her hope. She was being positive. Like Kirsten herself, she knew it was a long, hard road ahead for Richie. But somehow both of them knew he would make it.

8

Two months passed before Kirsten and Duncan found themselves in the nursery of the maternity unit waiting to take baby Richie home. These eight weeks had felt both long and short. During this time the stillborn babies were cremated and Kirsten had spent hours in the grey fog of her private sorrow grieving the loss of those wee, never-glimpsed souls.

For Duncan, the time had dragged, as he'd witnessed his premonition — of Kirsten becoming besotted by her one remaining son — coming true. Oh yes, he felt quite useless as he watched her sweep everything and everybody aside, including at last her own grief, so she could concentrate on being with Richie as much as possible. Duncan allowed himself a wry smile as he remembered how Kirsten had wangled a stay of fifteen days in the hospital. Even the nurses smiled at that, as all their other patients couldn't wait to get out in under the mandatory ten days. Then when she had to come home she persuaded her mother to put off going to Shetland until her precious Richie was home. This allowed her to visit the special baby unit first thing in the morning, later in the afternoon and last thing in the evening. In her maternal passion, she expressed so much milk that it was kept in bottles in the baby unit fridge and the surplus was used to nourish other premature babies.

Gazing down at her sleeping, contented Richie, Kirsten was unaware that the Sister had arrived. 'So, at last you are off home, Mrs Armstrong.'

Kirsten nodded. 'Yes, and I didn't want to leave without thanking you for all you did to help Richie to thrive. I can't believe how he's come to be so bright and healthy.'

'And within a year or so he will have made up all that he lost by being premature,' the Sister assured a beaming Kirsten. 'Word of warning, though . . . don't mollycoddle him. Let him decide when he is ready to take each of his next steps forward. Don't hold him back by being over-protective. Before you know it, he will be a big bouncing boy.'

Kirsten smiled and, cradling her son, she left the maternity hospital with Duncan.

Going home, they all were.

★ ★ ★

Two weeks passed before Kirsten felt that she should catch up with the Balfour Street 'mothers' meeting. Twice a week the mums with little children would make their way to Pilrig Park and, weather permitting, spend the afternoon knitting, gabbing and putting the world to rights. There were, of course, the mandatory Thermos flasks of tea and homemade scones, which they took turns to provide.

'Well, if it isn't a stranger coming into our midst,' Alice Greenhill announced when Kirsten pushed her pram towards the assembled group.

45

'Leave it be, Alice,' Molly Clark warned before going over to look in Kirsten's pram. 'And so here you are, little man, and pretending to be asleep at that. Let me lift you out and you can survey your kingdom.'

Before Kirsten could stop Molly she had lifted Richie out of his pram and, as she gazed down on his small crushed features, she crooned, 'And what a darling you are.'

Always when there was a new baby to be introduced the women took it in turns to hold the newborn and drool over the wee soul. Even so, Kirsten couldn't believe it when her friends decided Richie was a parcel to be passed around from one set of outstretched arms to another.

While her son was being admired, Molly, the group's unelected leader, spoke quietly to Kirsten. 'Are you coping, hen?'

Kirsten bristled, unmistakably.

Molly continued. 'All I mean is, three bairns with not much between them is more than a handful.'

'Just, I am. But you see, Richie is so small that I am feeding him on demand.'

Molly laughed. 'And he demands every half-hour.'

'Not quite, but he can be greedy.'

'Aye, but then it's true he hasn't had the best of starts. But of course he is loved and cherished and even although he looks like a dumpling in a hankie still, he is piling on the pounds, eh, hen?'

Kirsten nodded. 'He is my darling. The only one of my three who survived.' She sighed, tears glistening in her eyes. 'But I am so tired. You see,

46

he takes so long to feed and Duncan, well . . . '
Kirsten did not wish to be disloyal but she had
to tell someone. 'Well, he's not the doting daddy
he was when the girls were babies. Goes out to
the pub every night. He'd do anything rather
than help with any of the bairns like he used to.
Never picks Richie up or speaks to him, he
doesn't.'

'That's men for you. Cannae cope with
competition . . . even from their own son. But
my Ella is no' back at school yet, so . . . Here,
did I tell you she had another asthma attack?'
Kirsten shook her head just as Molly shouted,
'Ella, come over here, darling, and take wee
Richie for a walk in his pram. Just around the
park.'

Kirsten, propelled by feelings of maternal
protection, spoke up. 'Molly, that is kind of you,
but Ella is only twelve — perhaps she is too
young to take my baby for a walk. He needs to
be with me all the time.'

'Nonsense! You know that from the age often
it's nae bother for wee lassies to take babies for a
walk. Just as long as they don't cross with the
pram over busy Leith Walk. And as to Richie
being with you all the time . . . balderdash
. . . you need a break . . . time to be with your
pals. Have a giggle and a fag.' Molly laughed.
'Oh, I'm sorry, I forgot you dinnae smoke.'

Ella was now holding onto the pram handle,
waiting for Richie to be put back in his pram. As
soon as he was, he started to holler.

'There, there, wee man,' Ella crooned as she
lifted up a soft toy rabbit and shook it towards

47

Richie's face. 'Dixie see, Dixie see, Dixie see,' she crooned over and over again.

'That's an unusual name you have given the bairn, Kirsten,' Jodie Smith said. 'Is it a Shetland one?'

'What do you mean?'

'Dixie.'

'But his name is . . . '

Again Molly came to the rescue. 'No, it's not a Shetland name, it's a Balfour Street name. A very special name for one of its own.'

Kirsten started to protest but Molly ignored her concerns. 'Look, Kirsten, I think my Ella has got it right. Dixie is a special name for a very special wee lad who has beaten all the odds and held on to his own wee life.'

Kirsten nodded with a smile.

Molly now looked earnestly at Kirsten. Colourful September was just about out. She shuddered as she mused that a harsh drag of a winter was in front of everybody. A winter that might seem even longer, colder and harder for Kirsten than for anybody else. Molly could see that Kirsten was all skin and bone, which, as a new mother, she shouldn't be. All her energy was going into making sure that Dixie thrived. She would barely let him out of her sight, which meant she'd get very little rest over the coming months and even years.

9

1963

July saw a happy Dixie celebrate his third birthday with a home-baked cake and, yet more exciting, a little red tricycle from his doting Granny Armstrong. It was to everyone's surprise that he had come so far. True, he'd taken nearly this long to catch up with his contemporaries, but that was quicker than anyone had expected. Of course, there'd been a high price to pay for this triumph. It was a price that was not only paid by Kirsten, whose whole life now revolved around Dixie, but also by Duncan, Bea and Jane as the neglected outsiders in their family.

When Kirsten was being honest with herself, which wasn't often, she knew that there was resentment smouldering in Duncan. This bitterness very rarely boiled over, but Kirsten knew that to keep it in check they would have to find a bigger house. She knew that, like her, Duncan longed to have more living space. He longed to be able to afford one of the modern semi-detached villas with their white-pebbledash fronts that sat so snugly at the end of McDonald Road.

Often Kirsten and Duncan would take a walk with the children on a Sunday. Always, they ended up gazing at these homes, so different from the brick tenements of Leith, wishing they could afford one. Their main problem was that Dixie was such a demanding child — a state of affairs Kirsten had created herself, with her conviction that for all of his life Dixie must be wrapped up in cotton wool. Kirsten insisted that Dixie share their bed so she could always be near him; indeed the boy just had to sneeze and he was taken to see the doctor. What Kirsten understood, but couldn't seem to do anything about, was that her obsessive overprotection was creating a rift between her and Duncan.

What they required was a bigger house where they could have a bedroom to themselves again. Kirsten also wished to be close to her Balfour Street pals — her support, as she saw them. Especially Molly, who, when the rearing of Dixie had been so, so difficult, and Kirsten was at the frayed end of her tether, had always found time to help. She always seemed to be there to calm explosive situations.

But one explosive situation that Molly couldn't calm was Duncan's conviction that his marriage had reached a place of no return. On one of their walks along the Water of Leith to McDonald Road he announced that he was making a supreme sacrifice by signing on for the Merchant Navy again. Naturally, the shipping company he would be sailing with was the Ben Line.

Even though they were barely speaking, the thought of him not being with the family for at least six months caused Kirsten to panic. She could hardly contain the terror that rose up in her stomach and started to reach her throat and choke her.

'But, but — could you not have signed up with the Gibson Line? Remember, they do short-haul trips to the Continent . . . '

'Aye, but I have a good record with the Ben Line. Besides, I'm chasing the big money now. So I have to go deep sea. And I will either be requested to join the *Ben Nevis* or *Ben Cruachan*.'

'But these ships can be sent to the Far East.'

'Aye, that's right. But if I work hard I can do well with the company again.' Duncan was now rubbing his fingers together: *money*.

'But,' she spluttered, 'how will I manage the children, especially Dixie, without you?'

Duncan took her hand in his before replying, 'You will manage. The one thing I am sure of is that no matter what, you will find a way to cope. As to Dixie, he is fine . . . doing so much better than most three year olds, so he is. And just think, Kirsten, when I come home again with my pockets bulging with money . . . ' Kirsten bit her lip then shook her head. 'Look, love,' he cajoled, 'it's a chance to afford the deposit for the house of our dreams.' He hesitated but did not lift his eyes to meet hers before adding, 'Can't you see, darling, that we need to get out from under each other's feet. Maybe you can go on living in our nightmare but I can't.' She nodded and he wrapped his arms around her as she rested her head softly on his chest.

'Kirsten,' he said tenderly, 'I will look after you. I'll leave you a fortnightly allotment — enough to keep you and the children going until I come back.'

51

Kirsten smiled as she watched her children sup up their porridge. Admiring the sturdy little limbs of her eight-year-old daughter Bea, seven-year-old Jane and three-year-old Dixie, she felt she had a lot to be thankful for.

Yes, she admitted to herself, the last three years had seemed like a relentless winter. But now it was high summer — not only outside but also, she felt, in her life. Yes, she truly believed that the sunshine was heralding a happier time for her precious family.

She smiled when she thought that today she would pitch up at the Ben Line office in North St David's Street and collect the allotment that her loyal husband Duncan had signed over to her. She would then use this hard-earned money to pay the rent and the balance to keep her and the children until he came home. Duncan was making this sacrifice, she told herself, because he loved them and wished to provide better for them.

Yes, they needed space that would help them get back their loving relationship. She smiled coyly as she thought it would be good to be making love again regularly, not once in a blue moon, as it had been before he left on his long-haul trip. If she was being honest she truly regretted the breakdown of her fondly supportive relationship with Duncan. She knew that she had not been fair to him since Dixie's arrival — she shuddered as she reluctantly accepted the problems between Duncan and her had started when Dixie was born. When Dixie became her priority, everybody in the family had to take a back seat: she saw that now.

The girls were ready for school by the time she stopped thinking about Duncan's sacrifice to secure them a better standard of living. She saw them out the door with a smile, but Dixie, who didn't like his sisters to leave him behind, began to cry.

'There, there love,' she crooned as she lifted him up to comfort him. 'You and I are going on a nice meander past the houses, one of which could be ours in a few years. Then we will be off to the shipping office to collect our money. Think of it, Dixie, I haven't got a bawbee in my purse right now, but thanks to Daddy working so hard we will be able to have mince and tatties for tea tonight . . . Might even treat us all to a sugar doughnut.'

Pushing a go-chair was never a chore to Kirsten. She so loved taking her children for a walk. It was when she was walking that she did her reminiscing. Today, it was no different.

Thinking back was what she was doing as she wandered along the streets that would take her to posh uptown Edinburgh. She recalled what life had been like when Duncan and she had first fallen in love. She hunched her shoulders and smiled as she thought of how all that magic would be recaptured when he came home and they were living in their dream house, a lovely family together again.

★   ★   ★

53

On arrival at the Ben Line offices Kirsten found that five women were already waiting for their allotments. One of the women, Mairi Brown, looked surprised when she saw Kirsten.

'Didnae expect to see you here,' she said as she sidled up.

'Didn't think I would see myself here either, but my Duncan signed on for another long trip.' She giggled before adding, 'Likes the exotic, so my Duncan does. So I'm here to collect my share of his wages.'

Mairi still looked puzzled, but as the clerk called out her name she jumped forward and signed for her money.

Kirsten then moved towards the next available clerk and told him her name.

He scanned his list and said, 'Sorry, Mrs, now you did say Armstrong?'

Kirsten nodded.

'You are not on my list.'

'But I have to be. My husband signed on a month ago and left on his trip two weeks ago.'

'Look, please take a seat and once I've dealt with everyone else I'll contact upstairs.'

Every second that Kirsten waited seemed like an hour. At last everyone was paid out and the clerk turned his attention to Kirsten. 'Now, Mrs Armstrong, what is your husband's full name?'

'Duncan Armstrong, and as I said he signed on a month ago — left to join either the *Ben Nevis* or the *Ben Cruachan* two weeks ago. Look, I know my husband and he did leave me an allowance.'

The clerk did not reply, but he lifted up the

54

telephone and spoke to someone. After a few agonising minutes, Kirsten heard him say, 'So, you are saying he did apply and was taken on, but he then contacted you and withdrew his application? Thank you.'

Kirsten couldn't bear to hear the man repeat the heartbreaking message. Duncan had deserted her and the children. She stood still, rooted to the spot. Then as the grim realisation sank in, she began to react.

Without so much as a thank you to the clerk she bolted from the office. Her feet raced along the pavements, the go-chair bouncing in front of her. Why had Duncan left? Her mind raced, and she thought who, if anybody, would know where he was. She drew up abruptly.

His mother, that's who.

While she was deliberating what she should do next, she became aware of Mairi Brown next to her.

'See by your face you have just found out your Duncan has done a runner,' Mairi announced, almost licking her lips. 'And with a bimbo. Right slap in the face for you, Kirsten, is that no'?'

Kirsten didn't reply. She glowered at Mairi before turning Dixie's chair and starting to gallop towards Newhaven.

That was not her final destination, however; rather it was halfway between Leith and Granton — Granton, now the sprawling Corporation housing area where her mother-in-law had been allocated a garden flat.

Kirsten was making a beeline straight for Jessie's flat.

It was a dishevelled and breathless Kirsten who bolted into the passageway of Jessie's home. To add to her discomfort, she felt overwhelmingly warm. At first this heat had come from her anger at discovering that her supposedly faithful, loving husband had deserted her. Realisation of her desperate plight had then turned her anger into an engulfing, seething rage.

At the door of Jessie's ground-floor home, she made a grab for the outside door handle. When the handle did not budge, she realised the door was locked. Why, she wondered. In Admiralty Street no one locked their door, and most, when rehoused out of the slums, had carried on that tradition.

Taking some deep breaths gave Kirsten time to think. It really was beyond her comprehension how anyone could become a money lender and charge their 'friends' five per cent on the loan of a pound to see them through to pay day. But she knew that was what Jessie was doing. Perhaps that explained the locked door.

Slowly, Kirsten remembered how scheming Jessie had expanded her little earner when Duncan moved from the family home. It was now such a big mucky business that every Friday and Saturday she employed fierce Babs Copeland to assist her when her clients came with their repayments. Problem was, if it ever came to it, Babs, who by her looks could frighten the Free French, wouldn't actually be able to fight her way out of a wet paper bag. And so Jessie had decided she should get herself a guard dog. But Jessie didn't like big dogs, so she'd settled for a bad-tempered Jack Russell that she'd christened Brutus. Now, no way was Brutus any good at barking and lunging to terrify the punters, but he was an expert at yapping and snapping, and his jaws had to be prised open if he was ever swinging from anyone's coat-tails.

Thumping the door again brought Brutus charging up the hallway. His yelping sounded so fierce that Dixie began to scream and kick out.

'I'm coming, I'm coming.' Jessie's unmistakable gruff voice hollered down the hall. She grabbed hold of Brutus and lifted him up into her arms before yanking the door open.

'Well, would you look what the wind has blown in?' Jessie sneered when she realised who her visitors were. Letting go of Brutus, she bent down and stroked Dixie's face.

'No need to be frightened, my wee man. It's just Brutus and he really is a pussycat. Anyone could buy him with a biscuit. Mind you, don't you be telling my customers that.'

Pushing past Jessie, Kirsten spat, 'Look, I'm not here to idle away the day. I am here to find out where your son, my deserting husband, is and who he did a runner with!'

By now they were all in the living room. Jessie shrugged as she plumped herself down in her favourite armchair. 'You being so smart I thought you would have been here before now.'

'Didn't have a clue until I went to the Ben Line to get paid out and all they could say was . . . sorry.'

'Well, Kirsten.' Jessie stopped to look down at Dixie, who was sobbing. 'Look, my wee darling,' she said as she fished a handkerchief from her pocket and wiped away Dixie's tears. 'Let's get you calmed first. Now would you like a biscuit? Just wait and Granny will get them.'

Jessie being so fond of Dixie had come as a surprise to everyone. However, it was true that Dixie captivated everyone. Indeed, when Kirsten first took him out in his pram, everyone she met smiled when they looked at him. She'd lost count of the times the folk of Leith had dropped loose change into his hands.

While Jessie went into the kitchen to fetch the biscuit, Kirsten lifted Dixie out of the pushchair and sat him on her knee.

'Right, give the bairn here to me,' Jessie said when she returned. Before Kirsten could protest Jessie had taken Dixie into her hefty arms and sat herself down again.

'Now, I know, Kirsten, what my Duncan has done is wrong, very wrong. The blame, however, is not all his.'

'What do you mean?'

'Just pure logic, it is.' Jessie drew in a good sniff. 'A man has to be made to think that he is the only one that matters in the home. And Kirsten, since this wee chap arrived,' she now tickled Dixie's chest, making him chuckle, 'Duncan not only took a back seat but his bum was clean oot the proverbial windae. So, when Nessie Souter flashes her boobs in his face he naturally . . . '

'Oh no, please tell me he didn't leave me for

58

Nessie Souter. I mean she's . . . she's . . . '

'Afraid he did. Everybody kens she's the bottom of the barrel. And I ken fine how you must be feeling. Getting dumped for an Audrey Hepburn lookalike you can hold your heid up.' She paused. 'But an older, uglier version of Margaret Rutherford . . . well, that really is a kick in the teeth.'

Kirsten sniffed long and hard, daring her tears not to fall. Her thoughts then quickly turned from the insult of being dumped for Nessie Souter to how she was going to pay the rent and feed her children.

First, she reluctantly conceded, she would need to go to the Department of Social Security, but it would only provide funding at subsistence level. That would not be good enough for her bairns. So she'd have no alternative but to find employment . . .

While Kirsten was pondering, Jessie was rattling on about how the runaways were now on their way to Canada. But for all Kirsten cared they could be away on a one-way ticket to the moon.

'Jessie, never mind those two,' she heard herself say. 'I need to get the rent paid and money to feed the kids.' Her prime concern was her children, particularly Dixie.

Before answering, Jessie pursed her lips — a gesture that showed she was in danger of parting with money. She then huffed and puffed before spluttering, 'Well, I suppose I could lend you enough to get by. And seeing you are family I would only expect half the usual interest . . . '

'My three children, your precious grand-children, are about to go out on to the street and you want interest?'

Kirsten raising her voice caused Dixie to whimper. Jessie began to pat him.

'There, there, my darling boy,' she crooned. Kirsten couldn't believe it, but as Jessie looked down at Dixie's face she appeared to mellow and become entranced. Quietly and melodically Kirsten heard Jessie say, 'There, there. Cry nae mair, my precious bairnie. Seeing it's you that needs I'll gie your mammy the money she needs.' Jessie sniffed. 'Mind you, a *gift* this month, but like me when I got kicked in the teeth your mammy will have to go out and find a job or do whatever it takes to get next month's rent paid.' Jessie looked up at Kirsten now. 'Oh aye, when needs must, we all have to swallow our pride.' Kirsten huffed.

'You can huff all you like, but I can assure you that when your family are in dire straits you and everybody else will do whatever, and I mean *whatever*, you have to do just as long as you keep them afloat.'

10

After Kirsten left Jessie's home she felt cheap and useless. Jessie's words of warning — that if ever she came to borrow money again, she wouldn't see her stuck, but not to bring Dixie with her — had been a humiliation. The final straw, however, was when Jessie told her, 'I am running a money lending business, no' a charity!'

Needing time to calm down — and think about her precarious situation — Kirsten decided to walk home from Granton. As she meandered, instead of calm she felt rising anxiety and dismay. What kind of a future did she and the children have to look forward to? Indeed, did they have a future at all? Her feelings of unease seemed to unsettle Dixie too.

Kirsten had just turned off Bonnington Road and was making her way towards Pilrig Park when Dixie started to throw a tantrum. By the time she got into the park his screams were unearthly and Dixie was arching his back and kicking out his legs in all directions.

As soon as she could, Kirsten stopped at a park bench. She then tried to soothe Dixie, but her efforts only upset him further. Slumped down on the bench, unable to stop herself, she started to weep uncontrollably.

'That bad, is it?' she heard a refined voice ask.

Kirsten sniffed. 'Yes, it is,' she sputtered through her gulps.

A diminutive woman was now seated down beside her. Without another word, she leaned over towards Dixie. Her hands began to slowly massage his face. This action caused Dixie to calm. From his face, she moved her hands up to his forehead and two fingers from each hand started working on each side of his temple. Within a minute her actions had stilled and soothed not only Dixie but also Kirsten herself.

The woman then took Dixie's hands in hers and tenderly and expertly worked her magic on them too.

This action afforded Kirsten time to look at her Good Samaritan. She noted that she was a lady of breeding. Her dress — long flowing skirt and apricot-coloured silk stole — appeared to be from a past era. Kirsten also noted her subtle make-up, which instead of detracting from her quaintness only added to it. The woman completely captivated Kirsten and she now had Dixie so relaxed that he had fallen asleep.

Turning from the slumbering child, the lady focused her attention on his mother.

She moved closer to Kirsten. 'Now, my dear,' she began, taking Kirsten's hand in hers, 'what has upset you so terribly today? Is it just that your little boy was being a bit fractious?'

Before she realised it, Kirsten started to cry again and between each heart-rending sob she confided to the woman, a complete stranger, the whole sorry tale of Duncan's desertion.

'I see,' the woman replied as she massaged Kirsten's palm in an effort to calm her. 'Now, dear, my name is Stella Wise. I have been in the same situation that you now find yourself. But I made up my mind I was going to survive and provide for my two boys and myself.' She drew in a deep breath to indicate her satisfaction. 'And not only have we pulled through, but so very well at that.' She paused again. 'Men, well, we do require them because we are all just here for a short time. Just like all living things we are born, procreate and then die. What we do and manage between our birth and death is entirely up to us. You won't believe me but you will survive and flourish — provided you leave your scruples behind. Look, my house is just on the other side of Pilrig Street . . . Well, not exactly Pilrig Street itself. You see my house is on Rosebank Lane — tucked in at the top of the lane beside the boundary of the Rosebank Cemetery wall.' She shrugged and gave a polite giggle. 'All on its own, my house is. And the neighbours never say a word. They just arrive and get dug in.'

Kirsten almost smiled: Stella's neighbours were all in their grave, so how could they say anything?

'Now, how about you and I go over to my place and have a cup of tea? Have you eaten since breakfast?'

Kirsten shook her head.

'Right, let's go.'

They arrived at the secluded lane just as it dawned on Kirsten that Stella was guiding her towards what people in the district said was a brothel! An upmarket one, but a brothel all the same. Instinctively she drew up. 'But, but, is this not . . . I mean . . . are you saying this is your home?'

'Yes. It is my lovely home. The upkeep of such a large dwelling is hefty. That is why I have to sacrifice and rent out some of my rooms. Mark you, on an evening-only basis. But come on. Let me get some sustenance inside you.'

When she entered the downstairs drawing room Kirsten could do nothing other than admire the furnishings and curtains. To say they were luxurious would be an understatement. Her eyes then strayed to the corner, where a drinks cabinet stood. As she stared at the gantry she thought it was so well stocked it would not have been out of place in the first-class lounge of an ocean-going liner. Really, the house was like its owner; it too seemed to belong to a different time. When Stella became aware that Kirsten appeared fascinated by the gantry, she asked, 'What's your tipple?'

'Eh. Eh. To be truthful I only have a sherry on Hogmanay. Other than that I don't . . . '

Stella seated Kirsten in a lug chair before asking, 'Tea or coffee, then?'

'Either suits. However, I think I should be going. My girls will be home from school soon and I have to get a meal ready for them.'

'Of course, but before you rush off I was going to suggest that, as you will have difficulty finding employment that fits around your little boy . . . ' Stella stopped, as if to ponder. 'Look, I could teach you how to massage. That would not only help you earn a bob or two but would also be so useful, beneficial in fact, for your little boy . . . Does he have many of those wee tantrums?'

'He wasn't three pounds at birth, so it's just

that he needs lots of attention.'

Stella smiled. She recognised that Kirsten, like herself, was an overprotective mum.

Kirsten was now considering what Stella had said. Getting herself a job made sense. But caution made her wonder if this offer of assistance was Stella's way of enticing her into her business. No, she thought; no matter what, I could never stoop that low.

While she was deliberating, a woman, attired in overalls and a turban, came into the room. 'That's me got it all shipshape again, Mrs Wise. Mind you, the attic room again was a mess. Think it is time for you to tell the lassie that rents it that this is a first-class establishment and no' a hovel.'

Kirsten had to smother her giggles. Were these women real? The house was a brothel. It was beyond dispute that it was an upmarket dwelling; but, however posh the curtains might be, the house was one of ill-repute.

'Thank you, Mrs Baxter, for reminding me that lately you have been so busy putting things back as I like them you have not had time to do the shopping,' Stella said, then paused. Time ticked slowly by. She pursed her lips. Slowly a smile came to her face. 'I have just realised what I require is a housekeeper — a type of lady butler. You know, someone who will relieve me of doing the food provisions and the tedious paperwork. I find those two activities so dreary and time consuming. Now that I have decided on this, I think it would be a perfect job for you, Kirsten.'

'Grab it with baith hands, hen,' Mrs Baxter urged Kirsten with a wink and a nod. 'Mrs Wise pays good rates and you get wee perks thrown in.'

'Wee perks!' a bewildered Kirsten reiterated.

'Aye, like when my man was off for the Trades' Holidays she treated us to a week in Blackpool.' Dreamily she added, 'Food was good and the high jinks . . . Great holiday, that was.'

An uneasy feeling of being sucked in began to overwhelm Kirsten again. 'Erm, I am so pleased for you, Mrs Baxter.' She now turned to address Stella. 'You will need to excuse me. Time is marching on. As I said, I have to get home for my girls.'

Escape was now Kirsten's priority. Grabbing the handle of Dixie's pushchair, she headed towards the door.

'Oh, so you are leaving,' Stella said. 'Now, don't rush to give me an answer about my job offer. Take your time. Shall we agree I should let a week pass by before I advertise the post?'

★   ★   ★

On her way home Kirsten bumped into Molly. She knew this was providence; she was in urgent need of an ear — someone like Molly, who would listen, hear her out, before commenting or giving any advice. However, when she glanced up at the Pilrig church clock she could see that time — time that was needed to tell Molly *all* about her day — had run out. This being so, she suggested to Molly that she should come and

66

visit her after nine that evening, when the children were abed.

Molly could see that Kirsten was upset, so she naturally became intrigued. Even so, she did manage to agree to wait until later that evening in order to have her curiosity relieved.

★   ★   ★

Unable to keep her wandering imagination in check, it was no surprise that Molly arrived at Kirsten's just before eight o'clock. 'Seeing you looked so stressed I thought I would come early and help you get the children settled for the night.'

Kirsten, her mind in turmoil, nodded. To be truthful she was pleased to see Molly, as she so longed to unburden herself to someone: she would have accepted even one of her less discreet friends right now.

Eventually the children were bedded, night-time stories read. Lights switched out.

Now it was time for Kirsten and Molly to sit opposite each other at the kitchen table, drinking a mandatory cup of tea.

'Right then, Kirsten, tell me what happened today.'

Kirsten bit on her lip. Tears surfaced, but she sniffed hard in an effort not to appear a crybaby. 'The day started fine but once I arrived at the Ben Line offices . . . ' She stopped. Betrayal tears ran down her face.

Perplexed, Molly reached over and sought for Kirsten's hand. 'Just take it steady. We have all the time in the world. And I'll stay silent and just you tell me what happened today. Kirsten, love, what has distressed you so?'

It took Kirsten half an hour to tell her heartbreaking tale. When she was finished she lowered her head onto the table and sobs wracked her slender frame. Molly got up and went round to Kirsten. She lifted her distraught friend up into her arms.

'There, there,' she whispered as she bent down and kissed her hair. She hesitated while silently thinking, *Duncan Armstrong, you are an unfeeling, selfish bastard, that's what you are. You know how vulnerable Kirsten is. How she worries about Dixie. Every spare minute she has is spent on him. Then there are the girls — they are just bits of bairns still and to leave them — for goodness sake, man, they are your kith and kin.*

Molly, being astute, accepted that it was highly unlikely that Duncan would come back. He had gone to Canada with Nessie Souter. Nessie Souter, who had at last got a man to commit himself to her, would hang on to him like a leech. So where did this leave Kirsten? Finding work was the answer, if the four of them were to survive with any sort of dignity. That solution was impossible because Dixie was only three, and Kirsten would not allow him to go full-time to nursery. She had to have him with her. It was true that once he went to school — Molly sighed, as she acknowledged that was two years away — Kirsten would thankfully then *have* to stand back a bit. The plus in this was that it would mean she could go out and find work around the school hours. However, right now Kirsten had no — or very few — options.

Kirsten, still crying profusely, was contemplating her plight as well. She wondered where she could find employment that would allow her to take Dixie with her. She considered Jessie's suggestion that she go into money lending, but that needed capital. Money she did not have. Besides, there was something about lending money to your hard-up friends and charging them interest that made her squirm.

Slowly, her sobs began to subside.

'Nothing to make you feel better than a good cry,' Molly remarked with a wry chuckle. 'And now you have got that out of your system, time to think about what to do.'

'I know. I suppose I could uproot the children and go to Shetland.'

'Is that something you think you would like to do?'

'To be honest no, but if the alternative is landing out on the street — well, no, the children are my responsibility, so I have to stay here and just get on with whatever. I might even . . . ' She shuddered. 'No, I don't think I could ever do that.'

'Do what?'

'Sell my body.'

Molly chuckled. 'Yeah, like me, where we would never condemn a lassie that did it, it is not a road either of us would wish to travel.'

Kirsten nodded. 'No way! No. No. No way!'

'Having laid that to rest, would you consider

the housekeeper's job for this Stella woman?'

'No. That is the slippery slope. Well, as far as I am concerned it would be.'

Molly mused. 'Needn't be, and just think, her massage training would really benefit Dixie. You know how his tantrums have seemed worse of late.'

'They have and how.' Kirsten hesitated. 'It's strange, Molly, but he misses Duncan. Oh aye, even although his daddy has abandoned him, the poor wee soul can't forsake his daddy.' Kirsten paused, thinking that human nature was perplexing. 'Now, tomorrow,' she continued, 'I'll have to go, cap in hand, down to the DSS and register. At least from them I will get enough to pay the rent and scrape by at subsistence level. Then . . . I will have to look for work. Just take whatever I can get, just so long as they allow me to take Dixie with me.'

'Take Dixie with you! You are joking?'

'No. You see if I, like Duncan, was to go out of his life, even only for a few hours every day, that would be so cruel. The wee soul wouldn't cope.'

Molly just smiled. If any of them would cope, it would be Dixie, she thought.

11

Fourteen days passed. Indeed, it was a frustrating fortnight, which saw Kirsten desperately trying to find work. All she wanted was paid employment that would fit in with her parental responsibilities. Unfortunately, there was no employer who could or wished to accommodate her exacting terms. The Department of Social Security did provide her with enough resources to keep her afloat. But getting ends to meet was a never-ending struggle.

To add to her problems the weather became inclement. As bad as her financial position was, she was faced with the necessity of buying the girls wellington boots. Problem was, she had no money for such seeming luxuries. In sheer desperation she had to approach her mother-in-law for a loan. Jessie had at first *humph*ed and *haw*ed, before handing over the necessary cash. She then had the temerity to suggest to Kirsten that, as she couldn't find anyone wishing to employ her on her terms, she should go into some sort of business for herself.

'And what kind of business would that be?' Kirsten had asked.

'As I have already said, money lending is one option,' Jessie had retorted with a knowing nod of her head.

'So, you are again pushing me towards becoming a penny-pinching Shylock?'

'No. All I am saying is you should consider becoming a friend in need to your pals. No' just the folk here in Granton that are short of a bob or two before payday. Naw, naw, they are everywhere, even in Balfour Street.' Rubbing her hands and grinning, Jessie continued, 'See my customers when they've no' got the price o' a loaf of bread, they ken that they can depend on me to see them all right. And, Kirsten, they also ken I'll no' be asking any awkward questions. Nor do I ask them to sign on the dotted line.'

Kirsten did not reply. It was true that no one signed for their loan from Jessie. No, but it was also true that all the transactions were written down in Jessie's notebook. The same notebook that went everywhere with her — even to bed!

Unaware that Kirsten was lost in her own thoughts, Jessie continued speaking. 'And, Kirsten, they dinnae miss the penny or two when they pay back on payday. And don't forget twelve of those pennies make a bob.' She hunched her shoulders with delight as she cackled. 'And two hundred and forty makes a pound. And know what, that's the rent taken care of!' She paused to suck in her lips before adding, 'Or the bairns' wellington boots paid for!'

Kirsten got the message loud and clear. Yes, she was taking the moral high ground and implying that Jessie charging the poor interest on loans was immoral.

Nonetheless, when she required the where-for-all to put boots on her children's feet, she had no hesitation in accepting the ill-gotten funds from Jessie.

Kirsten cringed. She had to set her principles aside because her children were in need. Though she still thought money lending was one step away from what Stella Wise's girls did for a living.

The thought of Stella Wise had her considering the job she had been offered. Now, if she was going to lower her morals, would she not be better being a housekeeper? Surely, she argued with herself, managing Stella's affairs was a good few steps up from money lending and at least another two up from . . . True enough, but Stella had said she would only keep the job open for her for a week. A fortnight had now gone by.

★   ★   ★

Kirsten had to screw her courage to the sticking place. She tossed and turned all night, trying to find a solution to her problems other than taking up Stella's offer. In the end she had to admit there seemed to be no other option. In two years' time, when Dixie was five and away to school, she would then be able to seek more — she gulped — *suitable* employment. She couldn't worry about what other people thought. She alone was responsible for her children. Soon she would need to tell her mother that Duncan had deserted her and the children. And never could she explain to her mum that, to make ends meet, she intended to work for Stella Wise, who she had since realised was a woman known to the authorities for . . . She gulped again as she silently mouthed the words: *running a brothel*.

73

Even to hear such words spoken would shock her mother. Kirsten was well aware that her parents' Shetland beliefs meant that the family came first. This being so, Kirsten would be urged to round up her brood and make her home with her parents in the Northern Isles.

And so, here she was at the front door of Stella Wise's house. She hesitated. She knew full well once the door opened and she was faced with Stella there would be, if the job of housekeeper was still on offer, no going back. Her finger was poised to push the bell button when the door flew open.

'Well, well . . . ' Mrs Baxter, who was about to fling a pail of hot soapy water down the front doorstep, stopped, startled, and looked Kirsten up and down. 'You're two weeks late. But after the disaster we've had with the woman Mrs Wise employed when she thought you weren't going to take up her offer, you might still get the job.'

Kirsten smiled.

Wishing to alert Stella, Mrs Baxter turned her head to face the inside of the house and hollered, 'Here, Mrs Wise, you'll no' believe this, but that Kirsten lassie is here on the doorstep.'

Within a minute, Stella appeared. 'Oh, it's good to see you, Kirsten. And you have brought little Dixie with you.'

'Yes,' Kirsten stammered. 'I thought, that is if you don't mind me taking up your offer to teach me to massage . . . '

'Massage? Yes, that would be good for Dixie. But I was also hoping you would be interested in the job of housekeeper. Now, before you answer,

I am aware that you, like me, would not wish, nor ever could consider, the business carried out in my rented rooms.'

Kirsten nodded and Stella smiled. A bargain was made.

12

1965

So, to Kirsten's surprise, two years passed quickly with her working as Stella Wise's housekeeper. Years during which she learned to be independent and provide for her children. She learned, too, some of Stella's massage skills, which transformed Dixie's tendency to tantrum. But then, all too soon, August arrived and it was time for five-year-old Dixie to start his schooling.

The beginning of his formal education was a milestone not only for Dixie, but for Kirsten as well. Entrusting anyone with the care of Dixie, even her mother or Stella, was very difficult for her. Indeed, he still slept with her. So, how was she going to be able to hand over his daily well-being to strangers? At this present time, nothing would convince her that his teachers would understand what a miracle he was. That the bright happy child before them once only weighed two pounds fourteen ounces, that his two tiny siblings hadn't lived and his own survival hadn't felt in any way guaranteed.

On the morning that she had to take Dixie to Lorne Street Primary School, a well-run Edinburgh Corporation establishment, Kirsten was in a state of apprehension. Her mother, Aileen, had foreseen just how difficult this day was going to be for her daughter and had come all the way down from Shetland to support her.

Aileen took over getting the girls ready for their first day back at school after the summer holidays. This left Kirsten to get Dixie dressed. First, she donned his crisp white shirt and tie, then it was time to lift him into short, grey knee-length flannel trousers. While she was assisting him he repeatedly asked her why he couldn't just go over to the school with his sisters.

'Darling,' Kirsten replied ever so gently, over and over again, 'you are going to school for the first time. All the children in your class will have their mothers with them. Your sisters go to school with their chums.'

When she arrived with Dixie at the school, she was introduced to his class teacher, Miss Elliot. Shaking the woman's hand, and deliberately looking into her eyes, Kirsten couldn't help but be impressed. Here, she reckoned, was a woman who was not only very capable and dedicated but also seemed instinctively to know how difficult this day was for Kirsten. She would, without a doubt, strive to assist Dixie to reach his full potential in his first years in school. And so, with bittersweet gladness in her heart, Kirsten watched as Dixie took his new teacher's hand and sat at a low table alongside his classmates.

On arrival back at her home her mother could see that Kirsten was very emotional. Aileen recalled that when Bea and Jane had started school Kirsten had felt that she was no longer their universe, that others would now also play an important part in their lives. Going to school at five years old, that was the signal for all children that they were preparing to go out into the big world where they would one day make their own way.

Dixie going out the door that morning was even harder for Kirsten because she had sacrificed so much for him. Her whole world revolved around him and to hand him over to someone else, Aileen knew, was unbearable to her daughter. After all, had she not taken up the job with Stella Wise because Stella allowed her to take Dixie with her to work? Aileen smiled. That was all true, but now Kirsten could find work that would fit in with the school day — and she no longer had an excuse for staying in Stella's employ. Thankfully she could now move to something more respectable. A job where she could hold her head up and honestly say to people what her job was.

But Stella had become rather frail recently and now needed Kirsten just as much as Kirsten had once needed her. To Aileen's chagrin, she knew that Kirsten would remain ever so willingly in Stella's employ.

The bond between Kirsten and Stella had begun on that first day at Castle View House. This was because, unlike the previous job-holder, who had only lasted a week, Kirsten fitted in with Stella's wishes. Unlike her poor predecessor, who had thought that she could make more money for Stella by cutting down on not only the fees paid out to the girls but also on their food and general household upkeep, Kirsten from the very start had cottoned on to what Stella was all about. She quickly understood that Stella, although appearing eccentric bordering on bizarre, was a shrewd businesswoman. Yes, she was involved in a murky trade, but Stella tried to give *her girls*, her most *valuable asset*, good and fair conditions of employment. What she wished to achieve was that her *working girls* were the best in the trade. And so they had to know that they were appreciated and that their well-being was of importance. This being the case, she made sure her employees had regular medical check-ups and saved some of their earnings so that they would be able to leave the trade when they got better opportunities. She also insisted that the girls did not share their wages with any man. If she found out that they did, she would dismiss them on the grounds of gross misconduct.

Kirsten's view was that prostitution should not happen. But she also realised that it seemed to have always existed, since time began. If it wasn't going to go away, then surely Stella's approach was the correct one.

Kirsten, whose working hours were 9.30 a.m. until 1.30 p.m., had been working with Stella for six months before she came into contact with any of the *girls*.

She would always remember meeting Marigold Thomas, Stella's right-hand evening manager. Marigold was a statuesque lady of mixed race. Kirsten noted that her beautiful black hair was always swept up and held in place by two diamante-adorned combs. Her hair, however, although lovely, was not her main attraction. It was her soft, twinkling brown eyes that mesmerised you. Kirsten also thought that she must be a very warm person because the girls always turned to her if they had an issue to resolve. This estimation of Marigold was confirmed when Stella confided to Kirsten that, although Marigold was a working girl herself, she could rely on her to shepherd the other staff on duty. Under her watch, Marigold would not tolerate any of her charges to be abused or ill-treated.

Kirsten realised that Marigold, like Stella herself, accepted that their trade was, or could be, fraught with danger, but insisted there were standards they would always maintain.

Naturally, Kirsten wondered why Marigold, who appeared to have so much going for her, had chosen prostitution. Marigold herself was tight-lipped as to why she earned her living the way she did. There were reasons, but these were only known to Marigold.

★   ★   ★

MARIGOLD'S STORY

Marigold's mother, Trudy, to her parents' disgust, had fallen in love when she was just nineteen with Ahmad, a stately Nigerian student. Ahmad, who was studying medicine at Edinburgh University, appeared to be brilliant. First in his class, he was, at all his studies. Unfortunately, his memory did not match his intellectual ability. Thus it was that somehow he forgot to mention to Trudy that, on completion of his studies, he would be returning home to

Lagos, Nigeria, where he would be resuming marital bliss with his wife.

Admitting to her parents that she was pregnant by Ahmad was something for which Trudy would require courage. Unfortunately, this mettle evaded her. But then how many people would be brave enough to tell Bible-punching Alexander Thomas that he was about to become the grandfather of a mixed-race child? After all, Alexander, who would swear he was not racist, *knew* that his blue-eyed saviour was born in Bethlehem, with skin as white as the driven snow.

Knowing well how her father would react to her news, Trudy, who worked in Edinburgh as an auxiliary nurse, decided not to return to her home in Bathgate to await the birth of her child. The only alternative she could see was to go to Leith and find lodgings. Why Leith? Well, she had been led to believe that Leith residents were more accommodating and tolerant. Once in Leith, Trudy had been immediately befriended by Maggie Sibbald. Maggie, a forty-year-old matriarch, at once guessed that Trudy was pregnant. Like she would have done for one of her daughters, she suggested that Trudy could either go to an unmarried mother's home or stick it out in Leith, where she would take care of her.

Naturally Trudy opted for Maggie's assistance, and so the months passed before Marigold made her spectacular entrance into the world. There was no doubt that everyone who looked at her could see that she was a very beautiful child.

However, everyone could also see that, with the child being mixed race, she would, even in Leith, have a difficult time.

Marigold did indeed have a difficult childhood. And these difficulties were because her mother yearned to be married and was always looking for a suitable mate. Trouble was, she was not a good judge of character and always seemed to be exchanging one unpleasant or abusive partner for another.

Crisis point came when Marigold was fourteen. Her mother's then partner was Johnny Stuart, a roughneck seaman. His desire did not end with Trudy, however, and Marigold was soon frightened of this man and felt threatened by his presence.

It was true that Trudy was not the best of mothers, and when her partners had physically chastised Marigold, who could be truculent, she had turned a blind eye. But this was another matter.

Marigold, therefore, found herself being awakened at three in the morning, with her mother urging her to get dressed so they could make their escape.

The following year they moved to six different addresses in Edinburgh, always keeping one step ahead of Johnny Stuart. As bad luck would have it, Johnny did track them down. Trudy's reward for trying to protect Marigold was a severe beating. Even as she was losing consciousness she implored Marigold to run — to escape.

Marigold should have put distance between herself and Johnny, but she loved her mother.

Her devotion was such that she could not leave her mum to suffer any further physical abuse.

But in throwing herself over her mother in an effort to protect her, Marigold gave Johnny his opportunity. When dawn broke, a badly injured Trudy was rocking her distraught child in her arms. They remained huddled close to each other until they were able to make their escape.

From that time on, Trudy was unable to work and Marigold cared for her. She worked at any jobs she could get. By the time Marigold was eighteen Trudy was bedridden and the only way Marigold could care and provide for her was by selling herself.

This was not an easy course for Marigold, but one she knew she had to take. She asked around and, on hearing about Stella, she approached her.

Stella had a dilemma about Marigold. Her rule was that her girls had to be at least twenty and had chosen their path for themselves. Marigold was too young, but the position she found herself in was such that she needed to provide for her beloved mother. Taking these factors into consideration Stella acquiesced and allowed Marigold to become a 'renter'.

Stella was the only one who knew Marigold's secrets. Up until now, five years down the line, she had worked for Stella and Stella alone. Never did she tell anyone about herself or her mother. Indeed, no one knew that she cared and provided for her bedridden mother. As to Trudy, she believed what Marigold told her: that she worked as a night-duty nurse.

13

1967

Another two years galloped past for Kirsten. Bea, who was always hoping her darling daddy would come back into her life, moved on to Broughton Secondary School. Jane, who also yearned for her daddy, was preparing to follow Jane to Broughton the following year. Dixie, to Kirsten's delight, was moving upwards and onwards at Lorne Street Primary. Truth was, he had settled well. He had even found the first love of his life at school: Rosie, a bubbly lassie of similar age to himself. What was also dandy was that Rosie thought Dixie was just wonderful. Real inseparable pals, they became.

Kirsten, for the children's sake, always stayed in contact with her mother-in-law, Granny Jessie. Jessie would, from time to time, read them a letter she supposedly got from their dad. Always, she claimed, he was saying he was missing his children and that someday soon he would be coming home from Canada.

When Jessie read from the letter, Kirsten would just look up to the ceiling and roll her eyes. She knew that Duncan had not only deserted her and the children but also rarely contacted his mother.

It was time again for the children to see their granny and after the *letter reading* Jessie asked the girls if they would run to the shops for her. Seemed Jessie was requiring a loaf of bread and a packet of biscuits.

Kirsten was taken aback. She had just been in the kitchen and Jessie had sufficient bread and biscuits. So, what was afoot?

The door had just closed on the girls when Jessie signalled to Kirsten to come and sit closer to her. Kirsten thought she was about to impart some dreadful news about Duncan. However, she was bowled over when Jessie suggested in their secret tête-à-tête that, as Bea and Jane were getting to an age where they were able to work things out for themselves, it was time for Kirsten to get a decent job.

'Decent job?' Kirsten said with a huff.

'Aye. And I've thought of the perfect one for you.'

'You have?'

'Come into the money lending business with me. From the start it will be on a full partnership basis.'

Kirsten gaped.

'Nae need to look surprised. You're hearing right . . . a full partner you will be.'

Kirsten pondered. It could be argued that the money lending trade was a good deal more respectable than Stella's community service. But was it really acceptable? And why was Jessie being so generous as to offer her a partnership?

'Jessie,' she drawled, 'I'm no' daft. What's the catch here?'

Jessie humped her shoulders, shook her head and snorted.

'So, my thinking's right. Your offer to me has something to do with you wanting something for your son.'

'Okay, Kirsten, I did get a letter two days ago. He's asking me, no' begging, to persuade you to let him divorce you.'

'Him divorce me!' Anger mounted within Kirsten. She was about to scream when she inhaled and mellowed her tone. 'On what grounds?' she asked.

'Desertion!'

Kirsten's husky, unrestrained laughter echoed around the room. When it abated, she stammered a lie: 'Tell him he's too late. I've already started proceedings against him. Oh aye, Jessie, I just cannot wait to be rid of him.'

'That's just great.'

'You think so. Well, Jessie, my three bairns are your grandchildren. And at first, because I thought it important to keep a link with you and their dad, I came here.' Kirsten stopped, as if choked with emotion. She swallowed hard before continuing. 'And I've kept coming here because in the past you and I have not quite met eye to eye. So I thought for the children's sake we should build bridges.' She sniffed and brushed her hand under her nose. 'I now realise what a deluded fool I've been.'

Jessie seemed to get flustered. 'What do you mean?'

'Loyalty, Jessie, and friendship, is what I have given you. Did you appreciate them . . . no, you blinking well didn't.' Kirsten, now consumed by rage, spluttered, 'I came in here today to let you see your grandchildren and have a natter with you. And my reward . . . you try to buy me off with a share out of your mucky business. And all because you want me to allow your son to divorce *me*! You actually wish me to give him the means to make that trollop Nessie Souter respectable!'

'Naw, naw, Kirsten, you've got it all wrong. Nessie Souter came home last year. I mean, what else could the lassie do? Try and understand, Kirsten, my Duncan had dumped her for a native Canadian. A Cree, I think she is.'

'He's going to marry a Cree woman? Pull my other leg.' Kirsten felt helpless with shock.

'Yes.' Jessie nodded. 'Turns out he has found himself at last and he likes the lassie.' She paused. 'Look, do you want to read his letter? It's behind the clock.'

Kirsten's reply was an emphatic, 'No!'

'Look, Kirsten, dinnae get shirty with me. I'm only the messenger.'

'And the message?'

'Well, I think he must have told the lassie the break-up of your marriage was all down to you.'

Kirsten's eyes bulged.

'So, it would suit him if he divorced you.'

'No chance. Besides, as I have already said, I have started proceedings.'

'That's fine by me. So now let's get back to us. You're wrong about me trying to buy Duncan a divorce.'

'I am?'

'Yes. You see, Kirsten, our Bea and Jane . . . Look, they're getting to an age when they are beginning to understand.'

'Do you think that I don't know that?' Kirsten butted in, eyes blazing. 'After all I'm the one who has kept telling them that Daddy will be coming home soon . . . Now, I will have to tell them that callous swine is staying put.'

'Before you fire yourself into space again, let me finish. There is no one who will ever convince me that you are on the game. I know you're not. But with you being all palsy-walsy with that Stella dame . . . Well, there's some that are saying . . . Come on now, Kirsten, you didnae need me to spell it out what the gossip is. Do you want our lassies standing in the school playground being taunted?'

Kirsten's face fired.

'So that's why I thought that if I was to offer you a job with me. On an equal basis, that is. Can't you see how that would solve the problem for the girls and give you back some respectability?'

Before Kirsten could reply that if she really wished to get herself into high regard money lending wasn't the job for her, the girls, along with Dixie, returned. Immediately Jessie became the doting granny again and pulled Dixie on to her lap.

★   ★   ★

Kirsten had tossed and turned all night. Jessie, she conceded, was a rough diamond, but there was no doubt she loved her grandchildren and wanted the best for them. It was also true she was not a diplomat, but she had spoken the truth. Yes, it was time for Kirsten to move on. Get a job in a 'respectable' establishment.

'Mummy, Mummy, I am going to be late for school. Can I just go down with Jane?' Dixie, who was looking expectantly from the window, hollered up to his mum.

Kirsten smiled. Dixie was always pleased when it was Monday morning. He liked school for various reasons. First, he was clever, so class work was easy for him. Second, he liked socialising, especially with Rosie and his special pal, Mark. And third, he liked kicking a football about the playground.

Donning her coat, Kirsten said, 'No, maybe next year you can go over to school by yourself.' She then ruffled his hair because she didn't wish to remind him that he was, in her opinion and nobody else's, still delicate and had to be specially nurtured. Opening the door, they then set off for school, where Kirsten would safely see Dixie into the playground before she turned and made her way down to Stella's. Stella's — where this morning she would have to tell her boss that she would be leaving her employ.

* * *

When Kirsten arrived at Castle View, Mrs Baxter was scrubbing the front doorstep.

'Nice morning, Kirsten,' Mrs Baxter said. 'Catch up with your gossip at the tea break.'

Stella was in the lounge and Kirsten decided to be brave and say what she intended to say.

89

'Stella,' she began 'things are coming to a head and I need to — '

'Oh, Kirsten, please do not say that you are going to leave me. I depend on you so. We, that is, Marigold, you and me . . . '

Stella stopped as Mrs Baxter hollered, 'That's the mail, Kirsten.'

Stella smiled. 'And of course Mrs Baxter. I depend so much on the three of you. Couldn't imagine what I would do without you.'

Resolve started to wane. Kirsten realised this possibly was not the day to hand in her notice. But it was the day to ask for time off.

'No, of course I'm not thinking of leaving you,' Kirsten lied, before adding, 'Stella, you see today I have to go and consult a solicitor, and I cannot delay it.'

'Whatever for? Is someone threatening you?'

'You could say that. You see I have just found out that my husband wishes to sue me for a divorce, citing my unreasonable behaviour.'

'He what?'

'Stella, I still have my pride. I now have to beat him to it and sue him on the grounds of desertion and failure to pay maintenance.'

'That is exactly what you should do. So go right now, and if you have time come back and let me know how you get on.' More to herself she said, 'Men are such selfish individuals. Just walk off and leave you to paddle the canoe as best you can.'

And, as Kirsten left for her solicitor's appointment, Stella started to recall.

14

STELLA'S STORY

Life in the colonial service was so good for the wives of diplomats. Endless dances, tea parties and games of mah-jong. When it came to mah-jong, Stella excelled. But then she would, as it called for skill, calculation and strategy. These attributes Stella, although young in years, had in abundance.

Stella had just finished at her Swiss finishing school when she had been bowled over by Robert Wise. Rob, who was ten years Stella's senior, was tall, fair and handsome. Stella was immediately enchanted by his charm. Being full of joy and devilment added to his attraction. Within a year they were married. By the time the Second World War broke out Stella was the mother of two sons — Jamie and Lewis, who were five and four respectively. Luckily, she and Rob were home visiting her parents when the Japanese invaded Malaysia and the family therefore spent the war years in the safety of her parents' home in Edinburgh.

Rob, of course, was called up. Naturally, being a Brylcreem boy, he elected to join the Royal Air Force, even though he was judged to be too old to be trained as a pilot. However, he did enjoy being part of the ground control staff and acquired many new skills. Unfortunately, one of these skills, unknown to Stella, was gambling.

The gambling was not a worry when he was sitting in the mess just playing cards for a couple of bob. His addiction became a problem when they went back to Malaysia in 1947. Unknown to Stella, he started to gamble away most of his earnings. Then, probably because he was desperate to pay the boys' boarding school fees back in Edinburgh, he began to put his hand in the till.

The boys were now eighteen and seventeen, ready for university. Stella was delighted to learn from their school reports that both appeared to be doing well enough to be accepted at Edinburgh University. It was while she was still smiling at her sons' reports that she began to think that the social life in Kuala Lumpur was not what it used to be and perhaps she should spend more time at home in Scotland. She had missed her boys when they had gone off to school together and she knew she could not buy the years back. Willingly, and perhaps selfishly, she had given their entire development over to their teachers. She now thought that was a mistake. Perhaps it was not too late to build a relationship with them, if she became part of their university years.

The ringing of the telephone broke into her thoughts. Elated at the thought of spending more time in Edinburgh with her boys, and indeed her mother, as her father had passed on just a few months ago, she lifted the receiver and jauntily said, 'Stella Wise.'

'Stella.' It was the unmistakeable voice of

Crystal Parker. She allowed a long sigh to escape her lips — time hung in the balance — before eventually continuing. 'Look, Stella, you and I have known each other for donkeys years, so we both know I am not a fair-weather friend.' Stella had to stifle a giggle. Crystal was well named, in that she was all sparkle and not much depth. Unaware of Stella's opinion, Crystal continued. 'So, you know when I say if there is anything I can do to assist you until you get back home you just have to ask.'

Stella's mirth now changed to concern, but before she could ask Crystal what she meant the doorbell rang. Knowing that the servants were in the back of the house, Stella said, 'Look, there is someone at the door. Could you hold on, Crystal?'

When Stella yanked open the door she was faced with an errand boy who handed over a letter. Gazing down at the handwriting on the envelope, she realised it was from her husband. But why on earth was he writing to her? Had she not arranged to meet up with him at the club for dinner?

Deciding first things first, she must say goodbye to Crystal before she read the letter, she picked up the telephone receiver and said, 'Sorry about that, Crystal. It is just a letter. Now, you were saying.'

'Stella, I just wish you to know that it was not me that crossed out your name on our invitation list, it was my George. Believe me, I think it is a disgrace that you have been shunned for something your husband has done. Now, do you have your fare home?'

Without another word passing between the two women, Stella hung up. Ripping open the letter, she discovered it started with 'My Darling Stella' — as she read on, she knew it should have read 'Dear John' because that was exactly what this letter was.

According to the letter, he had been foolish — *foolish*! Funds were missing — more than he said he was responsible for, but as he was the last man to be treasurer he freed all others. Stella knew Rob, and she was in no doubt that he was responsible for the shortfall. He had admitted his guilt and he was now completely disgraced and on his way to the airport. He regretted that there were insufficient funds in the bank for her to get home, but he knew that her mother would send on the where-for-all.

Flopping down, she realised the powers that be would have purchased his ticket home. They would not wish the stink he created in their 'superior' ranks to linger a minute more than necessary.

Stella tried to calm her mind. She had to think. Luckily her father, who was never wowed by Rob, had decided to purchase a flat in Goldenacre as a wedding present for her. Dad, of course, had bought the property solely in Stella's name. So at least she would have a roof over her head. Problem was that her mother, who found Castle View too large to reside in alone, was now dwelling in the Goldenacre flat. Castle View was rented out to an Eastern European gentleman. Not to worry, there was enough room for two ladies at Goldenacre until the rental of Castle View expired and they could go back to their family home.

Sitting down at her writing desk, Stella lifted her pen. Tears stung her eyes. Emotion choked. Begging, she would have to do, not only for her fare home but the fees for the boys' school as well. Thank goodness she was an only child, and her mother would not allow her or her children to be affected by the disgrace of Rob's downfall.

★   ★   ★

When at last Stella arrived home in Edinburgh, she went straight to the flat in Goldenacre. She truly believed all she had to do was settle in there until the lease of Castle View was up and she could take over the house again. The house and the flat in Goldenacre were the main assets that her mother and herself now had. Loose change was something neither of them had much of.

Of course, she would need to think of a story to tell her boys. They would have to know why she and their dad had parted company. She didn't wish to burden them with the truth, but what if they heard it from someone else? Having been with the in-crowd in Malaysia, she knew how a dig in the dirt was what some people revelled in. Nothing the mob liked better than kicking a dog when it was down.

Telling the boys the truth, she thought, would be her first priority, but when her mother opened the door her heart sank.

'Mum,' she gasped, as she allowed her suitcase

to drop from her hand. 'What's wrong? Where is your old bright and breezy self?'

Moira Wise just shrugged before motioning to her daughter to follow her into the lounge. She then sat down on the couch and, as she bent over, she wrung her hands. 'Stella, my dear, just when you need me to be strong for you, I require you to be a stalwart for me.'

Stella was now sitting down beside her mother. Instinctively, she put one arm around her mother's shoulders and, with her free hand, she lifted her mother's head up. 'I will be as strong as you need me to be. Now, don't spare me. Tell me the truth. Exactly what is the problem?'

Biting on her lip, Moira nodded. 'Pancreatic cancer,' she whispered.

Stella was shocked. She knew it was a death sentence. 'How long?' she managed to ask, not really wishing to know.

'At the most three months. I know you won't believe me but I was going to ask you to come home and be with me until . . . '

'I'm here now. And everything else will be put on hold until . . . '

★ ★ ★

Tenderly Stella cared for her mother. There was lots of reminiscing and laughing. Mother and daughter made every precious moment count. The only thing they did not count was the days. These days were days of wine and roses. Both accepted that like all wine and roses days there would not be many, but nevertheless they were precious. They were days where the word goodbye would not be mentioned, but in reality they were days of goodbye and thank you. Treasured days that Stella would need to see her through.

Two weeks after her mother's funeral Stella decided to call on the gentleman who was renting Castle View. The term of agreement was up three months ago, however the rental continued to be paid. Because of her mother's illness the arrangement seemed to suit both the renter and Stella. That was then, but now Stella wished to take possession of her family home and put it on the market.

After ringing the doorbell Stella stood back before turning around to look at the gardens that her mother and father had once taken such pride in. Well, she thought, that is something that will have to change before the sale of the house. Why oh why, she thought, has the agent, who was supposed to see that the property was well maintained, allowed my parents' garden to become so overgrown and sad?

She heard a voice behind her. 'Do you have an appointment? If you don't, could I say that Mr Nowak doesn't take on lassies that knock on the door.'

'What do you mean?'

'Look, hen, he's got enough hookers. So you will just have to peddle your wares elsewhere.'

The woman, obviously a cleaner, was about to shut the door when Stella jumped over the threshold.

97

'Look, whatever your name is, I am no hooker. I am Stella Wise, and I own this establishment, so you go and get Mr Nowak immediately.'

'Are you for real?'

'I certainly am. And while I am at it, don't turn up for work here tomorrow because I will have taken my house back into my possession and you and Mr Nowak will both be looking for jobs.'

Five minutes elapsed before Mr Nowak presented himself.

'Look,' he said, 'I have a contract from my cousin which states that I can keep the rental of this house for another six months.'

'That right. Well, I have a will from my mother that states I, and nobody else, owns this house and your cousin's lease has expired. So, sir, you either vacate the property now, or I summon the police. And while I am at it, who gave you permission to use this house as a brothel?'

'Look, lady, there are twelve letting bedrooms — what else would you do with such a property?'

'That, sir, is a decision for me. Now, you have the telephone number of the agents?'

He nodded.

'Good. Now, could I suggest that you ring them and ask that they clarify the situation to you? And when you have done that, please depart from my premises.'

Mr Nowak laughed. 'I sure will get clarification for you. Until I speak to the agents, take a seat and then I will throw you out.'

But Mr Nowak wasn't laughing as he slowly replaced the telephone receiver. 'It would appear that you have the law on your side. Tell you what I propose — how about you and I have a refreshment and a business chat?'

'No! I have nothing further I wish to say to you other than please *vacate* my home and *right now* at that.'

'Don't be so hasty, madam. This wee business here is a gold mine. I could cut you in for a slice of the profit.'

Stella snorted. Rage engulfed her. Why on earth would she wish to have anything to do with this vile, unprincipled man? Truth was, she didn't wish to spend another minute in his company.

'Sir,' she hissed, 'I will not be leaving here today, but you will pack up your belongings and go. If you do not, I will contact the Vice Squad. I will, I assure you, advise them what has been going on and have them not only remove you from my house but also charge you with living off immoral earnings.'

'Vice Squad?' His uproarious cackle echoed around the room. 'Well, you do just that. And be sure to ask for Sergeant Price because he is the one that sorts that side of things out for me!'

Stella was back-footed. Was this man saying that the police knew what was going on here and that for a pay-off they turned a blind eye? She drew in a few long breaths. Keep calm, she told herself. This is your property and he has to go.

'That may be so,' she managed, with conviction, 'but you are on my property and I have rights, so please leave or I will summon the police.'

As it turned out, Mr Nowak was no match for Stella. An hour later, after a few frantic phone calls, the gentleman was packing his bags.

★   ★   ★

To Stella's dismay, throwing Mr Nowak out turned out to be the easiest thing she had to do that day. To her annoyance, she spent the evening explaining to the gawdy ladies who turned up on the doorstep that their services were no longer required. With the exception of none, this information led to the girls spitting out a barrage of abuse at Stella. Three were so incensed that Stella thought she was in danger of being physically assaulted.

If the annoyance of the women was difficult for her to deal with, it was nothing to the pure malice from a few of the *gentlemen* callers.

The news that Castle View had reverted to a dwelling house got around fast. By the third day Stella was no longer dealing with irate or disappointed girls or their punters.

By late afternoon that day she was feeling pleased that she had got things sorted out. This feeling of elation, however, was dealt a chilling blast when her eldest son, Jamie, breezed in and announced that he had been accepted to continue his arts degree in one of the east coast of America's universities.

'Why?' she asked.

He huffed and snorted. 'Because, Mum, the stink of Dad is holding me back.'

'Jamie, don't be silly. It is true that your father

made a few silly mistakes, but he is hardly Dick Turpin. Besides, what he did in Malaysia cannot affect you and Lewis here in Scotland.'

'It does. And how.'

'It can't,' replied Stella, who did not wish to concede that her sons' futures would be affected by what their father had done.

'For the young people I am studying with, it makes no difference. But their parents tell them that I am not to be invited into their homes. Weekend house parties and celebrations are not for us.'

Stella knew that Jamie must have thought long and hard about going to America. To be truthful, it was probably for the best. She also accepted that Lewis would follow him. So, thanks to Rob, she not only lost her way of life but she was also to be punished with the loss of her sons. America would be the place where they would make their home. But even so, they would need financial support. Rob was just two steps out of prison and she had never worked, so what could she be employed at now to provide for her boys? Money, money, money: that was what she urgently required. But where was she going to find that kind of money? She could do some training and then get a job, but Jamie was leaving this month. In the end, she had no choice. Only the sale of a property would release the necessary cash.

Jamie, having got his mum to agree to more than he thought possible, rose to leave. 'Mum,' he said as he pulled her into an embrace, 'I knew that somehow you would come up trumps. That you, being you, the best mum in the world, would find a way to finance Lewis and me going to America.'

Stella breathed in deeply. She couldn't quite believe she had agreed to sell one of her homes to finance her sons' initial years in America. She raised her head and kissed him on both cheeks. 'Off you go now. And Jamie, I will take care of you and Lewis and provide all you require. I am so sorry that you two boys are paying such a high price for your dad's mistakes.'

The door had just closed on Jamie when Stella sank down on an old comfortable armchair. Yes, she thought, I have agreed to sell one of my homes, but this house, where I was raised and was so happy as a child, I do so wish to keep. The flat in Goldenacre Gardens was pleasant enough, but it would not finance one of her boys qualifying, never mind both of them.

Dusk was falling. She should get up and close the drawing-room curtains, but somehow she lacked the enthusiasm to do even that. It was the stringent sound of the doorbell ringing that broke into her apathy. Thinking that perhaps Jamie had forgotten something, she opened the door with a fixed smile on her face. However, when she discovered that the caller was none other than Madge Snodgrass, whose name changed to the slightly more alluring Jasmine when she was working, her smile slipped.

'Now, I have already informed you that you and your like are no longer welcome here,' Stella began, clipping each word. 'And, as a matter of fact, as from today, the house is going on the market.'

'The house is going up for sale?'

'It certainly is.' Madge looked puzzled at Stella's news. 'And before you say another word I simply cannot afford to keep it.'

'Look here, Mrs Wise, let me come in and talk to you.'

Stella felt it was a mistake, but she stood aside and allowed Madge to enter. When they reached the drawing room Stella, being well mannered, indicated to Madge that she should take a seat.

Madge sat down. Her head sank forward. Ever so slowly she raised her head to look directly into Stella's eyes. 'Now, please let me finish before you shoot me down in flames,' she uttered. Stella nodded. 'We . . . that is . . . the top six of us that were working here . . . have had a meeting. As a result of that I am here as the spokeswoman of our group.' Madge paused.

Stella bowed her head so that Madge would not see that she was smiling. Her amusement was for the fact that Madge had just confirmed what she already thought. Yes, even among the ladies of her trade, there was a hierarchy — and she was informing her that the women she represented were top in that pecking order.

'We have an interesting proposal to put to you.'

The words had just left Madge's mouth when Stella's head shot up. 'You wish to what?'

'Put an interesting and *very profitable* proposal to you.'

'Such as?'

'The business carried out here provided a gold mine for that bloke you rented this house to. So

103

we thought, why don't we get you to carry on the service we provide and divvy up the profits between us?'

Stella was dumbfounded into silence. Only short gasps escaped her.

'Mind you,' Madge continued, 'as you have no experience in the business, and let's face it you are a bit long in the teeth to be starting now, we will run the actual business for you . . . naturally for a better slice of the cake.'

'Is that so? Well, I can advise you I have no intention of allowing you to talk me into continuing your sordid trade here and me becoming your madam! Allow me to repeat . . . this house is going up for sale. So could I suggest that you negotiate your ever-so-tempting offer with the new owner?'

The doorbell sounded again. Stella heard the door open before Jamie called out, 'Mum, nothing to worry about, it's only me. Forgot, I did . . . ' He was now in the drawing room and realised that his mother had company. 'Sorry, I didn't mean to barge in. Mum, could I speak to you in the hall?'

Stella rose and followed Jamie out of the room. Closing the door behind her, Stella then looked quizzically at her son. 'Mum,' he haltingly began, 'I should have asked if it was possible that you could give me an advance to help me buy some new clothes and for travelling expenses.' She nodded her assent. 'America is going to be just so great for Lewis and me. Clean off all Dad's dirt.' He hesitated before giving her a hug. 'I do realise that it will be so expensive for you

. . . possibly wipe out all your free cash. But that's you, Mum; you always put Lewis and me before yourself.'

Jamie grabbed for his forgotten hat and then Stella watched him sprint up the path; a young man full of the confidence that by tomorrow his mum would have the ready cash for him.

Stella then leaned against the portal and thought.

Having reached her resolve, she returned to the lounge. As soon as she entered Madge rose. 'I'll be off then,' she said.

'Wait, Madge, or should I call you Jasmine. It would appear that I will have to lay my principles aside and agree to your proposal.'

★   ★   ★

So, much to her chagrin, Stella allowed Castle View to continue as a house of ill-repute. But it should be remembered that, like all mothers, Stella had put the welfare of her children first and her reputation second.

She allowed a month to pass while she watched the ladies' every move. Then slowly but surely, she took over the management of the business. The girls knew better conditions. First, they saw a rise in what they earned. Then they were encouraged to save part of their earnings for any time they were not able to work. They also had regular health checks. Only problem for them was Stella discouraged them from sharing their earnings with a man, be him husband or pimp.

To accomplish all she had rewarded her girls with, the clients too saw a hefty increase in what they paid. As Stella informed them, 'I provide, not through myself, but through my ladies, who have chosen that way of life, a first-rate service. A service that obviously is lacking for you at home or elsewhere! And if you desire, I will even provide you with a nightcap before you leave our company.'

Quickly, the years passed. Madge had become romantically involved with one of her clients, on his part anyway. He had an ailing wife and when she died he decided to make an honest woman of Madge. Everybody was thrilled for her. Not only did she get a ring on her finger but also the comforts of a middle-class life. Madge's departure meant that Stella had to promote one of the ten girls, as there was now a night manager vacancy. She chose Marigold, who would turn out to be an even better manager for her than Madge had been.

The only drawback was that Stella, in her second year in business, had earned herself a criminal record. She was furious. She and her girls were, on occasion — when the council required money, she deemed — summoned to court and fined heftily, in the girls' case, for being prostitutes, and, in her case, living off immoral earnings. Yet the men who paid for sex were exempt. She thought this grossly unfair. She also objected to the girls never being able to get a job outside the trade. No way could their criminal record be expunged. Oh yes, no one would employ them even to serve up fish and chips.

15

It wasn't until she became aware of Kirsten asking if she was all right that Stella realised that, while Kirsten had been consulting a solicitor, she had been reminiscing for going on two hours.

'Sorry, Kirsten, as you age you catnap,' she lied. 'Now, how did you get on?'

'It would seem that I will have no problem getting a divorce on the grounds of desertion. Mr Dobbie, the solicitor who will handle my case, is very confident. I have just to leave it in his hands and he will contact me when he's got everything finalised. Quite positive he was about everything. Even the hefty cost. But it will be money well spent to be rid of Duncan. Now, would you like a cup of tea? By the way, thank you for giving me the time to get it all sorted. If there is ever anything I can do to repay you just ask.'

'No repayment required.' Stella beamed. 'Well done, you.'

★   ★   ★

But two days later when Kirsten arrived for work Stella seemed a bit upset. 'Problem?' Kirsten asked.

'Yes. But I am sure you will be able to help me out.'

'What is it?' Kirsten said, feeling suddenly panicked.

'Don't look so alarmed. It's nothing for us to worry about. Sad as it is, Marigold's mother becoming terminally ill is not unexpected. However, as you know, tonight is my Conservative Party meeting and I have to be in attendance. Next time round we must make sure we elect a Conservative government.' Kirsten was about to ask why, but Stella raised her hand to silence her. 'Your Labour lot always wish to take everything into public ownership. I bet you they would even try it with my business.'

Kirsten had to stifle a giggle, as she imagined the girls all being in a union of sex sellers and given fair and reasonable conditions of employment. Trying to control her laughter, she uttered, 'So you think our Labour government will be in power for a while?'

'I hope not. Mind you, they have their spies everywhere, so they know what we are proposing to get them out. And see that Martin Glover, who recently joined our group.' She now leaned over to confide to Kirsten. 'I am sure he is a Labour mole. Got to keep an eye on him. And so, I have a favour to ask.'

'Ask away.'

'It's just that as Marigold will be staying with her mother tonight, could you stand in and look after the shop?'

Kirsten's eyes widened. Her mouth gaped.

'Just from when I leave at seven until I get back at ten thirty, or the very latest eleven or thereabouts. Please don't say no, Kirsten. It's your patriotic duty.'

'Patriotic duty?'

'Of course. The country is in a mess and the Conservative Party need to save it! If I thought for a minute that your Labour lot had the savvy, I wouldn't ask. Besides, you do owe me a favour.'

Yes, Kirsten nodded, she did owe Stella. She was loath to do it, but her concern for Marigold, who was about to lose her mother, was the deciding factor.

★   ★   ★

That evening Kirsten arrived at Castle View at seven o'clock prompt. Stella smiled when she noted that Kirsten was dressed in a dark skirt and white tie blouse. Even her sensible court shoes gave the impression she was going to a meeting of the Women's Guild.

'Making sure that none of the punters think you are available,' Stella chuckled as she lifted her mink stole and slung it around her shoulders.

'Don't laugh! Molly couldn't do my child-minding, so I had to ask Jeanette. She is the salt of the earth, but I had to tell her I was going to a business meeting with my mother-in-law.'

'Why?'

'Stella, you just wouldn't believe how strait-laced Jeanette is. She is a dear friend but she just has never really approved of me . . . ' No way did she wish to insult Stella, so she hesitated before adding, 'Working here. She really is a . . . puritan.'

'Well, at least she's looking after Dixie and his sisters. Must be off,' Stella chanted, as she skipped her way to the door. 'Any problems tell them to wait until I get back at eleven.'

'Do you think there will be?'

'No. Problems are for others. Not me. They just irritate me. Toodle-oo.'

The door closed. Stella was gone. Kirsten was in charge.

★ ★ ★

The grandfather clock chiming ten caused Kirsten to smile. Everything had gone according to plan. The girls had all arrived for their shifts. Within an hour men were on the doorstep. Money exchanged hands before the clients vacated Castle View. It had all been so much easier than Kirsten had thought.

One hour was all that was left of her obligation. To pass the time she decided to be kind to Mrs Baxter and wash up some of the drinks glasses and coffee cups. The clock had just sounded ten thirty when the doorbell sounded.

Thinking it was Stella, and like everyone else who called at night, the door would need to be unlocked from the inside to allow her to enter, Kirsten dashed to open it. A broad grin came to her face as she turned the key.

'Your punctuality is just great,' she called out as she threw the door open. There, to her consternation, stood a uniformed police inspector and sergeant.

'Good evening, Mrs Wise. I am assuming you are Mrs Wise?' the inspector said, as he gave a polite salute.

'Sir,' the sergeant said, 'this is not Mrs Wise. This lady, I think, must be one of the girls. One I have never met.'

The inspector looked perplexed. True, he had experience of street prostitutes. But he never imagined he would ever meet one in a brothel who dressed like a Sunday school teacher.

'Look, before you get the wrong idea, please come in. I don't wish anyone to see me speaking to you on the doorstep.'

Once they were in the lounge, Kirsten blurted, 'I am just standing in for Stella. She is attending the Tory Party meeting tonight.'

'Be that as it may. We are here because there have been complaints from the residents in Pilrig Street.'

'Don't like the idea of what is going on in here, they don't. And they claim it reduces the value of their property,' the sergeant butted in.

The inspector raised his hand to indicate to the sergeant that he would lead proceedings. 'I am Inspector Eddie Carmichael. I have just been promoted into this division and my colleague is Sergeant Jack Weir. We are here tonight to issue a warning about the business that is being conducted here. The day shift should have issued the warning, but they were too busy. We will also be . . . ' He stopped as he became aware that the young woman before him was beginning to hyperventilate. He looked long and hard at her. She was now causing him problems. Feelings that he never thought he would feel for any woman again were rising up inside him. For goodness sake, he told himself, this woman is probably — no, is — a hooker. So how can I possibly be attracted to her? With difficulty, he got himself in control again. 'As I was saying, I am here to advise Mrs Wise, and any others that are in this establishment tonight, that they are going to be charged with either prostitution or living off immoral earnings.'

By now Kirsten's legs were wobbling like jelly. She couldn't stay upright and flopped down onto a chair. 'Are you saying that I am — ' She swallowed hard. 'That I am to be charged? Please, please try and understand I was only doing Stella a favour.'

'Now, where have I heard that one before?' Sergeant Weir sneered. He then gave a knowing look to the inspector.

'Doing a favour is all I am guilty of,' Kirsten persisted. 'It is true that during the day I keep house and do admin for Stella, but I have never, nor will I ever, do anything else.'

'So, you admit you are paid wages from the business that is carried out here?' the sergeant said.

Kirsten raised her hand to her mouth. She unwittingly had just given the police the evidence they required to charge her with living off immoral earnings. She just couldn't believe she had admitted that she was employed here.

Tears surfaced and, try as she might, she was unable to stop them coursing down her face. All she could think of was what Marigold had told her; that once you got a conviction for either prostitution or living off immoral earnings, then it was more than likely a social worker would be appointed by the courts to see to the welfare of your children. In most cases they deemed that the children, especially girls, were in need of protection, so they were immediately taken into care.

As Kirsten's tortured mind went into overdrive, the doorbell rang. Her natural reaction was to get herself up onto her feet but she was too paralysed with fear to move a muscle.

The person at the door now had their finger on the bell and they obviously were not going to lift it off until they were admitted.

'Look, if you are unable to unlock the door, then give me the key and I will ask Sergeant Weir to do it,' the inspector said.

Nodding to the inspector, Kirsten fished in her pocket for the key.

Sergeant Weir had just left when the inspector said, 'You are getting yourself into a right state. Try taking deep breaths and, as you calm, things will not look as bad to you.'

From where she got the surge of energy she did not know, but looking the inspector in the eyes she spat, 'It is all right for you. You are not a mother. I have three children who depend on me and me alone. Tonight I was doing Stella a favour. And by doing that simple favour my children could end up in care!'

'I think you have got yourself so overwrought that you are seeing the worst scenarios.'

'And what would be the best ones?'

The inspector shrugged. 'Firstly, that no action will be taken against you. Or secondly, you could, and I think most likely, be let off with a warning.'

Sergeant Weir re-entered the room, followed by a bewildered Stella.

'What is going on in here?' Stella demanded. She seemed to have forgotten that when dealing with the police she always gave the impression that she was a naïve, skittish character rather like the mother in *Pride and Prejudice*.

Eddie Carmichael immediately extended his hand to Stella. 'You and I have not met before. I have just been appointed to this division.'

'Good evening,' Stella replied, accepting his hand. 'Now, inspector, given the hour I do wonder if your visit is one of business or pleasure . . . '

'We,' flustered the inspector, 'that is, Sergeant Weir and I, are just doing our duty. Mrs Armstrong here has admitted that she is in your paid employ. Therefore it will be for the courts to decide what her job is and if she is guilty of living off immoral earnings.'

It was true that Stella was advancing in years to the stage where it could be alleged that she was not as bright as she used to be. However, she was still as sharp as a pin. Immediately she realised the problem for Kirsten, whom she could see was upset and anxious.

'Inspector,' she said in a modified tone, 'Kirsten tonight was helping me out. She usually works in the mornings doing shopping, banking, just generally seeing to the house.'

'Maybe so, but she is paid, it could be argued, by ill-gotten money.'

'Technically, yes. But, inspector, I pay her from my purse, so technically it could be argued

114

it is my personal money.'

Eddie pondered.

'Now, while you and I debate on the technicalities, Kirsten needs to go home and relieve her child-minder.' Stella turned to Kirsten. 'Come on, now. Home you go. I will sort all this out. See you in the morning.'

'And a member of the constabulary will also be calling on you to charge you with . . . '

Stella ignored the overzealous sergeant and propelled Kirsten towards the door.

★   ★   ★

It was one o'clock in the morning when Eddie got his break. This was because he had spent nearly an hour with Stella, who tried fruitlessly to persuade him to charge everyone except Kirsten. Time after time she had pointed out that everyone, except Kirsten, already had a criminal record, so one more line on their crime sheet wouldn't matter. Eventually, with great difficulty, he managed to get himself away from Castle View. It was then on to routine duties of meeting up with the beat constables and checking reports.

He should then have gone to the canteen to have some food, but he didn't. He started to walk down Leith Walk towards Balfour Street — a street outwith his divisional responsibilities.

One lower flat dwelling house had a light shining. On checking the number of the tenement, he saw it was the tenement that Kirsten had given as her address. He knew it was madness — he should not be trying to see if the light was coming from her flat. He checked the nameplate and was pleased to note that it read 'Armstrong'. Lightly, he tapped the door.

Within a minute the door slightly opened and Kirsten asked, 'Who the devil are you? And what do you want at this time of night?'

'It is Inspector Carmichael and I just wished to check that you are all right.'

The door was then flung open wide. Eddie was confronted with a pyjama-clad Kirsten. He saw that she was still furious and frantic with worry. 'No, I am not *all right* as you put it. And I am not going to be until I get . . . ' Her voice quivered.

Eddie then stepped forward: he knew he was crossing a line, and not just that which marked the threshold into Kirsten's home. He knew this house was not in his division. It was Leith and his division was Gayfield. He also knew he should not be following up an inquiry by visiting a woman at this hour without another officer present. But still, quietly, he closed the door. He couldn't believe that his instinct was urging him to take her into his arms and comfort her. He was close to throwing caution to the wind when a boy's voice whimpered, 'Mummy, where are you? I'm frightened.'

The change in Kirsten was instant. Running up the hall, she swept Dixie into her arms. 'There, there Dixie. There's nothing to worry about. Mummy is home now.' She then took the boy into the living room, where she sat down, before pulling him onto her knee.

Eddie followed her into the living room. He was then confronted with Kirsten cradling Dixie into her body, soothing him. This image of devout motherly love moved him. He was surprised that, instead of the obvious deep relationship between Kirsten and Dixie putting a damper on the feelings he was experiencing for her, it only inflamed them.

He pondered. 'Your husband?'

Kirsten tittered. 'Oh him, well, he simply didn't like responsibility.' Eddie looked askance. Kirsten then added, 'And, as he thought life wasn't hard enough for us, he did a runner. Left us penniless, he did.'

'You and your little boy?'

Kirsten nodded. 'And, as I told you, I also have two lovely daughters.'

Eddie gazed at the floor. He couldn't understand how any man could do that.

Unaware of Eddie's concern, Kirsten went on dreamlike. 'If it was not for my mother, my mother-in-law and Stella, goodness knows what would have become of us.'

'Are you divorced?' he asked. Somehow it was important to him to know that she was *available*.

'In the process. Then darling Duncan is going to marry another gullible lassie. A native Canadian, apparently . . . The marriage won't last but that's her concern. I have enough to worry about here.' She hesitated. 'Is there no way to stop action against me?'

He shook his head. He wished he could somehow lose the report. But that was impossible for him. For the last ten years all he'd

117

had in his life was his police career. He was an exemplary officer who was known to assist people wherever he could. He could bend the rules slightly, but losing the report for Kirsten would mean losing Stella's, and all her girls' records too. That action was impossible unless he was prepared to face the repercussions and censure. Oh yes, at the very least questions would be asked as to why a police decision to charge the miscreants was not carried out. Looking at Kirsten again, he was filled with a desire to protect her. But duty was duty, so all he quietly said was, 'I will try to put in your mitigating circumstances.'

She now rhythmically began to pat Dixie on the back. Dixie's eyes dropped and flickered. Try as he might to stave off sleep, it overtook him.

Glancing at his watch, Eddie was startled to see that he was now over his break time. He was loath to leave this woman who was having such an effect on him. However, duty called, so with the picture of Kirsten gently cradling Dixie now imprinted in his memory, he took his leave.

Walking briskly back up Leith Walk he became so engrossed in his thoughts that he did not notice two Leith constables on the other side of the road.

★ ★ ★

EDDIE'S STORY

Had it really been ten years since Eddie's life had been torn apart? He'd been a cop in A

118

Division then. Married he was to Anna, his school sweetheart. He tried to think back as to whether it was in primary or secondary school that he had fallen in love with her. He shrugged because when exactly he had begun to care for her didn't matter, only that he did.

He supposed it was natural for them to find each other. They both resided with their parents in the village of Longniddry in East Lothian. They first met in nursery school. Then it was on to the village primary school. Finally, they travelled on the school bus to their North Berwick secondary school. There was the parting of the ways for two years when they left school. Eddie had to do National Service in Korea. It came as a shock to him to find himself in a foxhole shooting at Chinese soldiers. There seemed to be thousands, but if he did kill any of them, by the morning there were no bodies lying about. Meanwhile, Anna started her training to become a physiotherapist.

On his return from Korea he met up with her again at the village midsummer party. It felt inevitable that they should get engaged and then married. By that time, he was a constable in the Edinburgh City Police and Anna, having finished her training, was working at the Royal Infirmary in Lauriston Place.

Three short years after they were wed, his beloved Anna was diagnosed with an aggressive brain tumour. A grade-4 type. When they realised she only had a few short months to live, they went back to Longniddry so her folks could assist him in nursing her.

The four months seemed, to her mum and dad long, too long for their daughter to suffer. But to Eddie and Anna, who wished to spend their life together, far too short. Before the end she had urged him to marry again. To find a lassie who would have his lovely babies. But marrying again was something he had vowed he would never do. He honestly couldn't see himself falling in love again. In the ten years since, he had never wavered. There had been offers — especially from the female police constables in the force. He chuckled as he remembered one of the most ardent, Betty Booth, who as luck would have it was now a sergeant in B Division. As he had also been promoted to B Division, they would probably meet on a daily basis.

He shrugged. He thought up until tonight no other woman would move him as his Anna had. Then out of the blue he came across Kirsten Armstrong. She was a beauty, true; but then so was Betty Booth. There was also the ever-faithful Sylvia, who partnered him whenever he required a social outing companion. Hunching his shoulders again, Eddie tried to think of what exactly it was that was pulling Kirsten to him. It was more than her turquoise eyes and long, soft brown hair. There was something about her. Hadn't he foolishly left the police station to go and find out if she was okay? That was madness. Truth be told, right now he really wished he was back sitting beside her. Taking her hand in his — trying to allay her fears.

Eddie was so engrossed in his thoughts that he really wasn't aware that he had entered the police station until he heard the station sergeant say, 'Evening, sir. Was there a problem you had to attend to?'

He shook his head. 'No, just needed to get some fresh air.'

Before the sergeant could respond, he took the reports the sergeant had prepared for submission the next morning and started flicking through them.

★ ★ ★

The night seemed to be never-ending for Kirsten. The policeman had just left when she got herself and Dixie into bed. Cradling him into her, she was filled with horror at the thought that he and his sisters, Bea and Jane, could be removed from her care. She just could not have that. No use beating about the bush. She was in deep trouble. Oh yes, she realised, to gain some sort of respectability she would have to leave Stella's employ.

'Dear God,' she silently prayed, 'when I arrive before the court, please grant me the ability to persuade the sheriff, or whoever is my judge, that I have never been a . . . ' She gulped before thinking 'prostitute'. She bit on her lip before adding, 'Yes, I will confess that I am guilty of living off immoral earnings because in truth I have. But, Father, I must make them understand that Stella's was the only job I could get that fitted in with my Dixie who needs me so.' She hesitated as she pulled Dixie in closer to herself. 'Dear God,' she earnestly went on, 'help me to get them to understand that I have given up working for Stella and am now . . . ' Now what, she wondered. A cleaner, a cook, whatever job I can get.

Saying Stella's name reminded her that after the children had gone to school she would call on her employer. Call on her not to carry out her duties, but to advise her that she could no longer work for her. She knew Stella would understand why she was leaving her. She knew Stella, like any mother, would know that her children's well-being was her first priority.

16

Bea and Jane had just left for school, and Dixie and Kirsten were already walking along the pavement towards Lorne Street Primary when Kirsten decided to let Dixie catch up with his pals. This allowed her to go straight to Stella's. After all, she had to face Stella and tell her of her decision. No point in waiting until later. The sooner she got it over and done with, the sooner she could be out looking for a job. She started to argue with herself again that if she got a job before her court case, then perhaps she would be kept on, then the thought that after her hearing she would have a criminal record panicked her again.

On arrival at Castle View she was surprised to find everything in order. When she entered the downstairs lounge Mrs Baxter, as usual, asked her if she would like a cup of tea before she got started.

Started? she thought. *After the nightmare of what had happened the previous night she wasn't ever going to get started in here again. She was leaving, and she hoped she'd be gone in the next half-hour!*

Of course, she could think all that, but what she did in response to Mrs Baxter's offer was nod, and before she could respond verbally, Stella breezed into the lounge.

'You're sharp,' Stella chirped. 'I thought with

you being late getting home last night you would be a bit later.'

'Well, with what happened, I thought I should come and talk things over with you.'

'Yes, we should. But I am awaiting a call at about ten before I wish to discuss last night's . . . How can I put it, other than fiasco? By the way, Marigold's mother died. Poor lassie is broken-hearted.'

Before Kirsten could respond, the clock struck the half-hour and the telephone rang simultaneously.

'Castle View,' Mrs Baxter yelled into the receiver. 'I'll just get her. Mrs Wise, it's for you.'

'Did they say who it was?'

'Naw. But he has a posh voice. Ye ken, bools in his mooth.'

After giving Mrs Baxter a warning glare, Stella took the receiver from her.

'Thank you for ringing back so promptly,' she said, with a purr. There was a long silence before Stella uttered, 'Thank you, sir. And I assure you that I will desist from asking another favour from you.' Another silence. 'Yes, and I will think long and hard about the position I have put you in. Next time you are in to visit Delores, do join me in a drink first.' Silence, then a cheery, 'Goodbye.' The receiver was then replaced in its cradle.

Stella turned her attention to Kirsten.

'That was the call I was awaiting.'

'Stella,' Kirsten interrupted. 'I came in this morning to say I can no longer work here. I must — '

'Kirsten, that telephone call I just took was from one of our clients and he has — '

'Please hear me out. I have to put my children's safety first.'

'My dear, there is no problem. You will not be going to court. Charges against you have somehow . . . disappeared.'

'How?'

'I called in a favour. In my type of work, it is wise to have a few favours in the bank.'

'That may be so. But you and I know that there will be a next time and a next time. And eventually the bank of favours will be bankrupt! Stella, please . . . try and understand that if I were to lose my children I would simply curl up and die. Your boys are adults and they live in America. Nothing here touches them except the money this place makes.'

Stella nodded. She liked Kirsten. She also understood that Kirsten, like her, had made sacrifices for her children. She accepted that, even although she had sorted this problem, Kirsten was right in thinking that this week or the next there could be an overzealous police officer who would charge her again. She sighed.

'So, Stella . . . ' Kirsten's eyes now implored her employer. 'Believe me when I say that I am grateful to you for giving me work. I now count you as a dear friend. Although I will not be in your employ I will still come to visit you.' She smiled before adding, 'And from time to time I will even bring Dixie because I know how fond you are of him.'

'Know something,' Stella smiled. 'If you had a

bob or two I could have steered you into a new business.'

'A new business?'

'Yes, there is a small family hotel in York Place that has come up for rent. You could make a go of it there. There's always money to be made between the sheets.'

'You mean you think I could start up a new . . . a new . . . place like this!'

'No!' Stella winked, but her tone was serious. 'There is money to be made from travellers and visitors staying the night. Ask any hotelier and they will tell you. Edinburgh is such an attractive city that it is always full of tourists.' Stella grew wistful, and more to herself she mumbled, 'Would love to have gone for it myself. Would have liked that, so I would. Get away from this.' She waved her hand.

'Why don't you?'

'Because, Kirsten, that bijoux of a hotel may be rundown but it has a liquor licence and because I have a criminal record I would not be granted the tenancy.'

If she was being completely honest, Stella could have added, *If my son Jamie didn't see me as a cash cow, I could have advanced you the money to start up there. I would, of course, have remained a silent partner.* Stella was, as she did every day now, thinking about Jamie. America had sent him packing back home two years ago. Evidently, they had enough spongers of their own; they therefore did not require any immigrants to add to their number. He had settled down in London on his return from the

USA. However, every week he pestered her for money. He was like his father. He would neither work nor want. As to having any scruples, again like his dad, they were in short supply.

Kirsten got to her feet. They both knew it was time for her to leave. Time for her to look for alternative employment. Firmly, they shook hands, and Stella wished Kirsten well. Her only regret was that she could not go with her.

Once outside Castle View, for reasons she would never quite understand, Kirsten decided that she would seek out the letting agency for the hotel. *Just suppose, she thought, that I could raise the setting-up money. Would that not be a great step forward? A little hotel in York Place that was, after all, in the centre of Edinburgh, so it could not fail as a business.*

★ ★ ★

Eddie had just reported for his night duty shift when the back shift station sergeant informed him that the chief superintendent was still on the premises. Not only that, but he wished, no insisted, that Eddie go up and see him immediately.

The chief super, Donald Nicholson, was an Isle of Lewis man. He was a strict Protestant who abhorred alcohol, sins of the flesh and he strictly observed the keeping of the Sabbath holy.

Eddie had worked under his supervision before, when Eddie was a rookie cop in A Division and the chief super was then a sergeant. He smiled as he recalled how Donald Nicholson had confided to him that the drinking of *alcohol* was going on in the pubs close to the police station. Eddie had thought then that the man was a bit too much of a zealot. So much of a zealot that whenever he was promoted he sold his house and bought one in the divisional boundaries of his new charge so he could keep an eagle eye on all that was going on. Now, as Eddie climbed the winding staircase up to the managerial floor, he wondered, no, *knew*, that for the chief super to have stayed on for a face-to-face meeting, something serious was about to be discussed.

He just finished rapping on the door when a gruff voice called, 'Come in.' Obeying the summons, Eddie was confronted by the chief super, who, by the expression on his face, looked like he had just swallowed a stinging nettle. Before Eddie could say, 'Good evening, sir,' Donald spat, 'Get this straight, I run a tight ship here, and I don't wish to be contacted by the commander of another division asking, no demanding, to know why one of my inspectors was visiting a house in Balfour Street at the unholy hour of one in the morning.'

'Sir,' Eddie interrupted, 'we had occasion to call at Castle View and the lady in Balfour Street — '

'Lady? There are no ladies employed at Castle View.'

'If you would hear me out, sir. The lady concerned is a lone parent. She has three children . . . one of whom, her son, seems to be very dependent on her. Naturally, when she saw last night how precarious her position was, she got very upset. To date she has no criminal record.'

'All that tells me is that this Kirsten Armstrong has worked for years for Stella Wise while the troops on the ground have been failing to do their job properly.'

'Again, I ask you to hear me out,' Eddie said, trying not to grow too frustrated. 'I called on her because I was concerned. She was so horrified by the thought of going to court that I just wished to ensure ... and I also wished to double-check that the correct procedures had been followed in her case.'

'Oh, so you thought perhaps you could have the case concerning her dropped?' The chief super smirked. 'And what would you have expected from her in return?'

'Sir, it is true that I have been a widower these last ten years, but never in that time have I misused my authority where women are concerned.'

The chief super huffed. In a voice full of scorn, he said, 'Your concern for the lady and her children does you credit. And I am pleased that you did not try and withdraw her report. But as to the lady ... ' He stopped to snort. 'I have to advise you, Inspector Carmichael, that she obviously has clients in high places because I have been asked, mind you not instructed, to somehow lose her summons.'

Eddie had not been asked to sit down but now, without permission, he slumped down on a chair. He was gutted. Someone on high had leaned on this Holy Willy in front of him. He knew it would be against the chief's strict principles to do what he had been asked to do, but still he would do it. Holy he was, but to the high command he was also a crawler. So, thanks to someone's intervention, Kirsten Armstrong would not have to appear before a sheriff to plead her case. Eddie heaved a sigh of relief as he accepted that the report on her was now in the confidential waste bag awaiting incineration.

'Is that all, sir?'

'No. Could I suggest rather than visit women of questionable character in the early hours you get yourself a respectable wife. Someone like mine perhaps?'

Please God, no, Eddie thought. He remembered, all too well, attending a wedding where Mrs Nicholson was also a guest. He almost smirked as he recalled her reaction when she caught a glimpse of the slightly merry young bride showing her groom her blue garter. 'What is the world coming to?' Mrs Nicholson had cried, as she feigned a half faint, 'When wives are showing their husband the top of their stockings?'

Eddie got to his feet, but the chief super was not finished. Waggling his beefy finger at Eddie, he added, 'As I have just said, get yourself a respectable wife. Stay away from that Kirsten Armstrong. She will stall your career.'

'Why would she do that?'

'Your association with her will be seen by those on high as unbecoming of a police officer . . . especially a senior one.'

After this warning, Eddie was allowed to make his escape. As he descended the stairs, his mind was in turmoil. Was he wrong about Kirsten Armstrong? She was lovely; in fact she was more than lovely, she was quite enchanting. And he was touched, too, by how very maternal she was. She had awakened feelings in him that he thought were dead forever. But she clearly had friends in high places. What friends? And how did they know her? He felt baffled, but it was clear that they obviously knew her so well that they were prepared to go out on a limb for her.

17

Kirsten spent the morning touring around Leith trying to find work. However, the jobs available — cleaner, shop assistant, usherette, undertaker's assistant — did nothing to inspire her. But then, she thought, they wouldn't. Not after Stella had waxed lyrical about her running her own hotel. *To hell with it*, she thought, *I'm going to the letting agent's in Queen Street. I'll ask them what exactly they're looking for in a tenant.*

If nothing else, her work at Stella's had made Kirsten bold. She charmed the agent's receptionist, and was delighted to learn that she met most of their necessary criteria — except, of course, the ready finance to upgrade the hotel. The sweet-natured lassie even suggested that she take the keys and go and look over the property.

As York Place was only a hop, skip and jump away from Queen Street, Kirsten gladly accepted her offer and made her way to the hotel.

As she mounted the five steps and stood in front of the large wooden door to the hotel — which, on closer inspection, she saw was in need of a lick of paint — Kirsten felt herself become bewitched.

She didn't dwell on the work that would be required to make the place habitable: all she could see was the potential. In fact, she could actually picture herself standing in the hotel lobby proudly welcoming foreign visitors. Indeed, she knew instantly that if she did not try and find a way to get the money to finance the upgrade, she would have failed herself.

But how? Who had ready cash? Who would oblige her with a loan?

Kirsten immediately thought of Stella. She could almost bet Stella would jump at the chance to be a silent partner in the venture. But then slowly she shook her head. Normally she would have asked Stella, but she'd noticed how, of late, even though her business was on the up and up, her former employer seemed always to be short of ready cash.

As she closed the door on Stella, Kirsten became momentarily despondent.

Then, as if touched by a magic wand, her shoulders relaxed. A broad grin came to her face. Of course, she knew where to go for a big fat loan. Where else other than Jessie, her formidable mother-in-law? With a literal skip about the entrance hallway, Kirsten was sure she would only have to say to Jessie that it would be better for the children, especially the girls, if she was in *respectable* employment and Jessie would, despite all the differences between them, help out.

When she returned the key, Kirsten assured the receptionist of her very real interest. She was only too pleased to give the lassie her particulars.

★   ★   ★

Kirsten wasted no time in hurrying on the bus to Jessie's Granton home, where she rang the bell.

It struck her as strange that there was no yelping and snarling, and no sound of Brutus charging up the hallway. After a few minutes the door opened ever so slightly.

'Who's that there?' Jessie demanded.

'It's only me. Kirsten.'

'Thank God it's you, Kirsten. Just wait until I take the chain off the door.'

Once the chain was removed Jessie flung the door open wide and grabbed Kirsten into a strong embrace.

Bewildered, Kirsten asked, 'What's wrong?'

'Sssh. Come in and shut the door. I don't want anybody to ken.'

Once they were in the living room, Jessie sighed. 'Oh, Kirsten, thank goodness my God answered my prayers and sent you.'

Kirsten had never before felt that Jessie was so pleased to see her. Amazed, she looked about the living room. Nothing seemed to be amiss, so what was the matter with her mother-in-law? Then she remembered the dog. Relieved, she smiled when she saw Brutus asleep in his basket. Going warily over towards him, Kirsten bent down to clap the dog. It was then she realised that something was wrong. Normally the dog would have been awakened by the ring of the doorbell; certainly he would have sensed company and begun to bark.

'Is Brutus ill?' she asked, turning to look at Jessie.

'Aye, awfy ill. So much so that he's deid!'

'What happened?'

'You ken how he likes chasing cars. Well, we

were out at the shops and on oor way hame he ran off the pavement to annoy a car.' Jessie sniffed. 'The swine saw him and swerved into my wee darling. I picked him up and he seemed okay. Carried him hame, put him in his basket. Later, he didnae seem to be moving. I lifted him up and I . . . oh, Kirsten, do you think he was deliberately hit because someone is coming to rob me?'

'Shh, no. Of course not.'

'Loved that wee rascal, so I did.' Jessie was now crying. 'He was my pal — my companion — my guard.'

This was a side of Jessie that always surprised Kirsten. She was hard as nails. But she could be so kind to an underdog. Kirsten nearly sobbed herself when she recalled the moment Jessie first saw Dixie; how she said, 'Oh son, we will need to get some meat on your bones.' From that first minute, there was no doubt she loved him — she had a special place in her heart for him, which meant she would always try to make life easier for him. And Brutus — well, he was her dog, but in truth he was a terrier, a bad-tempered one at that, and his bark was indeed worse than his bite. Kirsten shrugged before going over to rub Jessie's arm.

'Now steady on, Jessie, calm down. The first thing we have to do is wrap Brutus up in something and then bury him. Then we have to talk.'

All Jessie could do was nod.

An hour passed before Kirsten and Jessie were in the kitchen washing their hands. Brutus, of course, had been wrapped snugly in his best blanket before being buried in the backyard.

Kirsten smiled as she dried her hands; remembering how Jessie had asked if they should say a prayer and sing a hymn. Kirsten had suggested that a silent prayer from them both would suffice.

They had just sat down to settle themselves with a cup of tea together when Jessie said, 'Kirsten, are you sure I will be safe tonight? I still think that driver deliberately targeted Brutus so that he could come and hit me.'

'But, Jessie, do you not keep most of your money in the bank?'

'Bank? If I did that, they would ken how much I was making and I could end up . . . having to pay tax, and what's worse than that?'

'How much do you keep in the house?'

'All I have.'

'And how much is that?'

'Well, the last time there wasn't something decent on the telly I counted it and it took me three hours. Must be . . . '

'Thousands?' butted in Kirsten.

'Well, aye.' Jessie shifted uneasily. 'And I'm no' wanting robbed of it.'

Well, Kirsten thought, with a bit of luck you will be robbed, but by me, who will repay you every brown penny.

Kirsten smiled. 'To be truthful, Jessie, I came today to see if you could lend me some of that money. You see, I have a business opportunity, but I need a few thousand pounds to take advantage.'

'A few thousand! Am I hearing right?' Jessie hollered.

'Aye, but it's a good venture I would be putting it into. A wee rambling old hotel in York Place.'

'Kirsten, if you are saying you want to start up a brothel with help from me . . . ' Jessie coughed and spluttered. 'The answer is a definite no. I have my standards, and money lending to someone who is hard up is one thing but a — '

'Jessie, stop. You know me, so you know there is no way I would open up . . . well, anything like Stella's business. Besides, the powers that be might turn a blind eye to Stella's business tucked away in Pilrig, but no way would they allow such an establishment in the city centre.'

'That so? Well, what are you going to do with this old hotel?'

'Just as it says in the advertisement — look here.' Kirsten showed Jessie the details from the agent. 'I'll turn it back into a small, upmarket, friendly hotel. It was that, before it went a wee bit ramshackle, but it still has a licence.'

'A licence for what?'

'To serve drinks to the guests.'

Jessie contemplated. 'So, you are thinking you and I could go into the hotel business together?'

'Not exactly in business together,' she managed to stammer, wrong-footed. 'What I thought was perhaps you could lend the money for me to get started.'

A long silence fell between the two women. Eventually Jessie said, 'First of all, I will need to see this place you want to start up in. Second, I will put up the cash you require, but only on condition that you and I become partners.'

'What do you mean? You have a business here.'

'True, but I won't feel safe here now my Brutus has been murdered.'

'Oh, Jessie! He was hardly murdered.'

'And what do you call someone driving their car right into him? See, if I didnae want my customers to see the police calling on me I would have reported that swine.'

'So, because of Brutus, you're now thinking of leaving here and going into another kind of business?'

'Aye, Kirsten. You've inspired me. I can just see it!'

'See what?'

'You and I running oor ain wee hotel. All respectable! Mind you, I will hae to see it first before I put my life's hard-earned cash at risk.'

A long sigh escaped Kirsten. She could see it all now. She would submit an application to take over the hotel, even although it meant going into business with Jessie. She hesitated as she considered if it would be worth paying such a high price. But before she could give the situation any more thought Jessie produced two large pillowcases.

To Kirsten's amusement, Jessie then went around the house — into drawers, cupboards, tops of wardrobes, and even the bread bin itself, from which she pulled out bundles of money. The cash was then hurled into the pillowcases, as Kirsten held them open, as instructed.

* ★ ★

If Kirsten hoped there was a chance of Jessie changing her mind when she saw how much work had to be done in the hotel, she had another think coming. The minute Jessie put her foot over the threshold she too was captivated.

'Hmm,' she observed. 'The folk we would be renting from, are they no' responsible for squaring up any of the mess here?' she asked.

'Yes and no. According to the law the premises must be wind- and watertight . . . which they are. They also must ensure we have running water coming in and sewage going out.'

'And that's all?'

'No, they also must provide electricity,' replied Kirsten, before switching the light in the hallway on and off.

'How many renting rooms?'

'Ten at present, but I intend to subdivide four of the large rooms, so that would give us fourteen and the three attics.'

'Nae guests going in the attics.'

Kirsten shook her head. 'No, they'll be the live-in quarters for any staff that need it.'

After that there was the tour of the hotel, with very little comment from either Jessie or Kirsten. However, when they reached the attics, Jessie started to make clucking noises.

'Problem?'

'Naw, naw. No' a problem, Kirsten . . . far from it. Just thinking, I am, that the first thing we will do is get the biggest of these three attic rooms done up.'

'Why?'

'Because that will be my room and I need to move in right away.'

Kirsten gaped.

'Remember, I told you it was time for me to move on from Granton. Biding here,' she said, clutching a pillowcase in each hand, 'will suit me just fine. And think of the bonus, Kirsten. I will be on hand during all of the renovations. Keep an eye on everything, I will.'

How Kirsten longed to backtrack, to not agree to Jessie being her partner. That boat, she reluctantly conceded, had sailed. Besides, she was so keen to take up this hotel offer and build a new life for herself and the children . . . So much so that if putting up with Jessie every day was the price, it was a price she would be prepared — in fact, happy now — to pay.

After the hotel tour, Kirsten suggested that instead of Jessie taking home the money in the pillowcases it would be wiser, in fact necessary, for them to open up a bank account. Reluctant though she was to part with her life's earnings, Jessie agreed, so they crossed over the road to Picardy Place and entered the Bank of Scotland Green-side branch.

They dumped the pillowcases on the counter and, naturally, the manager was summoned. 'Where did you get this money?' he asked.

'My mother-in-law's life savings, that is,' Kirsten replied, as she pushed the bundles nearer the cashier. 'She is now afraid of being robbed so she has decided to deposit it here.'

'That's right,' Jessie emphasised, before giving

the bundles one last loving pat.

'You wish the account to be in both your names?'

'Aye, going together into the hotel business, we are, isn't that right, Kirsten?'

'Well, with a bit of luck we are.'

★   ★   ★

Anyone entering the estate agent's office would have thought that Jessie and Kirsten were strangers to each other. Both were sitting bolt upright, immersed in their own thoughts. Both were apprehensive — very apprehensive.

Kirsten was wondering, as the estate agent made his necessary enquiries, if anyone had suggested that she was of questionable character. She also was sure that the bank would have said that the account, although very healthy, had been opened only two short weeks ago. Meanwhile, Jessie was feeling bereft, now that her bundles of cash were sitting in the bank in Greenside. Sleepless nights, she'd had, since she was parted from it. She was now beginning to think she had been foolhardy.

'Mrs Armstrong, Mr Hamilton will see you now,' the receptionist said, wakening both women from their thoughts. They followed her to an inner office.

When Mr Hamilton shook her hand, Kirsten relaxed. It seemed to her that it was a friendly handshake. Jessie, by now, was in two minds. On the one hand, she hoped that Mr Hamilton would say that they were not getting the lease of

141

the hotel. She would then go immediately to the bank and ask for her money back. She missed the comfort it gave her when she counted the piles of worn notes and found it to be all present and correct. But, on the other hand, she would like to start up a business within that wee hotel. There she could maybe be somebody. Earn the respect she felt she deserved.

'Right now, ladies,' Mr Hamilton was saying, 'all that is required is for you both to sign the lease papers, then you can take over the hotel.'

Kirsten and Jessie exchanged worried glances before they embraced each other and chuckled.

'Now, are you intending to change the name from York Hotel?'

'We are,' Jessie replied before Kirsten could say a word. 'Armstrong we both are, and oor hotel will simply be Armstrong's.'

Before accepting Jessie's reply as fact, Mr Hamilton looked at Kirsten for confirmation. She could have said no, but that would have ended up with Jessie and her having their first managerial difference of opinion. She knew they would have plenty of those very soon, and that the name of the hotel was a trivial matter, so better to wait until a more serious issue arose. She nodded her head in assent and gave her mother-in-law a weak smile.

18

The monthly get together of B Division, or the 'greeting meeting' of the senior officers, was drawing to a close. All matters, concerns and special duties of the division had been discussed. Looking around the assembly, the chief superintendent allowed his bottom lip to protrude out and cover his upper lip. All around the table knew he was about to discuss with them something of serious concern.

'Gentlemen,' he began, 'before I get down to what happened at the chief constable's meeting at Police Headquarters yesterday, I wish to go over something that is going to seriously affect us.' He grunted before continuing. 'As you are all aware, the tenancy of one of the York Place hotels has been granted to the two Armstrong women. One who, in my opinion, is a Shylock, a money lender who held the poor, firstly in Admiralty Street and latterly in the Granton area.' He hesitated. 'Now, how can I put it other than held the poor to *ransom*. The other . . . ' He paused again to inhale and exhale deeply. 'The other was in the employ of Stella Wise. We have been,' he feigned a cough, 'persuaded to accept that this lady was not one of the prostitutes and did not realise that by being employed by Stella Wise, a 'madam', she was therefore guilty of living off immoral earnings. The foregoing being true, and as there was not one witness to accuse either women of any ... let's say, misde-meanour, when we were asked if there was any reason they should not be allowed to have the liquor licence transferred for the York Hotel to them, all we could say was that there was none.'

Eddie Carmichael's hackles rose. Why was this man so against Kirsten Armstrong? A solicitor, even a ham one, would have had her freed, with at the most a caution. The evidence wasn't there. Before he could stop himself, he said, 'Sir, I think in the case of Kirsten Armstrong the only thing she is guilty of is a certain naivety.'

Finlay McKenzie, who was sitting next to Eddie, shifted his foot to nudge Eddie's. Hoping, he was, that Eddie would take it as a warning not to interrupt the chief super when he was in full flight.

The chief super snorted before replying, 'Naivety of what exactly, Inspector Carmichael?'

All eyes were now on Eddie. 'In that she didn't realise the money she was earning at ... '

'The brothel?' interjected the chief super.

'Yes, sir, the brothel — would be counted as living off immoral earnings.'

Finlay again nudged Eddie's foot. This time Eddie took the warning and lowered his head in submission.

'Right, gentlemen, I trust I can now continue without any further interruptions.' He then coughed before saying, 'So, with regard the hotel in York Place, which is now to be known as Armstrong's, I wish you all, from time to time, to give discreet attention to what is going on in there. Not on my watch do I wish to find out

144

that under our very noses, and a mere three-minute walk from the station here, it has turned into another ... I think you get my meaning, gentlemen.'

Eddie wished to protest again, but as his right hand was now resting on the table Finlay covered it with his. This time the warning was a tight squeeze.

'That is all, gentlemen,' the super confirmed. However, before the assembly left the room he pointedly requested Eddie to stay behind, as he had matters he wished to discuss with him.

As soon as the last officer had left and the door was firmly closed the chief superintendent invited Eddie to come up to the top of the table. The super sighed. 'You know, Carmichael, I was pleased to accept you on to my team here. You and I have known each other a long time. Indeed, we have followed each other as we have progressed. I have always considered you to be an outstanding officer.' He paused. 'But your judgement over the Armstrong woman has caused me to question that.'

Eddie opened his mouth, but the chief put up his hand to indicate that he should remain silent.

'Now, I am instructing you to do as your fellow inspectors will do. I wish you all to keep an eye on the Armstrong ladies, and in particular that Kirsten one. However, in your case I am asking you — no, *instructing you* — not to call on their premises late on the backshift and never, do you hear me, never ever on the nightshift.'

Eddie was about to protest. But he knew any protest would fall on deaf ears, and so he just

145

shrugged before nodding his agreement.

On arrival in the inspectors' room Eddie was surprised that only Finlay McKenzie was still there.

'How did it go?' Finlay asked.

'Why on earth is he holding such a grudge against Kirsten?' Eddie expounded.

'Kirsten, is it?' Finlay bristled. 'Look, I know old Nicholson can go on and on about things ... especially if they are at variance with his strict religious beliefs. But, on the plus side, he is an outstanding officer. Never does he stray from the rulebook. Being asked — and before you say a word, we all know that he was asked — to lose the Kirsten Armstrong papers, that really must have rankled him. Believe me, his conscience must have been sorely tried when he binned that report.'

Eddie nodded. 'I know all that, but he is wrong about Kirsten Armstrong.'

'That right?'

'Aye. There is something about her.'

Finlay inhaled. He shook his head. He pondered. 'Look, Eddie, you and I have known each other since our football days on the force. So you know I am speaking as a friend. Ten years you have been mourning Anna and it is great that at last you're thinking about getting another woman into your life ... but Kirsten Armstrong?'

'I am not saying I am thinking of Kirsten in those terms,' Eddie protested. 'But if I was, what would be so wrong with that?'

Throwing his arms out in despair, Finlay

replied, 'Man, you don't need to ask me that, you already know what is wrong. Things where she is concerned don't add up. Even if you give her the benefit of the doubt where working for Stella Wise is concerned, who on earth is bank-rolling the upgrade of the hotel?'

'Her mother-in-law is bound to have built up a fair bank balance with the money lending.'

Finlay shook his head. He conceded to himself that trying to get Eddie to see sense at this moment in time was more than useless. He was smitten with Kirsten Armstrong. Wish to goodness, he thought, that there was a Divisional Dance coming up where Eddie could be paired off again with Sylvia Sanderson. The sweet-natured Sylvia, who had been following Eddie around like a lovesick puppy these last ten years. Everybody could see she was throwing her cap at him — everybody, that was, except Eddie.

'By the way,' Eddie said, keen to change tack, 'before we go our separate ways home, I wanted to let you know that, as I've been playing for the police football team for over a decade now, I've decided to hang up my boots.'

'Surely you're joking?' Finlay replied. 'Football has been the only outside interest you've had since, well, since Anna died. To give it up — is that not foolhardy?'

'No, you've got the wrong handle. I am not giving it up, just moving on and making way for the young lads to charge up and down the field.'

'What do you mean?'

Eddie grinned. 'I've joined the Football Committee as manager. My first outing will be to accompany the team when they go to Northern Ireland in three weeks.'

'You are going to Belfast with the team?'

'Yeah. And I can't wait for them to play the Belfast City team.'

'Does the chief know?'

Eddie rolled his eyes. 'Knowing how he feels about football, I've requested annual leave for the four days I will be absent. By the way, as you are treasurer, surely you will be going too?'

'Yeah, and I'm a coward like you. I've taken leave to cover the trip. The things you do when you hang up your boots, eh.'

19

As soon as Aileen found out that Kirsten and Jessie were going to go into the hotel business she was on the next ferry out of Shetland. The ferry, bound for Aberdeen, arrived on time, which meant that Aileen was quickly on board the train for Edinburgh. She was in such a rush to see that Kirsten was at last turning respectable that she nearly hailed a taxi in Princes Street. But then she remembered that money to do up the hotel may be short so there was no sense in wasting any. Besides, York Place was only a hop, skip and jump down Leith Street.

On arrival at Armstrong's Hotel Aileen smiled when she saw the overloaded skip on the street. It confirmed that all Kirsten had told her about her and Jessie being given the lease of the hotel was true. Thinking that finally Kirsten had seen sense and was at last going to earn her living in a proper and respectable way pleased her beyond belief.

Skipping up the five steps, she saw the door already stood ajar and walked inside.

The first person to greet her was Dixie. 'Grandma Aileen, Grandma Aileen!' he blurted as he hurled himself through the debris in the hall to greet her.

'Careful, my love,' Aileen said as she swept him up into her arms.

'Mummy,' Dixie shouted, 'Granny Aileen is here.'

Aileen had to choke back the tears. She was always emotional at how Dixie, no matter how long it had been since he had last seen her, was overjoyed at her arrival. To her he had achieved so much by just surviving those first difficult months. Kirsten had certainly smoothed his rocky road. Even though Kirsten had not been brought up in Shetland, where the children and their welfare were paramount, Aileen had been sure to rear her daughter in the Shetland way.

Before Aileen could reflect further, Kirsten arrived. 'Great that you were able to come to help us, Mum. Now, Dixie is a big boy so put him down.'

'I don't want down,' Dixie protested.

'Yes, you do! You're too big for those long cuddles. Besides, we're going to show Granny the hotel.' Kirsten now turned her full attention to Aileen. 'Don't look at all that requires done. Just use your imagination to think what it will look like when we have got it finished.'

Twenty minutes later Kirsten and Aileen arrived in the attics.

'So, you have one room nearly finished and someone is in residence?'

'Yeah, but Jessie is not yet quite in residence. As you can see there are still no curtains on the window.' Kirsten tittered. 'You know, Mum, for the guest rooms we are having the drapes made by Jenners.'

'Jenners! Have you won the pools?'

'No, but as we want the rooms looking first class we decided not to stint on the soft furnishings.'

'And the attics?'

Kirsten smiled. 'Mum, you know how you left your old treadle Singer sewing machine with me when you went back to Shetland?'

Aileen relaxed. She smiled broadly. She just felt so pleased with her daughter. At last she had got her act together. 'So, you are going to make the curtains for the attics yourself?' Aileen said, playfully nudging Kirsten.

'Well, not really. You see, since you gave me the machine, I have never used it . . . even to turn up a hem. But I thought if you went up to Remnant Kings at Newington you could purchase the curtain material for the attics and run them up before you go home, maybe?'

Aileen was about to protest but, as she looked around, she could see that it would be at least six months before the hotel was anywhere near ready for opening. This being so, she nodded to indicate that she would, indeed, spend her time sewing while she was here.

Within days the attic windows were looking smart and fashionable. And as Aileen had time she also set about making matching duvet covers. She smiled, thinking it was just like Kirsten to see that the recently introduced duvets from Scandinavia were the thing of the future and were therefore a must for her stylish hotel.

*   *   *

It was a bright, sunlit Saturday. Aileen had just returned to Shetland. Jessie was now in

151

residence in the attic of Armstrong's Hotel. And an overall-clad Kirsten was going over the subdivision details for the next week's work schedule with the foreman joiner. It was just then that Inspector Eddie Carmichael decided to call.

Kirsten looked up at him questioningly.

'I thought I would just check up and see how things were going with you,' Eddie said as he allowed his eyes to sweep about the litter-strewn entrance hallway.

Ignoring him, Kirsten instead turned to the joiner. 'Thank you. You have explained everything very well. I look forward to seeing the first of the four rooms to be subdivided. As agreed, if it works as I think it will, we will then go on and convert the other three. Now, as I have once more to deal with our constabulary.' She gave a long sigh before adding, 'Who it would appear has nothing better to do than check up that I am adhering to the conditions of my building warrant, I must bid you good day!'

The joiner took his leave. An uneasy silence fell between Eddie and Kirsten. Both appeared to wish to stay mute. However, Dixie bouncing a ball, scampered into the room.

'It's a goal,' he shouted, as he kicked the ball against the wall.

'You like football, son,' Eddie said, as he kicked the stotting ball back towards Dixie.

'Love playing it.' Dixie stopped before adding with a smile, 'I'm a Hibee supporter.'

'Oh, so you support the Hibernian. I'm going there this afternoon.'

Dixie's mouth gaped. 'Are you really going to

see the game? Could I come with you?'

'Sorry, son, I couldn't take you today. You see, I am on match duty. But in two weeks you and I could go and spectate at the Edinburgh derby together.'

'I don't want to spectate. I just want to see the match.'

Eddie grinned. Kirsten was fuming. 'Dixie, the policeman is a stranger and you know how I don't allow you to go away with strangers . . . especially officious ones. Now shush, please.'

'Look, please don't be angry. Try and understand that our chief just wishes us to make sure that your alterations are not going to cause any problems.'

'Such as?'

'Well, skips are traffic hazards.'

'Granted, but so far they have all been located outside on the road adjacent to the kerb — true?' Kirsten's eyes swept the inner area of the hotel. 'And certainly not on the pavement or in the hotel here!'

Eddie nodded. He looked at Kirsten. He could see she was no fool. Indeed, she had worked out that the chief was making sure that she was not going to be running a questionable establishment on his patch. No way would he tolerate a city centre hotel where there would be extras on offer. Like all other establishments in his division, Armstrong's would toe the line.

Eddie's eyes were now drawn to Kirsten's. They were, as he knew, the most attractive shade of turquoise. Today, because she was angry, they were even more enticing as they sparkled and glinted. It was true, her working attire, which was covered in muck, did nothing to enhance her youthful figure, but there was still something very attractive about her. As he appraised her, she tossed her soft brown hair. As it slowly spread out, the old magic that she cast over him started to again rise up in him. He wished to suppress it, but try as he might it was beginning to overwhelm him. Common sense then told him to flee, to put distance between himself and this madness, but he stayed rooted to the spot.

'Mum, I don't want you to talk about skips,' Dixie said, interrupting his thoughts. 'I need you to talk about football. Talk about the Hibees.'

Before Kirsten could reply Jessie, carrying a bucket of water, strode into the entrance area. As soon as she saw Eddie she exclaimed, 'Oh no, not another one. Look, Kirsten, have you robbed a bank or something?'

'No, nor have I disembarked from a spacecraft. But I am in danger of assaulting the next police officer who puts his size ten feet over our threshold.'

Sucking in her cheeks, Jessie nodded. 'I wondered how long it would be before you started to fight back.'

'And why would she require to be fighting back? By the way, I am Inspect — ' Eddie began before Jessie interrupted.

'Well, whatever inspector you are, let me tell you this, that ever since we took over this hotel there have been more police officers reporting for duty here than there have been at police headquarters.'

154

'Granny Jessie,' Dixie interrupted.

'Yes, son, what is it?'

'Mummy won't let this man take me away.'

Jessie's mouth gaped. Her eyes blazed. She allowed the bucket of water to slip from her grasp. As it slumped down on the floor water cascaded over everyone's shoes.

Dixie laughed. However, when Jessie started to jab Eddie in the shoulder, Kirsten became alarmed. 'And Mister Inspector let me tell you,' Jessie hollered, 'that you and the rest of your force will be in hell roasting before we allow you to take our laddie away from us.' Jessie paused before adding, 'And precisely on what bloody grounds?'

'Jessie, calm down,' Kirsten implored. 'You could be arrested for assaulting a police officer, and that would be the excuse they are looking for.'

'Me arrested for assaulting him? It is him who should be charged with putting us in a state of fear and alarm.'

'I am very sorry but I think you have misunderstood,' Eddie said, as he distanced himself from Jessie.

'No, you are the one who has misunderstood. That lassie, Kirsten, my daughter-in-law, is the best mother oor Dixie could have. Willed him to live when the nurses and doctors said he couldn't, so she did. And now you have the blinking cheek to come in here and try to take him away from her.'

Kirsten grabbed hold of Jessie. 'Look, all he suggested was that in two weeks' time he would take Dixie to see the Hibs and Hearts play.'

Jessie sniffed.

'And what upset Dixie was I said no. You see, I think he is too young to go to the matches. Long before half time he would be bored and wanting down on the pitch so he could kick the ball about.'

Jessie sagged as relief set in. With a laugh, she said, 'Aye, I suppose you're right. Mind you, with the way some of them played last week oor Dixie might be a good signing for them.'

Kirsten now turned to Eddie. She should have been seeing an overbearing officer, but as she looked at him she mellowed. Instead of wiping the water from his own shoes, he had bent down to comfort Dixie. The incident had distressed Dixie, who did not like people shouting. Kirsten too sank onto the sodden floor. Gently prising Dixie from Eddie's arms she cradled him in her own.

'There, there, my darling. There is nothing to worry about, everything is fine. We are all friends. Now, come on, you know what to do.'

'Long. Slow. Breaths.'

'That's right, Dixie. Now inhale for five. Hold for five. Exhale through your open mouth. Inhale for five. Hold for five. Exhale through your open mouth.' And soon Dixie's breath was under control.

'You're a wonder with him, Kirsten,' Jessie remarked. Still staring at Kirsten and Dixie she then directed her speech to Eddie. 'Said he wouldnae survive. But thanks to Kirsten he has made it and how.' She hesitated. 'So, when you

156

are thinking of coming in here to harass her you might think twice about it. What I am trying to get through to you is that she has enough on her plate providing for her three bairns. Oh aye, her only crime is to make life easy for them and harder for herself.'

'That's enough, Jessie. The wee lad can hear. See now that he is stable again how about you take him through to our back room and tuck him up on the couch. A wee rest will do him the world of good. Don't concern yourself about the mess here, I will square it up, then I will finish early and get him home.'

Jessie assented with a nod. Eddie was then amazed at the gentleness that overtook Jessie. Jessie who, when you looked at her, was the fierce street fighter of her reputation, but there was another side to her — a tender side. She was a loving, doting grandmother, and Dixie and his welfare meant so much to her.

'I'll go with Granny, but, Mum, about me going to the football matches?'

Kirsten shook her head. Jessie then left with a disappointed Dixie. Exhausted, Kirsten sank further down onto the floor. Her hands rhythmically began to pat the water. She wanted to cry, but she dared the tears to fall. No way did she wish any stranger, as Eddie was, to know how frightened she was for her children's future. Each night she prayed that she would not die until they were all adults and independent of her.

She was more than surprised when Eddie pulled her up onto her feet. Her buckling legs felt like jelly. Before she knew it, she had fallen against him. He knew he was courting trouble but the most natural thing for him to do was encircle her in his arms and he couldn't believe it when he heard himself speak. 'Come on now, it's going to be okay,' he said softly.

His comforting words were more than she could bear and she began to sob.

Once her weeping had subsided she drew back from him. She then practised a few of Dixie's breathing exercises, and as her breathing calmed she felt more able. Looking at him, she felt that he was a good man, a man of honour who understood that she just had to provide for her children.

'Look,' she began, 'Dixie is just too young to sit through a whole football match. I am grateful for your offer, but not this year. Next year . . . well, who knows . . . perhaps . . . '

'Are you finishing early today?'

'I finish early every Saturday. At the weekends I try to find time for my family.' She smiled. 'Easy tea tonight. I will dish up their favourite. Fish and chips from the chippie. Tomorrow, Sunday, I don't work.'

'For religious reasons?' he asked, unable to keep the sound of disbelief from his voice.

She began to laugh lightly. The magic started in him again. He felt an overwhelming desire to sweep her into his arms. 'No. I am not my mum or dad. Sundays to me are our special together days.' She smiled. 'Days of just my children and me. They go to Sunday School, then in the afternoon, no matter the cost, I dish up a roast dinner. Later, we go out for a walk and I treat them to an ice-cream cone.'

A silence fell between them. Both were deep in thought.

Eventually Kirsten said, 'I know that no one in the force believes it, but it is so important to me that my children have as happy a childhood as they can, that they know they are the most important thing in my life. I can't smooth all the rough roads that they will have to travel, but I can try to make sure they have childhood memories to hold on to when dark days come. Unfortunately, they do come for us all.'

Eddie remained stuck to the spot for a moment, before something triggered in his head. Time was marching on. He was on duty, and duty called. 'I must be going,' he said quickly. 'I cannot promise but I will try and convince the powers that be to give you some slack.'

She looked into his eyes and smiled. She remembered how he had done what Duncan had never done: bent down and comforted Dixie. He had been so tender towards her son that she was moved to look at him in a different way. He was tall, distinguished and handsome. The stirrings that affected him now rose in her. It was then she looked down and saw that he was wearing a gold ring on his wedding finger.

She sighed as she thought, that's life. Besides, even if he was free, what chance would there be of him taking on a woman with three children?

20

After eight long, weary months Armstrong's was opening. Jessie and Kirsten both weighed a stone lighter. Their bank book was even lighter, so much so they had had to go cap in hand for a loan. Thankfully, the bank saw them as a good risk and they were granted enough funds to finish the refurbishment. An unforeseen bonus was the growth of the respect between the two women. Both had done more than their fair share to get the place up and running.

All that remained to be done was for invitations to the grand opening to be sent out. Jessie and Kirsten had discussed every single one. There was, of course, the mandatory thank-you list for assisting, and they were in complete agreement on that list. Then there was the second lot of people: they had to be sure they hadn't left anyone off that list who may be able to put business their way. Kirsten did have to point out to Jessie that those who had been her best customers, when she had been in the money lending business, were hardly likely to know of anyone who would wish to stay in an Edinburgh hotel for the night, so there was no point in asking them.

Finally, there were the friends and officials. It was while drawing up that list that Kirsten suggested to Jessie that she could invite five guests. And she could use these invitations for family, or even her Granton customers. The only real disagreement they had was when Kirsten said that they must invite the police chief at Gayfield Square.

'Why?' Jessie asked.

'Because since Inspector Carmichael dropped by . . . ' She paused, pretending she wasn't quite sure of exactly when that was he had visited. In truth that day — the day she realised that she could still feel attracted to a man — was so important to her that not only did she know the month but also the very minute of his appearance. 'Whatever day that was, the police presence in the hotel has been occasional and always polite and casual.'

What Kirsten didn't know was that Eddie hadn't spoken to the chief about the check-ups on Armstrong's Hotel, but he had casually asked his colleagues to do the minimum of visits.

★ ★ ★

Armstrong's grand opening was upon them and guests started to arrive. Jessie was dressed up as if she was going to a wedding. Not only had she had her hair done by a Jenners hair stylist, whose prices made her choke, but Kirsten had advised asking a beauty expert about facial hair removal.

'Hair removal?' Jessie had queried. 'Whatever for?'

'Look in the mirror.'

'So, I have a moustache and the start of a wee

beard,' she said, pouting her lips. 'But then, what old women don't?'

'True, but it's not the image for our hotel. The customers won't wish to have their breakfast served up by a female Father Christmas.'

When Jessie had returned from her visit to Jenners she seemed, thanks to the hair and facial treatments, to have lost twenty years. She literally glowed.

'Here, Kirsten, see when the lassies finished with me I didnae recognise myself. I mean I look so good I could gie that Jean Simmons, you know the film actress, a run for her money.'

Kirsten had just smiled and nodded. Somehow she knew that in the future Jenners would be seeing a lot more of Jessie.

Most of the guests had arrived and were being served drinks by the newly appointed waiting staff. Bea, Jane and Dixie were serving the canapés. Kirsten paused for a moment: it was a scene that showed exactly how her children were with each other.

Dixie, who was doing his best not to let things drop off his serving platter, was dutifully trotting behind Jane. But then he would, because he loved Jane, and she loved him so much that it was never a bother to her to look after him. On the other hand, Bea from day one had resented Dixie. Bea liked the world to revolve around her. Kirsten had hoped that in time Bea would stop being jealous of Dixie and start loving him. However, when Duncan left, Bea blamed Dixie for his going. Somehow she'd understood that Duncan, like her, had resented Kirsten's focus

162

on her son. After Duncan's departure it didn't matter what Kirsten did for Bea; she remained sullen and aloof. Kirsten also had to accept that, even although Duncan had deserted her, Bea would never love her as much as she loved him. There was no thawing in Bea's attitude, but still Kirsten did try to make life as easy as possible for her. A futile effort, if ever there was one. Yes, no matter what Kirsten did she never managed to make Bea smile.

She was still looking at her children when she became aware of the arrival of another guest. The police representative. Kirsten smiled and glided over the floor to greet Inspector Carmichael.

'How good of you to come,' she chanted. 'I take it that your chief sent you in his place, as he abhors alcohol.'

Removing his cap and tucking it under his arm, Eddie replied. 'Our old chief did . . . But now he's no longer in the force. Retired he is, and escaped back to his beloved Isle of Lewis.'

Kirsten smiled. She was thinking that the retirement of the old chief couldn't be anything other than good news for her. 'And the new chief?' she said with a smile.

'He would have come today, but as he has just taken up his post he wishes to acquaint himself with his team first. After that he intends to do the rounds of getting to know the community he will be serving.'

'And so you drew the short straw?'

He laughed lightly. 'No. The admin inspector is off on sick leave. I am filling in for him today, so I volunteered.'

163

She smiled again. Both were experiencing the joy of this unexpected meeting. Kirsten was so engrossed admiring him that she was startled when she heard Dixie call, 'Does the football man want one of these?'

Before Kirsten could reply Eddie said, 'Well, hello again, young man. Are you still supporting Hibs?'

Dixie nodded furiously. 'They won last week.'

'They did. Did you see the match?'

Forlornly Dixie's head shook from side to side. 'No one to take me.'

'Well, if your mum thinks you are old enough now, perhaps she will allow me to take you to the next match.'

'Mum, are you listening? Has it been long enough?'

'I am listening, Dixie. But . . . '

'Look, why don't you let me take him to the next home match and see how it goes?'

'That is so very kind of you.'

Eddie chuckled. 'Just trying to keep in with the new chief. He is very keen on us not only serving the community but also being part of it.'

'Mum, are you really saying I get to go?'

Kirsten nodded. Jane, who had been standing patiently waiting to serve them some canapés, said, 'Mum, I have to circulate, so could you hurry and take one of these fish things?'

'Inspector, this is Jane, the youngest of my daughters.'

'Pleased to meet you, Jane,' Eddie replied with a smile. 'And, yes, I will have one of your delicacies.'

Jane blushed. 'My sister Bea is serving today, too. And our frocks are identical because our granny Aileen made them especially for today.'

Eddie's eyes scanned the room. Once he spotted Bea, he said, 'And very smart the two of you look in your red gingham dresses.'

Before he could comment further three ladies came in through the doors. Stella, flamboyantly dressed in an electric blue flowing gown and bright dangling parrot earrings, was first to grab Kirsten in a tight embrace. 'This place is just wonderful. It is all so tastefully furnished. My girl, you have done well. But then I knew you would.'

As soon as she was able, it was then Marigold's turn to congratulate Kirsten. 'You and your mother-in-law knocked that hovel I seen last year into this?' Kirsten was delighted to nod.

Then it was time for Mrs Baxter. Mrs Baxter, who must have a first name, but who was always just Mrs Baxter. 'Oh, Kirsten, I wouldn't mind mucking this place out. Like a palace, it is. Even up market from the wee hotel my man and I go to in Blackpool.'

Eddie's feelings, on seeing the three women come in, were mixed. It was good that their arrival confirmed what he'd assumed about Kirsten — that she did not forget past friends, even those who could no longer do anything for her. No, Kirsten was not a fair-weather friend. On the other hand, if the old chief had still been in residence at the Divisional HQ, the three women's presence at the hotel's opening party would have confirmed his prejudices about

165

Kirsten. In his nightmares he would have seen Armstrong's becoming a house of ill-repute. Then he would have not only increased but intensified the surveillance on the hotel.

While Eddie was deliberating, Aileen, who was at the other side of the function room, was weighing him up. She had noticed that when he came in Kirsten had literally preened. And she was sure that when he'd accepted Kirsten's hand in welcome he too had seemed more than pleased. Aileen did hope that Kirsten would find another mate one day but — she was so proud of Kirsten and the way she'd always managed to cope. She couldn't have averted the happenings in her life, but she did always manage to take them head on and she never allowed herself to be beaten or diminished by them. Wasn't Dixie proof of all that? *Ah, Dixie*, Aileen sighed. Someone wishing to take on Kirsten and the girls would be one thing; taking on Dixie, whom Kirsten had spoiled rotten because he was the apple of her eye, was another.

But still, the rest of the celebration went according to plan. Eddie, who was on duty, left early to report that Armstrong's appeared to be in excellent management hands and he could foresee no problems. That would be true where the hotel was concerned, but was he opening a can of worms, now that he'd promised to take Dixie to football matches from time to time? This would mean meeting up with Kirsten. He pondered as he acknowledged his attraction to her. Was he using Dixie as a means to get into Kirsten's good books? He hoped not.

21

When Eddie, dressed in civvies, arrived at Balfour Street to take Dixie to the match, he smiled. Dixie was all ready and eager to go, standing at the window. He waved and grinned when he saw Eddie. But, on entering the house, Eddie could sense that Kirsten was anxious.

'Inspector . . . ' she began.

'Could you call me Eddie? You see, I would prefer that Dixie calls me Eddie instead of inspector when we are at the game.' He smiled before adding, 'Just trying to avoid any trouble from supporters who are not keen on the polis.'

She nodded. 'It is just that, well, I hope he won't be wanting home and spoil . . . What I mean is, he doesn't like loud noises. Have you ever taken any other boy, perhaps your own son, to Easter Road?'

'I am not fortunate enough to have any children.'

On hearing this admission, she would normally have thought that it was a great pity. But it only served to give her hope. Hope that he was perhaps unmarried. Her gaze then flew to his left hand again. The wedding ring was still there, so even although he had no children he obviously did have a wife.

'Don't worry about Dixie,' Eddie said as he took Dixie's hand in his. 'He and I are going to get on just fine. By the way, I will be taking him to a seated area and not to the terracing.'

'You are? But is that not expensive?' She blushed. 'Of course, let me get my purse and I will give you his ticket money.'

Saluting her he said, 'No need. This is my treat.'

'But I insist.'

'Look, let's just see how it goes and then if it is to be a regular event then we can talk finance!'

★   ★   ★

It's funny that we all have dreams. Some of these dreams when they do come true are not really what we thought they would be. It was like that for Dixie at the match. From the start, the noise of the shouting fans scared him. Whenever a roar went up his hands flew to cover his ears. His lips trembled and he whimpered. The game had only been going for twenty minutes when Eddie reluctantly accepted that football matches were not for Dixie. Probably never would be.

Having decided he must do what was best for Dixie, he then annoyed the other supporters in the row by asking them to let him and Dixie pass out into the gangway.

Once they were out of the ground and into Albion Terrace, Dixie wrestled his hand free from Eddie's. He then began to gallop towards Hawkhill.

'Hold on, Dixie,' Eddie shouted to the fleeing figure. 'You are going the wrong way. Balfour Street is the other way.'

Thankfully, because of his football days, Eddie

was still fit and it only took him a few strides to catch up with Dixie. As luck would have it a taxi was passing at that very moment and Eddie signalled to the driver to stop. All he could do then was bundle Dixie into the cab and tell the driver to head for Balfour Street. On reaching home Dixie bolted from the cab and into the house.

After paying the driver, Eddie followed. Kirsten, who was enjoying a cup of tea and a natter with her old friend Molly Clark, was taken aback when Dixie hurtled through the door and into her arms.

'What's wrong?'

'The match went on too long, Mum. The noise hurt my ears. And boys were shouting bad words,' Dixie managed to splutter.

'Look, Dixie, calm down. You are home and safe now. But remember, I did explain to you that there would be noise and swearing. But you were to ignore all that and enjoy the game.'

Taking his left hand in hers, she began to massage his palm. It was then that she became aware that Eddie was now in the house.

'Sorry it didn't work out,' he said, looking sheepish. 'The noise and crowds frightened him.'

Kirsten nodded. 'I thought they would, but don't you feel bad. You tried and, like me, even though we hope things will work out they sometimes don't.' She hesitated before adding, 'But I am grateful that you put yourself out for my Dixie. On the plus side at least you will get home to your wife early.'

Eddie lowered his eyes. 'Yes, at one time that

169

would have been so good to do.' Now it was his time to pause. 'Unfortunately my dearly beloved wife Anna died eleven years ago.'

Kirsten felt a rush of horror at this news. Through Dixie, and the football, she had imagined she could build some sort of relationship with Eddie. Even today, when she was concerned for Dixie, looking at Eddie made her feel like a silly schoolgirl experiencing her first crush. Two minutes ago she'd felt that a door would open for them — but the reality of Eddie's feelings for his beloved wife meant that door must remain firmly shut. Kirsten shook her head. What was she thinking? Dixie and his sisters must be her first priority.

Eddie then turned to go, but on impulse he turned back and sought for her hand. All Kirsten's resolve melted away at his touch. Lifting her fingers to his lips, he murmured, 'This is not the time for us. At the moment you have your children to see to, but believe me I can wait. Yes, I truly believe our time will come.'

Kirsten, overcome by emotion, could only nod. She was just trying to order her thoughts when Jane and Bea arrived home. Jane smiled at Eddie, but Bea glowered.

Eddie stepped away quickly, and threw up his hands as if in defeat. After kicking the door shut behind his departing back, Bea turned her attention to her mother.

'What's going on in here?' she screeched.

Without raising her voice, Kirsten said, 'Bea, please don't shout at me.' She then told Bea that Dixie had needed to leave the football match early, and so Eddie would no longer be coming on Saturdays.

To Kirsten's astonishment, Bea jumped up and clapped her hands. 'Good, at last Dixie has done us all a favour.'

'In what way, Bea?' Molly asked. She was sitting quietly, drinking in the situation as it unfolded.

'In the way, Molly, that when my dad comes home he won't take kindly to another man in our house!'

'Bea,' Kirsten said with emphasis, 'your dad is never going to come home. I know how angry you are about that, but there was nothing anybody could have done to stop him leaving us. What I am saying is, please, you have to get over it. Stop blaming me, and most importantly stop allowing it to ruin your life!'

22

Two years later, Armstrong's hotel was turning out to be very successful. It had not all been plain sailing. Indeed, no. This was no surprise to Jessie and Kirsten: they'd dived in headfirst with no experience in managing a city centre hotel!

Every time Kirsten, who was on duty in reception, thought of how at the start she and Jessie had just muddled through, she almost laughed in disbelief. Of course, she had to 'employ' Molly Clark to see to the children in the morning. This was no problem for Molly, whose children were older than Kirsten's and now independent. The arrangement with Molly meant Kirsten could get to the hotel by seven in the morning, thus allowing her to get things underway. She smiled as she remembered how at first serving breakfast and dealing with guests checking out had been nightmarish. In particular, she recalled the infamous morning when the chef didn't turn up. Jessie, in addition to showing visitors to their tables in the dining room, had to cook the breakfasts. By the time she darted backwards and forwards between kitchen and dining room for the whole breakfast service she was exhausted. So was the supply of eggs. Twenty eggs were required for the guests, but between yolks getting broken and frying pans going up in flames, forty eggs were used. Somehow Jessie went right off fried eggs for a while after that. Then there was the time that Jessie had to summon Kirsten back to the hotel in the early afternoon. When a breathless Kirsten stumbled in the door, she was gasping. 'What is it? What's gone wrong?'

Jessie looked about furtively. 'It's room ten.'

'What's amiss with room ten?'

'Man booked in and paid for the night. He said that the lady with him was his wife, but it turns out she is his secretary and they came in at two then checked out at four.'

'Are you saying that they went for an afternoon nap?'

'Afternoon something, but it certainly wasn't a nap. What if Super Cop down the road finds out about them and their romp in the hay? Don't you realise, Kirsten, that that will be all the excuse he needs to shut us down?'

'Calm yourself, Jessie. I am sure if two people book in as Mr and Mrs and leave after two hours that is their affair. Besides, how do you know she was his secretary?'

'Heard her say to him, I did, would she go back to the office or could she just go home. He replied, 'I think anything else I officially require can wait until office hours tomorrow.''

Kirsten was still reminiscing when she became aware that someone was awaiting her attention.

'I am sorry, my thoughts were miles away. Can I help you?'

'I hope you can.' It was Eddie, dressed in civilian clothes.

Caught unaware, Kirsten mumbled, 'I heard you had been promoted to chief inspector in Leith Division.'

'I have. But today I am not here on police business.' He chuckled. 'I received a phone call from a man who addressed me as Mr Scottish Police Football. He then went on to say, 'My name is Olav Olsen and I am a detective with the Oslo Police. I wish to bring my football team to Edinburgh to play games with your Scottish teams.''

Kirsten laughed. 'You are joking.'

'No. And I have approached the chief constable about the request and he is very keen for us to accommodate them.'

'So, why are you here?'

'Well, they have asked me to book accommodation for them and their wives and girlfriends.'

'Wives and girlfriends? Are you saying the ladies obediently trot behind the football team?'

Eddie laughed and winked. 'No, I am led to believe they will be shopping. Shopping, shopping, shopping until they drop.'

'Why?'

'Norway is a fine country to live in, but the price of goods . . . let's put it this way, wives wouldn't be out shopping every Saturday on a police constable's salary.'

Now it was Kirsten's turn to laugh. 'So, are you here to book the girlfriends in?'

'No, the whole assembly.'

'But as I only have sixteen rooms, and that is counting the two attics. I wouldn't be able to house them all.'

'Yes, you will. Olav and the trainer and their

174

partners will lodge with me.' Kirsten looked perplexed. Eddie knew what she was thinking. 'Look, Norway is a modern country and if the girlfriends bunked in with their boyfriends at home, then who are we to say, 'No, you can't do that here'?' Kirsten grimaced. 'Look,' Eddie sighed, 'their sharing rooms will have no repercussion for you or your hotel's reputation.'

'I accept that,' Kirsten lied with a shake of her head. 'But we are just so busy with the festival being in full swing. So, apologies, but I cannot help you.'

Eddie winked again. 'Would the fact that they would be coming in November help ease your anxiety?'

So engrossed were Kirsten and Eddie in their conversation that they hadn't noticed that Jessie was now beside them. 'Maybe not hers, but it will suit me just fine.' She now spoke to Kirsten. 'You ken fine November and February are the two dead months of the year for us. Here is a chance for us to be full up for a week.' She stopped to rub her fingers to indicate money. 'Stupid it would be to turn it down. Now, Chief Inspector Carmichael, or is it plain Mr today?'

'Prefer Eddie, if you don't mind.'

'We will take the booking,' Jessie stated. 'Now, you do know we have a fully equipped function suite?'

'Yes, I trust they will have dinner here, except the team on the nights they are playing in Fife, Aberdeen and Inverness. Also . . . ' He seemed to ponder. 'Would you be able to do the official welcome dinner?'

'For how many?'

He started to count on his fingers. 'Well, between their team, our teams, wives and partners, invited guests . . . ' He shrugged. 'Even all of them won't add up to more than a hundred.'

'A hundred!' exclaimed Kirsten.

'Don't see why we cannae do it,' enthused Jessie.

Stunned, Kirsten interjected, 'Please don't tell me you are agreeing that we do a full dinner for one hundred!'

'Aye, I am.' Jessie playfully nudged Kirsten before adding, 'Look, I know one hundred to dish up for is frightening you.'

'Yes it is, because remember the chaos when you and I did a couple of weddings for seventy-five.'

'That was when it was just you and me and we didnae ken what we were daeing.' Jessie drew herself up to her full height. 'But we are the management now and have experienced staff to do the kitchen and dining room duties, so it'll be a doddle for them.'

Kirsten was still shaking her head.

'Look,' Jessie insisted, 'I promise you that you and I will be mingling with the guests. I can see it now, both of us all dressed up to the nines and we won't have to wash as much as a cup all night.'

And so it was that the Norwegian footballers — and their female companions — were booked to stay at Armstrong's.

★   ★   ★

After the frenzy of August's festival season, November came all too soon. Both Kirsten and Jessie were in the foyer to greet everyone when they arrived for the official Saturday night welcome dinner.

Eddie was there a little early. 'Just making sure everything is going to plan.'

Kirsten nodded. 'No worries on our part,' she said, giving Eddie her warmest smile. Indeed, there were no concerns on Kirsten's part until a rather stylish, good-looking lady arrived. Eddie immediately went up to her and kissed her on both cheeks. He then turned to Kirsten. 'Kirsten, I would like to introduce Sylvia Sanderson. She and I have been colleagues since we joined the force. We accompany each other on all our official, and indeed private, outings when we require a partner!'

Kirsten's smile remained fixed on her face, however her insides felt as if they had been invaded by a bag of squirming ferrets. Up until now she had no idea about the role Sylvia played in Eddie's life. What she took from Sylvia's stance was that she saw herself as the next Mrs Carmichael.

Kirsten was abruptly snapped back to the present when Sylvia extended her hand to her. 'I have heard so much about you,' Sylvia said, her eyes locked on Kirsten's. Then with a stilted smile, she stared long and hard. In that moment Kirsten knew Sylvia was wary of her. She then thought that perhaps Sylvia had guessed there was chemistry between herself and Eddie. Whatever it was, Kirsten thought, without a doubt, Sylvia would put up a fight, a tough fight, to stake her claim to Eddie.

The Norwegians who had arrived three days earlier and had two games behind them were now starting to assemble in the foyer. Up until then everything had gone according to plan. The lady-loves, as Jessie called them, were all very nice, polite Norwegian ladies. The only problem was Olav, a very large man, who had a voice that matched his stature. It literally boomed and echoed. In addition to this he had obviously been taught English by someone to whom the F-word was an acceptable adjective. Loudly he would laugh and slap Eddie on the back as he shouted, 'You are a good f**king friend. So pleased I am that I was lucky enough to f**king find you, Mr Football.'

Still unsettled by meeting Sylvia, Kirsten got through the dinner duties as if she was on autopilot. She, like Jessie, was just so pleased that there had been no hitches and now it was time for the speeches. The depute chief constable, who was the most senior officer in attendance, was first to speak. He welcomed the Norwegians and said that he hoped it was the beginning of a long-lasting friendship between the Oslo and Edinburgh City police. Olav then stood to respond. He first thanked the depute and then he went on to say how wonderful the tour had been so far. Yes, problems had popped up but thanks to capable Chief Inspector Eddie being on hand they hadn't become no f**king problems.

The depute's wife, who had chosen to forget

that she had been born and reared in Leith, fell back against her chair in dismay. The depute turned to Eddie. 'Is there no way you can get Olav to understand that that word is very offensive?' Eddie replied that he had tried, but he would try again.

Later in the evening Eddie took Olav aside and explained once more about the F-word. Eddie suggested that Olav should just say, 'When my friend Eddie gets involved there are NFP.' Olav nodded enthusiastic agreement; 'NFP' it was from now on.

The evening progressed to the dancing. Kirsten, who was still on duty, felt her heartstrings yanked when Eddie took Sylvia on to the floor. It was obvious from the way they glided so perfectly around the room that they were used to dancing together. They looked so at ease in each other's arms that Kirsten thought in time they would marry. She knew she needed to put some distance between this heartbreaking scene and herself. Glancing at the clock, she was relieved to see that it was gone ten o'clock.

Immediately she sought out Jessie. 'Think everything went very well.'

'It did that,' Jessie replied with a giggle. 'In fact, there were NFPs and isn't that thanks to Chief Inspector Eddie and, of course, you and me.'

Now it was Kirsten's turn to laugh. 'Right now I was thinking, as I have to relieve Molly from her child-minding activities, that I will just get myself off. And as tomorrow is Sunday it is my day off. Now, will you manage?'

'You know fine that I always manage Sundays. Tomorrow will be no different. We have some really good and capable staff now.'

Kirsten nodded. Once she was out into York Place itself she hailed a taxi.

The taxi had just done a U-turn and was heading down Leith Walk when, back at the hotel, Eddie approached Jessie. 'I've just been looking for Kirsten, but I can't see her anywhere.'

'You won't, she is away home to look after her bairns. And she won't be in tomorrow either.'

Crestfallen, Eddie heard himself say, 'That's a pity.'

'Is it?'

'Yes, you see I was just going to ask her to dance.'

'Well, you're too late. And I think you should know that nothing or nobody would have stopped her getting home to her bairns. No' not even a birl round the floor with you.'

★　★　★

The children were asleep and Molly had just left when Kirsten kicked off her shoes before throwing herself down on the settee. She was so tired that she was sure within seconds she would be fast asleep.

However, exhausted as she was, slumber seemed to be eluding her. Her thoughts were on how handsome Eddie had looked as he guided Sylvia across the dance floor. She grudgingly acknowledged that, given the years that had

180

passed since they first met, a lasting relationship between herself and Eddie Carmichael was a non-starter. This being so, why had she experienced such pangs of envy from the minute she was introduced to Sylvia? Eddie, after all, had been a widower for so long now, it was only natural that he would be courting or flirting with one, two or three ladies. Sylvia obviously had hopes where Eddie was concerned. She was extremely nice looking, respectable enough to enhance his career prospects and she didn't come with baggage in the form of a divorce and three children.

All the foregoing was true, but everyone, she conceded, has the right to dream. Her dream was that somehow Eddie and she *would* get together. But how?

Her thoughts were disturbed by a tearful voice from the room next door. 'Mummy, where are you? And why are you not with me?' Rising, she thought not only would Eddie have to take on three children, but understand that Dixie would only sleep if she'd tucked him up in bed and stayed until he was sound asleep.

★   ★   ★

Once the Norwegians left for home Eddie rang Armstrong's to say that he planned to call in and settle any unpaid bills. Kirsten told the receptionist to say that Olav had taken care of everything before he left, so there was no requirement for him to call.

He then asked if he could speak to Kirsten.

181

Reluctantly Kirsten accepted the receiver. 'Good morning, Chief Inspector.'

'Why so formal?'

'I understood this was a business call.'

'It is, and it is not. I just wished to ask if I would be welcome to come into the hotel and have a coffee and chat with you.'

'About?'

'Well, I think your function suite is just what I need to hold the after-match hospitality meals for visiting teams. And so I was wondering if we could come to some sort of arrangement. An arrangement that would be beneficial to all concerned.'

Kirsten was about to say an emphatic no, but business was business, and if Jessie found out that she had turned a lucrative deal down, well . . .

Truth was, such an arrangement meant she would get to see Eddie regularly. But, she promised herself, good as that would be, she would keep him at arm's length.

23

1972

February was cold and bleak. It was true that so far there had not been the usual snowfall in Edinburgh, but that month had been windy, changeable and dreich. As Kirsten dished up her children's porridge one morning she shivered. *Well*, she mused, *it is true that February is the coldest month of the year. Must be getting old. I honestly feel the chill is going right through my bones.*

'Mum!' Jane, who had just come into the kitchen, began. 'Are you remembering that Bea and I will be going to the St Valentine's Youth Dance up in the church hall tonight?'

'Gosh, I forgot it would be St Valentine's Day soon.'

It was just then that the sound of the letters dropping on to the floor through the letter box had Jane scamper out of the kitchen to collect them.

'Oh, Mummy,' she enthused when she returned with three envelopes in her hand. 'I've got one Valentine already and Bea's got two.'

Kirsten's heart sank. She knew that both girls would receive a card from their dad. Ever since he'd deserted the family he had, on St Valentine's Day, sent his daughters a card to say how much he loved and missed them. To

Kirsten's vexation, he always had the cheek to add that he would come home to sweep them up into his arms very soon. It was also repugnant to Kirsten that Duncan never sent Dixie a card — not on his birthday, not at Christmas, never. This deliberate omission led Kirsten to accept that as far as he Duncan was concerned Dixie did not exist.

'Mum, where're my cards?' Dixie asked through a mouthful of porridge.

Bending over Dixie to wipe his mouth, Kirsten replied, 'You will get yours, darling, on Monday, when it is St Valentine's Day. These cards have arrived early.'

'But no early one for me from Dad?'

'No, on Monday you'll get one from . . . '

Kirsten was just about to say 'me' when Dixie shouted, 'Rosie!'

Seventeen-year-old Bea had now taken her place at the table. 'You and that Rosie. Don't you realise nothing will ever come of your obsession with her.'

'What's an obsession?'

In response Bea rolled her eyes and shrugged.

Dixie snorted. 'Well, whatever it is, Rosie and I love each other.' Dixie now turned his attention to Kirsten. 'Mum,' he said through a mouthful of food, 'how old do I have to be to get married?'

Kirsten was caught on the hop. 'Married, Dixie? You are far too young to be thinking of that.'

'Sixteen, you have to be,' Bea advised, as she ripped open her second valentine. 'And I am old enough.' She then smiled and giggled.

184

Kirsten reached forward and snatched the card from Bea's hand. Scanning the card, she gasped. 'This card is from Patrick Kelly . . . and in case you don't know it, he's the Port of Leith's Casanova.' Bea shrugged. 'Shrug all you like, Bea, but in addition to running for Lover of the Year, his mother is convinced that he is going to be a priest . . . You know, a minister in the Catholic Church, and they are not allowed to marry, even if they father children with someone as gormless as you!'

'I am far from gormless,' Bea said with a smirk. 'Which reminds me, how much longer do Jane and I have to slave up at your hotel at the weekends?'

'As I've told you,' Kirsten said, bristling. 'Until you leave school next year and you have either got yourself a job that keeps you or you go to college.'

'Well, as I don't want to be a skivvy like you, or a doormat like Granny Aileen, I'll be going to college. Social worker, I am going to be.'

Kirsten could not contain her laughter. 'Bea, to be a social worker you require a heart and a desire to help those less fortunate than yourself. You know, people who have problems, like no roof over their heads or insufficient sustenance . . . '

'I do that up at your hotel,' Bea replied. 'Always I'm asking the guests if they have had enough to eat.'

Kirsten flung her hands in the air. 'I rest my case.' Before she could continue Dixie interrupted.

'Mum,' he wheedled, 'I do love Rosie, really. I have to get her a Valentine's card and a box of Milk Tray ... Could I have the money for them?'

'Dixie, are you sure Rosie's mummy would like that?' Jane said as she stood up.

'No,' Dixie said with a grimace. 'She will be angry. She told Rosie that we would have to wait until she dies before we can get married.'

'She said what exactly?' Jane questioned, before taking Dixie's hand in hers.

'That Rosie and I could only marry over her dead body.'

A silence fell in the room. Kirsten slumped down on a chair. *Dear heavens, she thought, where did I go wrong? I mean, here I am with a naive seventeen year old who thinks she is ready to marry Patrick Kelly. She was my firstborn, so like her dad that she will desert the guy if — no, when — the going gets rough. Then there is Jane. Dear Jane, who worries about everybody and tries to make everybody happy. Dixie is so special to her that I am afraid she will stay with us when she should be out making a life for herself. Then there is my Dixie, who was short-changed at birth, but is now a strapping twelve year old.*

But then, Kirsten conceded with a smile, Dixie loved everybody and everybody loved him. Of course he could have the few coins it would take to buy his Valentine a gift.

Finally, she thought about her own life. There'd be no Valentines for her. It was true that in the two years that Eddie had used

Armstrong's for his after-match functions she had grown more in love with him. Often in her daydreams she would imagine that someday they would be together. Be husband and wife. But, in truth, she knew she had put that dream to rest.

★ ★ ★

St Valentine's Day. The girls and Dixie had left for school, but Dixie turned back and dashed into the house.

'Mum,' he spluttered, 'you let me forget the card and chocolates for Rosie!' Picking them up, he turned to face his mum. His grin now went from ear to ear. 'Look,' he said. 'I have them both here now.' He hesitated, then in a whisper added, 'Mum, when I give them to her, do you think it will be all right if I kiss her?'

'Don't see why not.' Kirsten smiled. But she thought to herself, *Oh, it is a sad day for a mother when her boy loves someone more than he loves her.*

Dixie, who was now running from the house again, turned back towards Kirsten. 'But I do still love you very much,' he emphasised as he returned to fling his arms about her. 'And I promise I always will. You're the best mum in the world.'

Kirsten stroked his hair before she bent to kiss the top of his head. 'Yes, but one day you may go and live with someone else like . . . Rosie.'

Dixie nodded. 'But I will come back every day to see you.' He turned to leave, calling back, 'Bye, Mum, see you tonight.'

Kirsten moved over to the window. Full of

pride, she watched her Dixie race to catch up with his pals.

After Dixie left, Kirsten set about tidying up the house. She was singing away to herself when the doorbell rang. On opening the door, she gasped. All she could see was a large bouquet of red roses.

Don't tell me that that loser Patrick Kelly has sent these blooming flowers to Bea, she thought. But then the roses were lowered and a uniform-clad Eddie stood before her.

'Court appearance today,' he explained. 'I am on my way there. But as I have time to spare before I am due I thought . . . Now, look, I know it's St Valentine's Day, but don't get the wrong idea,' he said. 'I thought I would bring you these flowers as a thank you for all you have done for the football team.'

'Come in,' she managed to reply.

To say that his statement was a disappointment to Kirsten was, well, an understatement. She cringed inside at her foolishness. She would have so loved to be his Valentine. To be truthful, the more she knew him the more she desired him. But with all the baggage she would bring with her, a relationship with Eddie was never going to be.

Just then a picture of possessive Sylvia jumped into her head. This image had her throw caution to the wind. Standing on tiptoe in the hallway, she lightly kissed him on the cheek.

'Thank you so very much,' she murmured, her face close to his. 'I do so love roses . . . especially red . . . '

Before she knew what was happening he encircled her in his arms. Passionately, he kissed her inviting lips. She willingly yielded to the moment, but as luck would have it the harsh sounding of the doorbell brought her back to reality. Like a naughty child being discovered doing wrong, she roughly pushed him from her. He caught the look of guilt in her eyes, but something else too — fear. But what exactly was Kirsten afraid of?

Patting down her hair, she rushed to open the door. There stood Molly. 'Saw the police officer at your door,' she stated. 'Is everything okay?'

'Yes, come in. The chief inspector was just delivering some flowers . . . a thank you from the football team.'

'Mmm,' was all Molly said as she followed Kirsten into the living room.

The minute Molly entered the room Eddie knew that Kirsten was going to use her as a chaperone. Looking directly at Kirsten, he nodded his indication to her that he knew she was asking him to leave — that already she was regretting allowing him to overstep the mark.

★   ★   ★

It was nearly lunchtime when Kirsten arrived at the hotel. Jessie was already in the dining room giving one of the waitresses her order. Kirsten smiled because this was something Jessie so enjoyed doing — being the lady owner and having the staff run hand and foot on her. She, of course, maintained that it was a good advertisement for the business if the guests saw that the owners liked to dine on the premises.

'Join me,' Jessie said, as she patted a side seat at the table.

'Think I will. I just seem to be chasing my tail today. A breather before I get started in here is just what I need.'

While they were waiting for their lunch, Kirsten took the opportunity to look at Jessie. She had for some weeks now thought that Jessie's health was failing. She was no longer the dynamic physical worker she used to be. So hard working she had been in the past that when she rolled up her sleeves she could make mere mortals like Kirsten seem inadequate and pathetic. Those rolled up sleeves made Kirsten's thoughts stray to when they first started to get the hotel shipshape. It had been a revelation to her to witness the strength of Jessie. Kirsten accepted that her mother-in-law was mentally still as sharp as a needle; physically, however, she was becoming weaker than a baby. The deterioration had started about six months ago but now it was accelerating at such a pace that week by week you could see the further decline. And today, to add to her frail appearance, there was something in her facial expression that caused Kirsten concern. She just couldn't put her finger on it. It could have been fear, apprehension or deep regret. No matter what it was, Kirsten could see that it was troubling Jessie deeply.

Before she could contemplate further the waitress placed a plate of soup in front of Jessie and herself. Jessie, as if in a dream, began to lazily stir her soup. Perplexed, Kirsten asked, 'Something amiss?'

'No. No, not really.'

'Now, come on. I know you so well, what's up?'

'Nothing other than the girls were saying they got a Valentine's card from their dad.' Jessie paused as she now covered Kirsten's hand with hers. 'I also got . . . '

Kirsten spluttered and withdrew her hand from Jessie's grasp. To stifle her giggles, she then placed her hand over her mouth. After a moment she said, 'Now, don't tell me he is so far gone that he sent you a Valentine too?'

'No. Not a Valentine, but a letter . . . a heartbreaking letter.'

'Heartbreaking?'

'Aye, you see . . . Oh, Kirsten, our poor Duncan. My poor laddie.'

'Is he seriously ill?'

'Worse than that, it's his wife.'

'Is it terminal?'

'No. But she does seem to have changed.'

'Changed? In what way?'

'Well, according to Duncan's letter, from Morning Star to Shooting Star.'

'What do you mean?'

'Shot off, she has, and left our poor Duncan in the lurch.'

Kirsten couldn't help but burst into uncontrollable laughter.

'Here, Kirsten, what's been done to my Duncan is no' a laughing matter.'

'It's not?'

'No. I mean, have you any idea what he is suffering? His letter says he just got up one morning expecting his breakfast and all he found on the table was a Dear Duncan letter.' Jessie hesitated. 'No' fair to do that to someone, so it is no'.'

Kirsten did not respond, but as her laughter abated she thought, *I wonder if he feels as bad as I did when he deserted my bairns and me?* A minute passed and then she again burst into laughter. So hearty it was, that she ended up crying.

Jessie was so concerned about her son's dire straits she seemed completely unaware of Kirsten's true reaction, but she did note her tears. Placing her hand over Kirsten's again, she forlornly said, 'Oh, Kirsten hen, like me you are so sorry that my poor son is now penniless and homeless.'

Kirsten swallowed hard. Trying most earnestly, she was, to control her merriment. Not for Duncan's sake, but she could see that Jessie was cut up about what had happened and she really didn't wish to hurt Jessie, who was now brushing away her tears. Kirsten thought she could control herself until Jessie ruefully confided, 'No' even got a place to lay his head now, so my laddie hasnae. Kirsten, he hasn't even got a paillasse to sleep on!' These revelations about Duncan were all too much for Kirsten. All she could now do to stifle her hilarity was to stuff her serviette into her mouth. 'And who says,' she thought, 'that life doesn't eventually come around and bite you on the bum.'

Minutes then ticked by. Neither of the two women spoke. Both were deep in their own thoughts. Jessie, naturally, was concerned about the plight of her son. Yes, he had made mistakes, but he was broken now and Jessie was wondering what she could do to help him get back on his feet. Kirsten was concerned as to what Jessie would do to assist Duncan. It was true that the hotel was more successful and more profitable than anyone thought it would be. This meant that Jessie had been paid back half of what she had put in to finance the start-up of the business. Kirsten too had profited to the extent that, when she was offered the chance to purchase her Balfour Street home, subject to tenant's rights, she had jumped at the chance. She didn't even have to ask the bank for a loan.

She smiled and shivered with delight when she thought how good it had felt that she had squirrelled away enough of her earnings and profits to buy her little Leith haven right out.

That was then when Jessie and she were on the crest of a wave. Now, though, the worry was what exactly Jessie was going to do to help Duncan. Kirsten grimaced when she acknowledged that her mother-in-law, although a hard-headed businesswoman, could be a pushover when her precious son was in need.

'Thinking of sending him a bob or two to let him get by until he decides what to do,' Jessie said.

Kirsten could only nod in agreement, and say a silent prayer that this wouldn't be the start of her ex-husband's return into her life.

24

Four months had passed since St Valentine's Day. Now that June was bursting out all over and the warmth of the sun beat down, it seemed to cheer everyone. Kirsten felt the light airy warmth had even heartened Jessie. She did seem to be so much brighter now, her wintertime deterioration abated. Really, it was as if somehow she had come to terms with Duncan's difficulties.

Dixie too loved the sun and long bright days. Kirsten smiled when Dixie said, 'Mum, are you remembering that this is my last year at Lorne Street School? Be going to the secondary after the school holidays.' Kirsten nodded. 'And you are remembering that today is also our last sports and picnic?'

'Yes, I am. That's why I have made sure your plimsolls are in your bag along with your packed lunch.'

'Good. Mark and I are going to run the three-legged race together,' Dixie boasted. 'Bet we will win.'

Kirsten smiled. Unlike Bea, who would need the crown jewels presented to her every day to make her smile, Dixie's essential requirements were simple. Porridge with the top of the milk for breakfast, getting to school to play with his pals, and stealing an occasional wee kiss from Rosie — Rosie, whose birthday it was today. Dixie had already told her how lucky she was to be getting the present of a new bicycle from her parents.

Naturally, Rosie had promised Dixie that he would be the first one to get a shot on her brand new Raleigh. Thinking of this, Kirsten smiled before saying, 'Now, after you have seen Rosie's new bike, Jane is going to bring you up to the hotel for your evening meal.'

Dixie threw his arms around Kirsten. 'Tell you all about my day when I see you.' He then stood back to back with Kirsten. 'See, Mum,' he laughed. 'I am nearly as tall as you.'

'So you are. Now, off you go and you can tell me all about your exciting day when I see you.'

*   *   *

When Kirsten arrived at the hotel, it was busy. But then it was June, and the tourists were very much in evidence. She had just checked up with the reception staff when Jessie appeared. She seemed bright enough, but Kirsten sensed that she was a bit preoccupied, so she was not surprised when Jessie asked, 'Time for a coffee and a wee natter, Kirsten?'

'A quick one. You are remembering the accountant will be here in twenty minutes for our monthly meeting?'

Jessie nodded.

As soon as they were seated in their own office, the coffee arrived. Kirsten had just started to pour out a cup when Jessie said, 'I am not going to beat about the bush, Kirsten. I've had another letter from Duncan. This time it's good news.'

'So, his runaway wife has reappeared?'

'No. He knows that that chapter in his life is closed.' Jessie started to rub her hands as she gave a shrug of delight. 'Kirsten, wait until I tell you. He says he could come back home and help us here in the hotel.'

'He what?'

'Aye, you see, I wrote to him and told him how well we have been doing. Truthful I was with him, and I also said that I am not as able as I used to be. By return of post, Kirsten, I kid you not, by return of post he writes back to say that he could come back and take some of the burden off us. What a boy! What a hero!'

Kirsten was aghast. She was tempted to shout out, 'Let me tell you, your boy will only put a foot into our hotel over my dead body.' But she decided that falling out with Jessie would just aggravate the situation. Better to box clever. Quietly, she said, 'Are you saying, Jessie, that you would like to stand back a bit and be a sort of silent partner?'

'Something like that. But I do want to stay on living here in the hotel.'

'Why?'

'I am somebody here, Kirsten,' Jessie said, almost in a dream-like state. 'I am the co-owner. I get respect. Never had respect before I came here. See, lassie, try and understand that folks in Leith and Granton just saw me as the miserable old money lender.'

'Hmm. But could you not do like me and buy yourself a wee house? You can more than afford it and that way you could split your time between the hotel and your new home.'

Jessie shook her head. 'Naw, I want to stay here until I go out in a wooden overcoat. But I'm no daft, I ken fine that I'm no' pulling my weight like I used to . . . So I think we accept Duncan's offer and let him come back as an assistant to you, Kirsten.' She paused to suck in her bottom lip. 'Now, I dinnae wish to build your hopes up, honestly I don't, but he was asking very kindly for you and the girls. Think he still fancies a second chance with you.'

Kirsten's mouth was now agape and she could feel her eyes begin to bulge. Anger and panic mingled. Was she hearing right? The man who had left her and her children to fend for themselves was thinking that now she was a good meal ticket he could come back into her life, get his feet under her table! Well, no he couldn't. No matter what happened she knew she could provide for herself and no way would she allow Duncan to come back into her life, not even as a paid employee of Armstrong's hotel. It was true that Jessie had worked hard too, and if she wished to give her profits to Duncan that was one thing, but it was Jessie and she who had the partnership. Their signed agreement was that if one wished to leave then the other, after a financial package had been agreed, became overall owner.

A long silence followed. Jessie was imagining Duncan coming home and how wonderful that would be. She really never had come to terms with him emigrating, but now she was feeling a bit weary wasn't it just great that he would be

197

back in her life? In her naivety, she saw him reconnecting with Kirsten and the family being reunited.

Kirsten, on the other hand, was boiling over with anger and trepidation. She believed that she had come to terms with Duncan's desertion, but the injustice and hardship of it still rankled. As to Jessie thinking that she would welcome him back as a loving husband — never ever would that happen. She owed Jessie, so what she did not wish right now was a blazing row with her — she required time — time to think of a strategy.

Whatever else, the biggest stumbling block was Jessie. She still had to be repaid the second half of the money she had ploughed into the business — money that Kirsten did not have. She could borrow to buy Jessie out, but by doing that she wouldn't be able to finance her children's further education. Her mind was in turmoil.

Thankfully, she was saved from further deliberation when the accountant knocked on the door. His appointment meant Kirsten could delay saying anything to Jessie until she had time to think things through thoroughly.

★　★　★

The grandfather clock in the hallway was chiming four o'clock when Kirsten had her next break. She reflected on how, again, the accountant had shown them that the business was doing exceptionally well. Some of the profits would be advancing to both Jessie and Kirsten. Unfortunately, good as that was, the funds being transferred were still a long way short of what Kirsten would require if she wished to buy Jessie out.

Thinking that Jane and Dixie would soon be coming in, Kirsten made her way into the dining room. She had just asked the waitress to set up a table for three when a white-faced Jane rushed into the room. 'Mum, Mum,' she cried hysterically.

'Jane, whatever is the matter?'

'Oh, Mum,' she gasped, distraught, 'they wouldn't let me or Rosie stay with Dixie . . . Mum, they have taken him away.'

'Who took him away? And where did they take him?'

'Ambulance men! I tried to get in beside him, but they said the best help was that I should go and get you.'

Kirsten flustered. 'Look, calm down,' she said, trying to contain the surge of panic rising in her heart. 'Start again by telling me what happened and where they have taken Dixie.'

'All I know is what Rosie said.'

'Okay. What did Rosie say?'

'Just that she, Dixie and Mark were each having shots of her new bike. Then when it was Dixie's turn he was racing as fast as he could. Oh Mum, she said he lost control and just seemed to catapult over the handlebars. He couldn't save himself and his head bounced off the kerb. Lost consciousness, he did, and there was blood. People tried to help him and someone phoned for an ambulance.' Jane was now weeping tears of distress and horror. 'Oh

Mum, one woman said she thought he was . . . dead. Please God, don't let him be . . . '

Kirsten was now hyperventilating. 'Oh no,' she whispered, 'I cannot lose you, my darling Dixie.' She then sought for Jane's hands. 'Quick, Jane, think now, did you hear anyone say which hospital they were taking him to?'

'I think Leith Hospital. The police came. You know, that man who was the chief inspector, but is now the superintendent in Leith, well, he was there and I am sure I heard the ambulance driver tell him that he was taking Dixie to Leith Hospital.'

'You are sure?' Kirsten called, as she started to race out of the door.

'Yes, I am sure. I saw the policeman take Dixie's hand in his and he said, 'Hang on in there, son.'' Jane was shaking with sobs, her tears profuse. 'I wanted to go with him, be with him, but they wouldn't let me. Why? Oh why? Oh why?'

The commotion had alerted Jessie and she arrived in the entranceway just as Jane and Kirsten were about to leap out into York Place.

'What's amiss?' Jessie called out to the fleeing figures.

'Something has happened to Dixie. Hit his head off the pavement. We are away to the hospital,' Kirsten called back.

'Maybe so, but you will need your purse to pay a taxi driver.'

Kirsten drew up sharp, wheeled round and went back into the hotel. She grabbed her handbag before catching Jane by the hand and

200

making off again into York Place. Thankfully Jessie had had the sense to go out and call for a taxi. She yanked open the door so all Kirsten and Jane had to do was jump in.

Jessie couldn't help but remember how her husband had died in a similar unexpected, awful accident, and so when she spoke to the taxi driver she alerted him to Kirsten's urgent need to get to the Leith Hospital on Mill Lane as soon as possible.

The man then drove off, expertly twisting and weaving his way through the traffic. On approaching the traffic lights at the Pilrig Junction he willed the lights to remain green, but as they ignored his plea and started to turn to red he pressed his foot hard on the accelerator. Kirsten was so immersed in her thoughts, her desperate need to see her son, that she didn't even hear the horns of the protesting drivers who had to swerve out of the pathway of the speeding taxi.

On arrival at Leith Hospital Kirsten opened her handbag to fish for her purse. 'No need, missus, the old lady gave me the fare and more when she hailed me,' the taxi driver assured her.

Dashing through the swing doors, Kirsten then bounded up the steps to the Accident and Emergency department.

'I am Dixie Armstrong's mother, where is my boy?' she cried.

A rather over-starched uniformed Sister laid her hand on Kirsten's arm. Rhythmically patting it she said, 'There, there, calm down. Getting hysterical is not going to do anything for . . . It is

201

your son you are looking for?'

'Yes. He fell off his friend's bike on Leith Walk. Dixie Armstrong is his name.'

'Ahhh. The doctors are with him now. So just take a seat and as soon as we know how he is we will come for you.' The Sister then turned and called out to a nurse. 'Ross, could you arrange a cup of strong tea for Mrs Armstrong?'

Kirsten took a seat, but she was bolt upright when the nurse arrived with a cuppa. 'I do not wish any bloody tea, strong or otherwise. I want to see my son!'

Thirty slow minutes then dragged by. Trying to find comfort, Jane, who was seated next to her mother, slid her hand under Kirsten's. All Kirsten was capable of doing to ease Jane's anguish was to squeeze her hand tightly. Eventually a young doctor came to speak to them.

'Your son,' he began, as he swallowed hard, 'has sustained severe head injuries.'

Kirsten's hand flew to her mouth. 'But you can do so much nowadays, so what will you be able to do for him?'

The doctor shook his head. 'What I am trying to say is that he is very poorly and it would appear we can do nothing to resuscitate him.'

Looking long and hard at the young man, Kirsten's breath came in ragged, urgent gasps. Fighting to speak, she managed to utter, 'But he is just a boy.' She paused, gripped with horror at what she was saying. 'He has his whole life in front of him. He loves his life. I know he wants to go on living it. Surely there is something you can do? Please let my boy live.'

'Mrs Armstrong. I am sorry, but what I am trying to say to you is that there is *no* brain activity.'

Kirsten swayed in her chair as emotion overcame her. 'Are you saying that there is no hope?'

The doctor nodded. 'He is being kept alive by artificial means. If you and . . . '

'My daughter, Jane.'

The doctor nodded towards Jane, kindness and sympathy in his eyes. 'If you could please follow me, I will take you to your son.'

Nothing could have prepared Kirsten for the shock. Her Dixie was unconscious and his breathing laboured. Machines and monitors attached to him hummed in the background. Just as when he was born, Kirsten had to fight to suppress the desire to haul out all the wires so she could hold him in her arms. Tell him she was there. Tell him that she loved him. Will him to awaken from his deep, deep slumber.

Time passed. Jessie, Bea and Molly all arrived. They stayed awhile, weeping and clinging to each other, to say their goodbyes, then they left in a small huddle of grief and shock. Only Kirsten and Jane completed the vigil. Twice during his shift Eddie called in. He was in the background when the doctor said, 'Could I suggest that when you are ready, and I will give you all the time that you need to say your goodbyes, you give me permission to shut off Dixie's life support. It would be best now to let him slip away.'

'Do you mean,' Kirsten said between sobs, 'that I *have* to let him go?'

'Yes, because he will not recover. I am so sorry, but only the machines are keeping him alive.'

Kirsten could only shake her head.

'Mrs Armstrong,' the doctor continued quietly, as he sought Kirsten's hand, 'I know how hard the decision is for you. All I can say is if he were mine, I would let him go.'

'But I love him so very much.' She faltered. 'Dixie has always been my special gift. You see, I cannot face the agony and misery of life without him.'

The doctor nodded and silently held her hand.

Jane came over to stand beside her mother. 'Mum,' she pleaded, her face wet with tears. 'I love him too. I love him so much, but if he cannot be as he was, laughing, singing, loving Rosie, then I know it is right to say goodbye.'

★ ★ ★

Thirty minutes later the monitors were switched off. Their sounds changed to a long drone. The zigzag line changed to continual flat. On either side of Dixie were Kirsten and Jane. Just holding his hands, they were, as the machines stilled. Kirsten then threw her body over Dixie.

'No. No,' she sobbed. 'Oh my darling, you never asked for much. You taught us all how to love. Mummy loves you so. I needed you so. My life will be so empty without you. Who will now fill my life with laughter, now you are gone?'

Jessie, who had arrived back at the hospital, then gently said, 'Kirsten, you have done all you could. I know he knows you were there. So, come on, lass . . . It is time to leave. And believe, like I do, he won't be alone until we join him in heaven. He will be with his two brothers. I can just imagine the three of them playing together. So, come now, Kirsten, it is time to leave. Our Dixie has gone.'

Kirsten shook her head, her hands still holding onto her son. 'No, I will stay until he is prepared for the . . . ' She couldn't say the word. 'But, Jessie, our Jane is all in, so please take her back to the hotel with you. She will be better with you tonight. Comfort her all you can.'

'What will you do?'

'Just stay with him until . . . ' She paused, unable to speak.

Jessie embraced her and took Jane from the room. She knew that Kirsten would stay with Dixie until the undertaker from McKenzie and Millar came and took over. Then Kirsten would tell them all she wished them to do for her precious Dixie.

★   ★   ★

And so, Kirsten accompanied Dixie over to the undertaker's. By the time she had made them aware of her wishes, it was gone half past two in the morning. She stepped out into Great Junction Street and decided that, even though the hour was late, she would not hail a taxi, but just walk home. With a bowed head, she had just

205

taken her initial steps when she became aware of someone alighting from a car.

'Please let me drive you home.'

Raising her head, Kirsten was shocked to find herself looking at Eddie. 'Where did you spring from?'

'I went back to the hospital when I came off duty. I intended to wait there until . . . Kirsten, I am so very sorry about Dixie. He was such a loveable boy. His laughter was so infectious.' She nodded. 'You brought him up so very well.'

'Please,' she pleaded, 'don't say nice things to me. If only he had regained consciousness long enough for me to say goodbye. I will miss him so very much.' She braced herself, as if trying already to get her feelings in check. 'But the memories of my Dixie will live with me my whole life through.'

'Come now.' Eddie offered her his hand. 'Let me get you home. Don't suppose you have eaten?'

'No, but I'm not hungry. A cup of tea and then all I want to do is curl up in bed.'

When they got to Balfour Street, Eddie made Kirsten a cup of tea. Slowly, as she drank it, she became lost in her memories of Dixie.

Thinking that he had done all he could for her, Eddie rose to leave.

'Where are you going?' Kirsten asked, as she staggered to her feet.

'Home.'

Kirsten reached up and placed her hands on his shoulders. This confused Eddie. It was something he always hoped she would do, but now he wondered why on this night of all nights. He was still trying to fathom out what was happening when a sobbing Kirsten uttered, 'No, Eddie, please, please, don't leave me. I just couldn't bear to sleep alone tonight. I am so bruised and torn. I have lost my son and I am heartbroken. I want . . . no, I need to feel the warmth of another human being. I can't bear to be all alone. Not tonight, when I have lost my son. My son, love of my life.'

Looking into his eyes now, she went on. 'Please understand this is not a whim on my part. Eddie, for years I have loved you. Wanted you. Tonight you are the only one I wish to comfort me. To be truthful, I know you are the only one who can.'

Taken aback, Eddie fished in his pocket for a handkerchief, which he used to gently mop her tears. 'There, there, love,' he said. 'If you are sure, really sure, that you wish me to stay with you tonight . . . I will. But, Kirsten, everything has a cost. The price of me accepting your invitation is that I will not be able to go back to you and me just being friends. I know you are a warm and loving human being. You would never be knowingly cruel. But to open the door to the possibility of us having a proper and lasting relationship and then banging it shut in my face would be so unbearable.'

Kirsten nodded. Life had been so cruel to her today. It was unimaginable to her, but now even in her grief, she simply wished for someone else she loved to soothe her. Someone who could, by their touch, warmth and closeness alleviate some

207

of the relentless, dark pain — help her live with her deep sense of loss.

★ ★ ★

Eddie was up and dressed when the doorbell rang. He answered its summons and, to his surprise, on the doorstep stood Molly.

'Oh,' she exclaimed. 'I just called to see Kirsten. Offer her not only my condolences, but all her chums condolences too.' Her hand went backwards to indicate all in Balfour Street. 'All around here, our deepest condolences. Poor, poor Dixie. We are in such shock. How is she?'

Molly did not wait for Eddie to answer, or for him to invite her in. Invitations to Kirsten's home she did not require. Before Molly could speak further Eddie became aware that her eyes were red and swollen. She had obviously being crying and quite profusely at that.

'Dixie will be a great loss, not only to Kirsten,' he said.

Molly pursed her lips. 'Yes, he was such a happy, lively lad. You know . . . ' She held out her hand. 'When he was born, you could have laid him there, and there was room to spare. Then he thrived and became Dixie. The lad who was always smiling, laughing and singing. Wanting to tell you a joke. And the way he and Rosie, who were too young to be in love, would just walk along the road hand in hand.' She stopped. Tears welled.

'Forgive me, but I will need to be going. I am on duty at two o'clock.'

Molly looked directly at him. 'I take it you spent the night here?'

Eddie nodded. 'Well, the early morning anyway.'

'That so? Fine, but let me say this to you, Kirsten will be so fragile for a while now, so please don't mess her about. She has been kicked in the teeth quite often enough. And losing Dixie is the hardest blow of all.' She paused and looked at the wall. 'Worked so very hard, she has, to provide for her bairns.' Turning, she stared right into Eddie's eyes. 'And, sir, I have known for some time that she was carrying a torch for someone. Somehow this morning I have the feeling that it is you she dreams about . . . has hopes about.'

Eddie could only stand and listen to Molly's words; he could sense that he'd be wise to heed them.

'Now, take fair warning, she is not the type to be used. She is honest and upright. If she loves you and you return that love, no one will be happier than me, but, sir . . . ' Molly did not finish her sentence. She did not need to — he had got the message loud and clear that if he were to break Kirsten's heart Molly would do what she could to wreak revenge.

'Has the funeral still to be arranged?' Molly went on, now that they understood each other.

'Yes, Kirsten did speak to the undertaker's, but that was just about how they should treat Dixie while in their care. But as to the funeral itself, of course that has still to be arranged.'

'It will be a big occasion,' Molly told him. 'So

209

much bigger than Kirsten will be imagining. Dixie was loved, not only in our street here, oh no, all over Leith, and wherever he went Dixie made friends. People loved him. He was always so happy, he brought out the best in us.'

At which point, Kirsten called out from the bedroom. 'Eddie, are you still here?'

Eddie did not respond verbally until he went back into the bedroom. 'Yes,' he said quietly, as he leaned forward to stroke her hair. 'But, darling, I have to go now. No need to worry, though, Molly has arrived to be with you.' He hesitated. 'She is, I believe, going to go with you to make arrangements for Dixie.'

★　★　★

As Molly predicted, Dixie's funeral was well attended. Kirsten had decided, like for his brothers, that Dixie should be cremated and his ashes scattered in the Garden of Rest. As the mourning cars followed the cortege down Leith Walk, along Duke Street, and then on towards the crematorium, the occupants noted that the sides of the streets were lined with people. People stood and waved or saluted a cheerful wee boy that they had known and admired.

At the crematorium Kirsten, flanked by Bea and Jane, sat in the front row. As the other mourners filed in, Kirsten turned to notice that a weeping Rosie and her mother were among them. Rising, Kirsten went up to Isabel Thomson. 'Isabel, as Rosie was such an important friend to Dixie, would you please both

210

join us here in the front row?'

Isabel nodded her consent and the two women linked arms as they moved into the seats together.

As soon as Rosie was seated, she turned to Kirsten and said, 'Do you cry a lot because Dixie has gone away?'

Kirsten nodded. 'Know something, Rosie?' Rosie shook her head. 'I think I have wept an ocean since he left. But aren't we lucky that we knew him . . . loved him. Just think what we would have missed if we had never met him.'

The after-service tea was held in Armstrong's; for Kirsten it passed in a strange haze of sorrow and tears. Then, once all the guests had left, Kirsten, Bea, Jane and Jessie sat together.

'Think it all went well, Kirsten,' Jessie remarked. 'And could I say you did a great job on Dixie. Remember, I do, that he wasn't promised two hours at the start of his life. But you and your attention to him brought him on and he thrived. Twelve good and happy years you bought for him.' She paused when she saw Kirsten's eyes fill with tears. 'Here,' she continued in a lighter tone, 'did you see that big police guy, you know that Chief Eddie Carmichael, the one that runs the football team, was there. Nice of him to think about us.' Kirsten nodded, and Jessie moved on, as if talking would hold their grief at bay. 'Look, don't be hurt, but Jane is not keen on going home just now. Says, she does, that she's not ready to be at home and Dixie's things being there and him not.'

'And, Bea, what about you?' Kirsten asked, turning to look at her daughter.

'I think I will come home. You never know, now that Dixie is away, you might notice that I am alive!'

Kirsten bristled, startled that Bea would say such a thing. But as her daughter's remarks sank in, she saw them as a wake-up call: she reluctantly had to face the fact that she had made mistakes. Not intentionally, but nevertheless very damaging mistakes. Some might argue that she was guilty of neglect — neglect of Jane's and Bea's needs. Always she had put Dixie and his welfare before theirs. When he was born, they had only been children. Children of the tender years of four and five, who needed to know that she loved them, valued them. Jane, who was a different nature from Bea, had coped by becoming another carer for Dixie. And care for him she had. Bea, on the other hand, was like her father, an attention seeker, and whereas Duncan had up and left to lead a different life, Bea had only been a child and therefore she had had to stay and endure. These facts, Kirsten now acknowledged, had turned her into the selfish, truculent teenager she now was.

Kirsten bit on her lip, thinking back to Jessie's mention of Eddie. After spending a night with him, she knew that she really loved him. He was tender, caring, loving — and even today she was longing for him again. Before Bea had spoken she somehow hoped that they might be able to marry very soon and all would be well. This she now knew was a pipe dream. She had to make sure that her girls were her priority. No way could she even suggest bringing a man into their lives. They both needed her attention — they had lost a brother, a brother who had taken all their mother's attention — and as much as she wished, no yearned, to be Eddie's wife, she knew that it would have to be put on hold. For how long she didn't know, but if he loved her then when she explained to him about the girls he would perhaps wait for her.

As if she was reading Kirsten's mind, Jessie now sprung another turn to the conversation on her.

'Kirsten,' she said, 'could I ask you to remember what we were discussing about me, Duncan and the management for the hotel before our Dixie . . . '

Kirsten's head shot up. 'No, Jessie, you absolutely can't get me back to that discussion.'

'But we have to talk about it,' Jessie insisted, 'and right now at that.'

'No! Now is not the time.' Kirsten could hear the alarm in her own voice and paused to let her panic subside. 'But as I don't wish to fall out big time with you, I promise that I will actually give it much thought and consideration in let's say . . . ten years' time.'

25

As if in a trance, Kirsten meandered her way into Pilrig Park. She had just gone on a further few feet when the sun glinting through the trees made her draw up. It was not so much the trees themselves that made her wonder, but their leaves — their leaves that appeared to be on the verge of turning red and gold. If this was so, she reluctantly conceded it must be September. The start of autumn. But if it was September, where did July and August go?

Standing motionless, she tried to recollect the summer. Painful as it was, she went back to late June. Never would she forget that month. That was the month when she had had to say goodbye to her special boy — her darling Dixie. Time from that moment seemed to stand still. Yet here she was in September and still her grief was raw. It was true that family and friends had supported her. These relatives and friends had tried to comfort her — be there in her bleakest times.

She paused to acknowledge that it was also true that during the last three months Eddie had become a very important part of her life. Indeed, without him and his tender love, understanding and care, she doubted if she would have been able to go on. Reluctantly, she remembered the day Dixie was cremated. That was the day she had been honest with Eddie. Told him as gently as she could that because of her need to now spend time with her daughters — time to ensure that they knew that she loved them — their being together in the eyes of the law, and of society, would have to be put on hold, indefinitely at that. She was not sure, because the expression on his face did not alter, when she had acquainted him with her decision, if he was disappointed or not. One thing she was certain of was that, no matter what he thought, it did not stop him seeing her. Indeed, on his days off she would also take time off — precious time for them to be together. She smiled as she recalled how they would go down to his home in Longniddry — a place where they could be assured they would not be disturbed — a special place, where at every opportunity she was passionately cosseted. She hugged herself with delight as she thought how it became their special place — a place where they could make-believe.

Without realising it, she had taken her eyes from the trees and had started to slowly stroll through the park and on to Pilrig Street itself. She had been so deep in her thoughts she had to literally give herself a shake. It was time, she reminded herself, to stop thinking back because today she was on her way to visit Stella. Stella, who had frequently called on her after Dixie died. Dear loyal Stella, who would just sit and not comment when she had railed against Duncan's injustices to Dixie — Dixie, who had so enjoyed life, and who had been denied the chance to go on living the life he so clearly cherished.

Still half-oblivious, Kirsten had diced her way

through the traffic to the far side of the road. That main road then took her into the lane where Stella's house stood. On seeing the house come into view she smiled. She was now thinking that today, as promised, she would sit down with Stella. They would then discuss something of great importance to Stella. Her grin widened when she thought that today it might be her turn to listen and stay tight-lipped.

Mrs Baxter, as usual, opened the door to Kirsten. Also, as was customary, she asked Kirsten if she would be having tea or coffee. 'Tea, please, Mrs Baxter,' she replied while advancing towards Stella's lounge.

'Bang on time, Kirsten,' Stella observed before laying down the *Scotsman* she had been reading.

Kirsten nodded. There then followed a chat about this, that and nothing at all, until Mrs Baxter had served them their tea and diplomatically taken her leave.

Stella sighed. 'Right, Kirsten, my dear, what I require is your ear.'

'Why?'

Stella chuckled as she lifted her arthritic hands up and waved them towards Kirsten. 'Ten out of ten to you, Kirsten, for being very diplomatic and not mentioning the fact that not only am I growing old but I now look it. Hands are like my face now — all twisted and wrinkled.'

Kirsten tittered before saying, 'Yes, but you are still sprightly . . . and you are so vivacious and lively that you belie your age.'

'True, I still have all my marbles, but physically I am just so sick and tired.'

216

'Of what?'

'The hassle.'

'Don't tell me the police pressure has been stepped up again.'

Stella nodded. 'Never really went away.'

'But I thought there had been a decrease in their attention to you since . . . '

'They threatened to close me down and I took them on?'

'Yes.'

'It is true that there is no longer an eviction notice hanging over me . . . ' Stella sighed. 'But every chance they get they pull me up for every petty misdemeanour, and that is whether I have committed it or some other person six streets away. Honestly, Kirsten, it borders on blatant harassment.'

Kirsten bit on her lip to control her laughter. 'But surely you expected that after you called that press conference?' she said.

'I had no alternative but to call that conference! And always putting as much business as I can towards you, I even hired your hotel for the meeting!'

Kirsten squirmed. 'Yes, but when you stated that your most regular and loyal customers were the clergy within all our religious groups within our city, well . . . '

'Truth hurts.' Stella snorted and shrugged. 'Especially those who believe they are the keepers of the truth.'

Kirsten stifled a smile before quipping, 'And I don't suppose the landed gentry were too happy to be mentioned in your despatches.'

'Hasn't, I can assure you, affected their attendance at Castle View!' Stella stopped to ponder. 'In fact, most have stepped up their visits. Think the notoriety we were given has added to their titillation and excitement.'

'Okay, I accept that you are being harassed.' Kirsten took a sip of her scalding strong tea. 'But you are not in danger of being put out of business, so why have you asked me here today?'

Stella drew her chair closer to Kirsten's. 'Having assessed the situation and the fact that I am weary, I have decided . . . Kirsten, I wish to get out of the business.'

'Good. So why don't you sell up?'

'Certainly I could do just that. But, Kirsten, there are others dependent on their living from . . . ' Her right hand encircled the room.

'If you are concerned about dear Marigold and the girls, surely they will be kept on by whosoever takes over the business.'

'Not just Marigold and company.' Stella fell silent. Kirsten could see by the way she was biting her lower lip that Stella had another worry. 'There is also my son in London. Through no fault of his own, he has inherited his father's flair for being . . . a waster, really. Would you believe that he completely depends on me to keep him afloat?'

'I see,' said Kirsten, as realisation sunk in. 'So, the money you would get from the sale of Castle View would soon be eaten up?'

'At the rate Jamie squanders money, believe me it would all be gone and I would still be here. But I have a plan that would help us all.'

'A plan?'

'Yes, a wonderful plan.' Stella was now quite animated. 'One that I require your assistance with,' she added with a chuckle.

'My assistance!'

'No need to look alarmed. I just wish you to advise me.'

'You require advice from me . . . about exactly what?'

'How to turn this house into an upmarket bed and breakfast.'

'You're thinking of turning this place into a small hotel?'

'No. You see a hotel, as you know, requires a liquor licence and I wouldn't get one. Powers that be seem to think I am a reincarnation of Lucrezia Borgia, or someone yet worse, and therefore I am not a fit person to pour up a dram.'

Kirsten giggled.

'You can laugh, but it is true that they see me as some sort of hellcat. As you know all I do is provide a service. A service that I do not advertise, yet men, some of whom dream up the rules we must abide by, queue up at my door to take advantage of.'

Kirsten was going to reply, but she hesitated. This gave her time to allow her eyes to sweep the room. She could see that Stella's proposal had merit. Castle View at one time must have been the multi-roomed seat of a very distinguished family. Now it was an upmarket — and notorious — house of ill-repute. But anyone could see that if it were gutted and refurbished,

219

it could become a pleasingly superior bed and breakfast accommodation. This would mean that Stella could keep her home and still provide an income for her spendthrift, wayward son. Only snag Kirsten could foresee was, would the Edinburgh Corporation grant a 'change of use' for the house? But then Kirsten smiled inwardly: of course they would, nothing would please them more than to get this thorn in their flesh pruned right back — right back to respectability.

Stella interrupted her thoughts. 'Nothing to say?'

Kirsten nodded. 'Of course I have plenty to say. Oh yes, Stella, I can see clearly what you mean. And I agree that your home would make excellent bed and breakfast accommodation.' Kirsten stopped to weigh up the obstacles. 'But have you considered that there will be a considerable loss of income?'

Stella nodded.

'Also what are you going to do about Marigold and the girls?'

'The girls I will give warning to.'

'Warning?'

'Yes, in that I will advise them to consider their position. I won't beat about the bush. I will tell them straight out that in three months' time this house will no longer be accommodating their clients. It will then be up to them either to carry on with their trade under a different roof and management or find alternative employment. I admit that neither option will be easy for them, but if they are determined, they will find something to suit. Now when I say *them*, that means everybody except Marigold.' Stella smiled. 'Where she is concerned, you and I will see to it that we train her up to run the bed and breakfast.'

Kirsten nodded — such a role would fit Marigold like a glove. 'And your son?'

Stella sighed. 'He will have to get used to providing some of his needs by himself.' She then added, more for her benefit than Kirsten's, 'And that won't be a bad thing. No. No, the time has come for me to advise him to stop sponging from me for his every need. I accept that it will come as a shock to him that his playboy days are over.' She paused and grimaced. 'And, even worse, he will now realise he will have to equip himself with some earning skills. Skills that will see him survive when I am gone.'

'But, not wishing to be morbid, when you go, will he not just sell up here and live off the proceeds?'

'If he were left my home, he could. But that is something else I have to see to.'

Kirsten looked at her friend, quizzically.

'I am going to make a new will. My sons will get any loose change I leave lying about, but as you can leave your home to anyone you wish . . . some people, including my sons, will be in for a surprise, a big surprise, when I go.'

'So that is that, then?'

'Yes and no, Kirsten. You see, I wish you to keep us right on what our new customers will expect from Marigold and me as landladies. Also, if you could please help us by advising on the refurbishment.' Stella stopped to look

221

Kirsten directly in the eyes before adding, 'And, of course, I expect you to return the courtesy I paid you when I hosted my press conference at your hotel.'

'Sorry, Stella, I don't quite get your meaning here.'

'Put your surplus business my way . . . just at the start, that is.'

Kirsten chuckled. 'You wish me to direct those I cannot accommodate at Armstrong's down here?'

'Yes, dear. And also the ones who cannot afford your inflated room charges.'

Kirsten bristled at that. 'Stella, I'm sorry but I would like to point out that Armstrong's provides a first-class service and we only charge what is fitting for that service.'

Stella laughed at her friend's indignation. 'Yes, I accept business is business. However, there will be those who,' she coughed, 'like here, cannot afford the exotic and have to settle for the . . . ' She hesitated, a wicked grin playing on her lips. 'Let's just say, less appealing.'

Kirsten nodded. She got the message loud and clear.

And so it was that Kirsten was co-opted in to assist with the long overdue change of use for Castle View. She knew that the decision to make these changes would not only be welcomed by the neighbours in Pilrig Street and beyond, but also by the ever-vigilant constabulary.

★   ★   ★

222

Assisting with the renovations of Castle View gave Kirsten a much-needed distraction from her mourning. But then that had been the first of Stella's objectives — albeit her secret one. The second reason was that she knew from experience that Kirsten, like her mother Aileen, had a flair for colour and design where curtains and bedding were concerned. Her third objective, probably the most important one to her, was she wished to tap into Kirsten's expertise where running a hotel was concerned. After all, hadn't Kirsten, and Jessie to a lesser degree, dumb-founded those who thought that Armstrong's would never become the profitable hotel it now was.

At the beginning of December Kirsten advised Stella that she would be standing back from assisting her from now on until after the first week in January. This was to allow her to be on hand in York Place for the festive season. She smiled when she added, 'And Stella, both Jessie and I are delighted that we are fully booked out with office lunches, dinners, dances and Hogmanay revellers.' She winked before she said, 'And in December next year I hope you too will do equally well.'

Nonetheless, Stella was piqued by the fact that Kirsten wasn't going to be around. This was because it was her intention to open Castle View for the Hogmanay celebrations. Indeed, she had hoped that she would have her precious change of use for the property in hand to start her new business and be making money when the bells heralded in the new year of 1973.

What Stella did not quite appreciate was that

Kirsten really would be disappointed not to be there for the grand opening. However, much as Kirsten would wish to assist Stella on that occasion, she had to put the needs and obligations of Armstrong's first. After all that was her bread and butter.

As 1973 loomed ever closer, Kirsten's thoughts turned to Bea. Bea, her firstborn, would be eighteen soon. Kirsten drew up and smiled as she thought, *That is what I can do that might help to break the ice between us — give her a present of anything that she would like for her very special birthday.*

Kirsten wondered whether Bea would say that she wished to get a passport and go on a foreign holiday, and so she decided to approach Bea at the earliest opportunity.

Sunday, the family day, when neither Kirsten nor Bea would be working at the hotel, seemed to Kirsten to be the ideal time to speak to her daughter. However, like most teenagers, Bea liked to sleep late on a Sunday, so it was approaching lunchtime when she surfaced from her bed, her hair a tangle and her eyes sleepy.

'I suppose I've missed breakfast, and lunch will be awhile,' Bea remarked, as she strolled into the lounge.

'Yes,' Kirsten replied, 'but I could make you a bacon roll.'

'Thanks, Mum,' Bea snorted. 'Suppose it will have to do.'

While Kirsten was in the kitchen busying herself frying the bacon, she called back, 'Bea, since it won't be that long until you are eighteen

I was wondering what you would like for your special birthday? Don't be scared to ask for anything you *really* would like!'

'In that case I'd like to ask — no, demand — that I can stop working in your damn awful hotel! Mother dear, that is all I wish for. And before you answer, let me remind you that you said when I was eighteen I could leave school and either get a job or go to college. And whatever option I plunked for I would no longer be obliged to work in blasted Armstrong's!'

Before Kirsten could reply, Jane came into the living area. 'Mum,' she called through to the kitchen, 'could you stop cooking? The smell is . . . ' She swallowed hard. 'Oh, Mum, I think I must have got that sickness bug that is going around the school.'

Kirsten entered the room with a bacon roll on a plate and a mug of tea, both of which she handed to Bea. Going over to Jane, she said, 'Oh, darling, you do look a bit peaky. Have you been sick?'

Without warning, Jane started to flee towards the bathroom. 'Not until. Oh please, please let me make it . . . ' she called out as she sped.

All that could then be heard was Jane vomiting violently.

'Well, if that is not enough to put me off this cremated bacon roll, I don't know what else is,' Bea said before stomping into the kitchen and dumping her belated breakfast in the bin.

Kirsten was now knocking on the bathroom door. 'Jane, please unlock the door and let me help you.'

'It's okay, Mum, I'm on my knees cuddling the lavatory. Best place for me, as I feel so . . .' Kirsten could hear her throw up again.

Kirsten couldn't help but smile. That was Jane all over. No matter what happened to her she never wished to be a bother to anyone — never really complained. She was so unlike Bea, who whinged her way through life. Without further ado, Kirsten returned to the living room, where she found Bea lounging on a chair.

'So, you were saying, you no longer wish to work in my hotel?'

'That's right. I will be going to college. And before you ask what I will be studying, I am now thinking of doing something that would cover family relationships.'

Kirsten did not rise to the bait. 'That's just so good to hear, dear,' she simpered. 'So glad you have made up your mind. And I will finance your fees, accommodation and books. Which means you will *only* need to earn your pocket money.'

'But — but you said I wouldn't need to work in Armstrong's.'

'Indeed, but with the experience you have gained at the hotel I am sure you will soon find some other employer to take you on.'

Before Bea could reply, a very sickly Jane came back into the lounge. 'Mum,' she said as she breathed in deeply, 'sorry, but I can't go out with Rosie today.' She paused to burp. 'Could you explain to her what's wrong with me?' She gulped again. 'Hope you don't mind, but right now I just want to climb back into bed.'

'That's what you get for eating school

226

dinners,' Bea said, her face hard. 'If you were like me and bought a sandwich you could have carried on being the wee toady you are and sucked up again to Rosie's mum by pretending you're Rosie's friend.'

Kirsten glared at Bea. 'Look, Jane, let me get you through to bed.'

'But, Mum, I still feel sick.'

'That's okay. I will put a basin by your bed.'

'Thanks, Mum. And I will try and be okay by tomorrow. You see, the other girls in my class who have had it were better after a day.' She hesitated and sighed. 'But a few were two, even three days.'

'Don't worry, darling. We all understand. Now, off you go.'

Once Jane had left, Kirsten turned to Bea. 'Since you hate the hotel so much, would you like to stay off this week and look after Jane for me?'

'And who,' Bea asked, will you draft in to serve in the restaurant?'

'Myself. I have done it many, many times before so it won't be a problem.'

'That's all settled then.' Bea smiled, or was it a smirk, before wheedling, 'Where the hotel is concerned. But, Mum, you were saying I really could have anything I wanted for my birthday?'

Kirsten looked at Bea and beamed. 'Yes, dear, anything at all.'

'Then how about letting my dad back into my life?'

Again, Kirsten was wrong-footed by the sharpness of her daughter's response. 'What do

227

you mean? Your dad left us; we did not leave him. As to why he did a runner, your guess is as good as mine.'

Bea huffed. 'We won't quarrel about why he went. But he now wants to come back into our lives and Granny says that you are the one who is stopping him!'

Hearing Jane being sick again saved Kirsten having to answer Bea. To be truthful, she really didn't wish to respond. What was there to say or do? Bea had always believed that if Kirsten had handled things differently Duncan would not have left. That stubbornness meant that Kirsten had to accept that Bea's attitude to her was never going to change, and the passing of time didn't seem to make that any less hurtful.

★   ★   ★

Unlike her classmates, Jane's sickness did not last for a day or two or three. No, the virus appeared to have grown in its duration and ferocity, so four days passed before she was up on her feet again. Bea, during this time, decided not to sleep in the same room as Jane as she did not wish to also become ill. However, what we hope for and what we get sometimes are two different things. So, as Jane got up on to her feet again, Bea was in the bathroom encircling the lavatory as she threw up.

Bea seemed to be affected more seriously than Jane. Like Jane, she was four days into her ordeal, as she saw it, before she stopped being sick. However, she was into her sixth day before

228

she could be persuaded to get out of bed. Naturally, when she tried to take a few steps, she was very wobbly on her legs.

'This is all down to you, Jane, that I am dying,' she wailed, before catching a glimpse of herself in the dressing-table mirror. 'Oh my goodness,' she continued, before sinking down onto a chair. 'I look like a survivor of the Great Potato Famine. What is Patrick going to say when he sees me?'

'Talking of Patrick,' Jane said, 'he called to see you, but Mum told him you were infectious and that he should stay away until you were feeling better.'

'Mum did what? And where is Mum, by the way?'

'Think Mum now has the bug . . . Close your eyes, that's her being sick now.'

Unlike her daughters, Kirsten's sickness did not abate. She felt so wretched that on the seventh day she consulted her doctor. The physician was sympathetic and her advice was that Kirsten should go home and make sure she took in as many fluids as she could. Kirsten then asked if there was anything the doctor could prescribe that would allow her to go to work. The doctor shook her head. Kirsten, however, was determined to get some sort of medication to help her, so she then explained that she had a hotel to run and it was the festive season, so she just had to be there to supervise. On hearing this further plea the doctor explained that, as the bug was highly contagious, it would be deeply irresponsible for Kirsten to go to work and put her customers at risk.

Kirsten tried again to argue her case, but the doctor was adamant. She pointed out that a few, a very few, like herself seemed to be taking that little bit longer to recover from this particular virus, so it was in everybody's interest that Kirsten should go home and go to bed.

Kirsten now began to feel sick again. All she wished to do was get home and crawl into bed. This being so, all she could do was admit defeat with a nod of her head. The doctor advised Kirsten that if she didn't feel a hundred per cent by the following week to contact her again.

For the next ten days Kirsten's sickness continued. Eddie, who called in to see her every day, became so concerned that he suggested that, as he was on annual leave for seven days, he would take her down to Longniddry, where he would look after her.

Kirsten, of course, said no. To go down with him to Longniddry for a stolen afternoon was one thing, but to stay for a week was something else. She explained to him that the girls were not fools. If she left to stay with him for a week, they would soon cotton on that they were lovers. Her lips quivered as she went on to say that she just couldn't have that.

'Scared to death, I am,' she said, 'that Bea would use my affair with you as an excuse to invite Patrick to stay the night here at Balfour Street!'

By the time Kirsten had endured the virus for what felt like weeks on end, she was so weak that she could barely stand unaided. No matter what

230

she did to alleviate her symptoms it seemed there was no let-up. Indeed, to her dismay, she continued to be plagued by persistent vomiting. This being so, it had brought on the added problems of dehydration and weight loss. It was not until she began to experience raging headaches and rapid heartbeats that she not only allowed but welcomed Molly calling in the doctor.

The same doctor she had already consulted was now very thorough in her examination of Kirsten. Before taking blood and urine samples she confirmed that, however smitten Kirsten had been by the sickness virus, that was not the problem now. This revelation caused Kirsten to sit bolt upright. 'And what do you think is wrong with me now?'

'Almost sure, I am, that you have hyperemesis gravidarum. These tests I have just taken will confirm that one way or another. I will call back later in the week.' Then, with a confirming nod, she added that she was almost positive the tests would confirm her diagnosis.

The doctor's words terrified Kirsten. 'It can't be that,' she found herself saying. 'I am thirty-seven years old.'

'So,' the doctor said as she prepared to take her leave, 'there is nothing to worry about. The sickness will settle and, did you know, some are of the opinion it is a good sign.' Kirsten wearily shook her head. Exhaustion was overtaking her. She was not convinced when the doctor went on to say, 'I know you feel bad, rotten in fact, but believe me in a few weeks you will be feeling so much better.' The doctor stopped to smile before

231

adding, 'In fact, positively glowing!'

The doctor's prediction was spot on. However, it was the beginning of February before Kirsten, though not looking at her best because of her weight loss and dehydration, felt well enough to return to work.

She was, of course, amazed that Jessie had managed the whole of the festive season, not exactly on her own but with the assistance of Bea. And, to Kirsten's disbelief, they had coped so well that the profits of the previous year were not only matched but exceeded.

Another bonus was that at long last Bea seemed to display some concern for Kirsten. Kirsten, if she had had the strength, would have been gobsmacked and delighted when Bea said, 'Look Mum, I am worried about you. You are so ill, so please, please just lie in bed and get better. Now, I know you will be worried about Armstrong's, but don't.'

Kirsten had protested. 'But I must go up and help Granny. She can't do it all on her own.'

'No, Mum, you can't go, but I can. Yes, I will go up to York Place and do all I can to help Granny. And to really be of assistance there, I will leave Jane here to look after you and I will move in at the hotel.'

Kirsten was still thinking about how wonderful it was that at last, despite the odd circumstances, she and Bea were friends, when Eddie arrived for his daily visit.

'Oh, so you are up, hair washed and dressed,' he said before going over and taking her in his arms.

'Yes. Today it is Wednesday, and on Sunday I intend to go up to the hotel and start to pull my weight again.'

'Well done you. And wait until I tell you, I don't know what it means, but I have been invited by the depute chief constable to have an off-duty drink with him in Valentine's on the High Street.'

'Is that the hostelry just round from Police Headquarters?'

'Yeah. Mind you, I hear on the grapevine that the new HQ they're building at Fettes will be ready next year and it is to be opened by the Queen.'

'Oh, so I won't be required to do the honours,' Kirsten quipped.

'No,' Eddie replied with a chuckle. He was just so pleased that Kirsten was feeling well enough to start wisecracking again. 'But the following year when we, that is Edinburgh City, Berwick, Roxburgh and Selkirk, Lothians and Peebles constabularies become the one force of Lothian and Borders, you might get a guided tour of those grand new Headquarters.'

Kirsten grew pensive. 'Here, darling, with the depute asking for a meet, do you think there is a promotion for you on the horizon?'

'No. Promotions are decided by the chief, and right enough others are consulted, but the depute would not be saying anything to anyone on that score. Prerogative of the chief, promotion is.'

'Why the meet then?'

'The depute is a football man and the chief favours rugby, so I suppose it has something to do with what we will do with the football teams when we become the one force.'

★　★　★

Eddie had been nursing a half-pint for ten minutes when the depute, Bert Stock, dressed in a civilian jacket, entered.

In deference Eddie got to his feet and held out his hand. 'Good afternoon, sir.'

Warmly shaking Eddie's hand, Bert replied, 'Good you could make it today. Oh, you have a drink,' he chuckled before opening his jacket to display his white police shirt and black tie. 'I am still on duty.' He turned then to call over to the barman, 'Just a coffee, milk with no sugar for me, Billy.'

While they were waiting for Bert to be served his coffee, the chat was light about this and that. His coffee had just been laid before him when Bert consulted his watch. 'Now, I have half an hour, so let us get down to business.'

Now it was Eddie's turn to laugh. 'So, it is official now.'

'What is?'

'That you are here today to talk to me about what we will be doing with the football teams when we become the one force of Lothian and Borders Police?'

'Wish it was that, but no.' He paused. He strummed his fingers on the table before saying, 'Friendly chat is what I am here for.'

Eddie, taken aback, looked questioningly at Bert.

'Look, Eddie, you and I have been colleagues,

234

mates really, for so long that you know I do have your interests at heart. So I was asked — no, it was suggested to me — that I acquaint you with a few facts.'

Eddie, suspecting that he was about to be told off for some misdemeanour or twisting of the rules, suppressed his anger.

Bert, unaware of Eddie's growing concern continued. 'Now, in two years, when we amalgamate with the other forces, there will a large number of changes. Some of these changes will happen before the official date.'

Eddie held up his hand. 'Just a minute, sir, as my hat won't be in the ring for chief constable, depute or assistant chief constables, what has all this got to do with me?'

'True, you will not be at that point in your career, ready for promotion to these senior ranks, but you will be in a good position before that to be promoted to chief superintendent.'

'Yes, but that will be up to the chief to decide.' He smiled. 'I know things are changing, but I do not think that they have changed so much that you are able to offer me a promotion in your coffee break.'

'True. But as I have said, there are promotion appointments to be made before the amalgamation. Oh yes, chiefs will be looking to have the best officers they can in their promoted positions.'

Eddie shrugged and nodded. He wasn't entirely sure where this was going.

'Look, let's talk hypothetically, say our chief decided to make some small changes now like . . . ' He paused. 'Let's say he has . . . has decided to take one of the present chief supers into HQ to supervise the changes. That would leave a division ready for a promotion. Now he looks at the superintendents that could fill the vacated post of chief superintendent. Perhaps he thinks that one stands out as being ready to take over his own division. Again, let's just suppose that the one whom he would like to promote, a certain officer who is, let's say a . . . a widower, and is therefore free to marry but he chooses to have a . . . mistress. In addition, the mistress has her working establishment in the division where the promotion is.'

Eddie didn't require Bert to elaborate further; he'd got the message. He could be considered for promotion, but not if he still had Kirsten as a mistress. He shuddered at the suggestion. Kirsten wasn't his mistress. She meant more to him than that.

Bert brought him back from his thoughts when he leaned over towards Eddie and spoke quietly and forcefully. 'This is me as your buddy. Either marry the woman or forget going further in your career.' Bert mused, then added, 'An even better option, why not wed Sylvia Sanderson? You've been dating her on and off for years. She's probably our best female officer and will go far in the force.'

Eddie simply nodded.

'So back to where we were . . . I can't make you give this Kirsten Armstrong up, but it is crunch time if you wish to go further in your career.'

Eddie could do nothing more than nod again.

Bert consulted his watch. 'Oh, we have ten minutes left and since all the chief wishes to discuss is rugby, how about you and I talk over how the new football teams will be arranged? Know whatever we do we will never match the wonderful team who won the British Football Cup. Now, what year was that?'

'That was 1955, sir, as I am told so very often . . . In fact, on a weekly basis. The opposing team was Cambridge and the match was played at Cambridge United football grounds. Constable Sandy Jack was the overjoyed manager of that glorious team, and our chief at the time, Sir William Morren, was so proud that his Edinburgh City Police football team got to the final that he journeyed all the way to Cambridge to watch the match.'

Bert got to his feet and offered his hand to Eddie again. 'This meeting was a friendly chat about football and nothing else.'

Without another word Eddie indicated with a deferent nod that he got the message loud and clear. Bert then smiled at Eddie before giving him a friendly pat on the back. The meeting was over.

The door had just closed on Bert when Eddie sank down into his seat again. *Nothing else for it*, he thought, *than to nurse what is left of my beer and contemplate.* He acknowledged that if he had never met Kirsten he would in all probability now be safely married to a female officer. But he did meet Kirsten, and from when he first set eyes on her he was smitten. She was the only person for whom he could move on from Anna. All that had really mattered to him since Anna had passed away was 'the job'. Policing for him was more than earning a crust; it was a vocation. Rising through the ranks was the only thing, before Kirsten, that ever gave him a sense of satisfaction. Bert had now given him a glimpse of what the future could hold — commander of his own division — B Division. Working in that division had in reality given him such satisfaction, but there was a price to be paid for dreams coming true. Now, what was the price here? Kirsten. He wished to marry her, but would she ever be free? Just now it was her daughters who were putting a hold on them getting together, but would Kirsten ever be ready to move on? He shook his head, wearily: Kirsten's family would always be more important than their happiness. Time, he thought, to do what was best for himself.

What he really wished for was both his career *and* Kirsten — but could he have both?

Eddie swallowed the last of his beer.

Time to bite the bullet, to make a decision.

26

Not only was Kirsten up bright and early on Sunday morning, so was the shining February sun. A promise, Kirsten thought, that spring was only a month or two away. Today she decided, as there was no frost or snow on the ground, that she would walk up to the hotel.

Strolling up Leith Walk gave her the opportunity to think. She had decisions that she had to make. No matter what she did it was going to be a revelation for some and a shock for others. She had just reached Elm Row, the part in her journey that led her past Gayfield Square Gardens, when she noticed some snowdrops that had pushed their brave little heads above the ground. Proof, she thought, that no matter what, when it was necessary, you had to put your head above the parapet.

Strolling on, she reached the bank in Picardy Place, which was nearly opposite Armstrong's. She stopped then to lean against the wall and have a necessary breather: she didn't wish to arrive out of breath and buckling at the knees. While she rested, she glanced over at the hotel. As she admired it, she breathed in a long breath of satisfaction. That smart little hotel, she thought, was now such a success that it did not matter what she decided — she and hers would never want.

Pulling herself together, when it was safe to do

so, she lightly skipped across the road. Then with willed agility she ascended the five hotel steps. Resting her hand on the door, she felt full of a deep sense of harmony in herself and achievement. Eight weeks it had been since she had been here; two months, during which she had been so ill at times that she did not care whether she lived or died. But that was then; today she was back, not quite fully fit but on her way to being so.

Making sure there was a genuine, warm smile on her face, she pushed open the door. Her eyes went immediately to reception and she called out to the male receptionist who had his back to her. 'Good morning.'

When the man turned towards her, he replied, 'Good morning to you too, and what may I do to assist you?'

Kirsten's smile switched immediately to an open-mouthed gape. 'What in the name of heavens are you doing in my hotel? And what idiot employed you?'

'Oh, it's you, Kirsten,' Duncan replied, coolly. 'I hardly recognised you. You look so done in. Frankly I am not sure you should be out of bed.'

Strength she did not know she had surged into her. 'Never mind your opinion of what I look like. I asked you what the hell you think you are doing in my hotel!'

'Not just your hotel, Kirsten. I think since my mother bankrolled this place that she is the senior partner.' Duncan now surreptitiously pressed the under-counter buzzer, which would summon his mum. 'And might I add, because of

240

your absence, my mum asked — no, begged — me to come in and help her keep things afloat over the festive season. Taken to it like a duck takes to water, so I have.'

Kirsten was thinking fast. Who else knew of Duncan working in the hotel? She felt her knees wobble. Oh no, Bea. So that was why she was so obliging and considerate. At last she had got her father back into her life. Kirsten could have wept as it also dawned on her that Bea had deliberately deceived her by never saying to her about her dad being back and staying at the hotel. Kirsten drew herself up, but then trembled as another shock revelation surged into her thoughts. This time it was Jane. Her Jane, whom she knew had been up here in the hotel in the last two months . . . Okay, Kirsten conceded, only occasionally because she had been at home looking after Kirsten herself. But, Kirsten bit on her lip as she thought, often enough to know about Duncan's return. Her Jane, who she thought was so loyal and dependable — had she also colluded with the rest of the Armstrongs to deceive her?

Before she could deliberate further Jessie strode into the reception. 'Oh, it's you, Kirsten. Good to see that you are back on your feet.' Jessie chuckled. 'A bit on the scraggy side, but nonetheless back on your feet.'

'That so? Well, I might be scraggy, but I am not the pushover you all seem to think I have suddenly become.' She now turned from Jessie to point at Duncan. 'So, out he goes, and in case you would like me to spell it out to you, I am back and your prodigal son's reign in our hotel is

241

over. By tonight I want his bags packed and him out on the street.'

'Look, Kirsten,' Jessie said with a firm shake of her head. 'I think that you, I and Duncan too, should retire to our office, where we can discuss our and the hotel's business in private.'

Kirsten started for the office, her face rigid with fury. Once the trio were inside Kirsten and Jessie both took a seat. Duncan stood with his back to the door.

Jessie opened the proceedings. 'Kirsten, I do not think that you are in a position right now to demand that Duncan leaves our employ.' Looking Kirsten in the eye, she continued, 'What we, that is both you and I, desire at this moment is for the hotel to be in safe management hands. You have not told anyone about it yet, but I know you have a problem. And,' Jessie continued before Kirsten could protest, 'we both know it's a problem that isn't going to go away in the near future.'

Kirsten shifted uneasily in her seat. 'I do not quite know what you are getting at,' she said, primly.

'Come off it, Kirsten. I know what is wrong with you. And because I am loyal, the only person I have discussed it with is Duncan.' Kirsten's bottom lip quivered. Jessie went on, her tone more kindly now. 'Come on, lassie, don't get upset. The only three people that need ever know are the three of us.'

Kirsten felt as if she had entered some unreal world of fantasy. What the devil was Jessie saying — implying?

242

'Duncan here admits he did wrong by you, but he is willing to try and make amends.'

Duncan nodded, but his eyes stayed fixed on the carpet as if fascinated by the patterns he found there.

'So he is going to bring back Dixie,' Kirsten cried, 'and tell him he loves him and will provide for him?'

'No, Kirsten, but let's go back twenty years and remember when you made a mistake and ended up thinking you were pregnant. Duncan, even although you entrapped him, stood by you then and married you. You've made the same mistake again, only this time you *are* pregnant and he is willing — no, happy — to marry you again. We accept the child is not his, but he will take it on and we can all work and live together, well, as one big happy family.'

Kirsten was flabbergasted, but she was determined to hold her own. 'Well, Jessie,' she replied, 'tempting as you and your son's offer is, it unfortunately is not for me. Firstly, because I do not require anyone to marry me, and secondly you, Duncan' — she now turned her full attention to Duncan — 'even if you were the only man on earth I wouldn't stoop so low as to marry you.'

Gasping, Jessie said, 'You've had an abortion! Well, I never thought you would do so such a thing.'

'What I have or haven't done is my business and not yours. Now, will you give your son notice or will I?'

'Neither of us will.' Jessie crossed her arms,

243

her street fighter pose still formidable. 'If you refuse my offer then what you can do is buy me out and then Duncan, Bea and I will go and start up somewhere else.'

Gulping, Kirsten slowly replied, 'But you know I haven't got that kind of money, and to borrow such a large sum would leave me struggling for the rest of my days.'

'I accept that, and as you have turned down our fair and generous first offer, how about we give you a handsome pay-off and *you* go and start up somewhere else?'

Kirsten immediately realised how easily she had been tricked — she'd been played for a fool and no mistake. The second offer was the one that Jessie and Duncan had steered her towards. Both of them knew her so well. They knew before the conversation started that there was no way she would tolerate Duncan in her life again, not even on the reception desk at Armstrong's.

A wave of deep fatigue swept over her, washing away her resolve. Weakened, she decided to leave the hotel for the day. In her heart she knew she would perhaps never be in Armstrong's again; well, not as a co-owner. Jessie and Duncan had been devious and, when she was too fragile to put up a fight, they had taken advantage of her.

Well, she thought, *I have survived worse and lived to fight another day. Pay me off, will they? Well, I will take them for every single penny I can.*

Before she could leave, a tap came on the door. Duncan answered the summons. 'Oh,

Mum, if it is not our Bea.'

The moment Kirsten and Bea's eyes met Kirsten felt a keen sense of betrayal. 'So, you have been coming to the hotel to help your dad pull the rug from under my feet?' she challenged her daughter.

'I haven't pulled the rug from you. You did that for yourself.'

'What do you mean?'

'Tried to replace my dad with that high and mighty policeman, Eddie Carmichael, you did. But Dad and I have found each other. We have got to know each other . . . understand each other. We are a proper father and daughter now.'

'Enjoy it, Bea, because your togetherness won't last,' Kirsten couldn't help but snipe. 'Your dad has a record for not staying the course. And by the way, miss, when he left you high and dry with homelessness a real possibility and nothing to eat on the table at teatime, who was it then that provided for you?'

'Nonsense,' Bea spat. 'My dad has explained to me that what happened was your entire fault. He had to get away from you and your constant drooling over Dixie.'

'Don't you dare bring Dixie into this,' Kirsten snapped, horrified that anyone would take her son's name in such vain. 'And has Jane been beguiled by your precious dad too?'

'No, Jane says you have always looked after her and so she'll stand by you. Don't worry, she has refused point blank to be part of us getting you out of our hotel.'

These words filled Kirsten with mixed

245

emotions. Jane's loyalty to her had her wanting to cry. Bea's ingratitude and disloyalty was so hurtful that she had to clench her fist to stop herself from smacking Bea hard across her gloating face.

She knew, too, there was nothing more to be said that would make Jessie change her mind. Both women then looked long and hard at each other. Kirsten read in Jessie's stare that she was saying, Duncan is my son. He has made a mess, and how, of his life. Like you, Kirsten, did for Dixie, I have to give him every chance to have a good life. A life where he can earn his living, be valued and respected.

Kirsten knew she was beaten. Jessie as a business-woman she could fight and win. Taking on Jessie as a mother, when her pride and devotion would see her become a brawler again, was an entirely different matter.

★　★　★

The sun had hidden itself behind a cloud when Kirsten found herself standing in York Place. She turned and looked back at Armstrong's.

'Pull yourself together, girl,' she inwardly urged. 'It is just a hotel that you can live without.' She shrugged. Yes, without the hotel she could go on, but now she felt she had lost forever Bea, her firstborn. Loyal, loving Jane she knew she would always have. But, as she turned to walk over towards Picardy Place, she placed her hand on her stomach, wondering if she should do what was against her nature, keep the

246

urgent appointment with the clinic. That squirming in her stomach, was it a protest? A physical reminder that someone else also had rights, had the urge to survive against all odds?

★   ★   ★

When Kirsten arrived home in Balfour Street she felt tired and useless. Crunch time in anyone's life is hard to face. Today she had so many dilemmas that she was not sure which way to turn or which one to deal with first.

Kicking off her shoes, she thought a sit down with a cup of tea was her first priority. As the warm liquid trickled down her throat she thought, what is my problem? She sighed as she conceded that it was not one problem, but in actual fact so very many. Given this state of affairs, she knew she now had to assess not only each problem individually, but its impact on others. She also accepted that to get any idea of the best way forward, she would have to reason in a calm, *very calm*, manner.

But, despite her resolve, before she had managed to list in her mind what her quandaries were, she started to feel queasy. Surely, she thought, that blooming sickness is not going to return. If it is, then I will without a doubt know what I am going to do about it. Her stomach heaved in frightened protest.

Kirsten had just started her peace-inducing breathing exercises when the doorbell sounded. The outside door then opened and someone entered. Immediately, any sense of peace deserted her and she began to fluster. She knew it could not be Jane, because ever since Dixie's death, Jane always spent time on a Sunday afternoon with Rosie. Where they went and what they did, Kirsten did not know. She just was aware that the loss of Dixie was so hard for Jane to bear that she liked keeping in touch with the great love of Dixie's short life, his Rosie.

Without anyone asking for permission to enter, the living-room door then opened. An expectant Kirsten frowned as she wondered who the visitor might be. As soon as she saw it was none other than Eddie, in his uniform, her frown was quickly replaced with a welcoming smile. A smile that lit up her whole face when she heard him say, 'I'm just so glad I caught you in.'

'You are?'

'Yeah, you see I took the chance even although I thought you might be still up at the hotel.'

'Have you just finished your early shift?'

'Yes, I was going to go home, but . . . ' He hesitated. 'Everything go according to plan up at the hotel?'

She lowered her head. The happenings up at Armstrong's were still so very raw that she did not wish to discuss them with anyone — least of all Eddie. Eddie, whom she thought would be so sympathetic. She did, however, have an urgent matter she wished to discuss with him — a situation that affected them both. This was so important; she knew that if they reached the wrong decision, the consequences, for both of them, could be catastrophic.

Raising her head, she knew she had to speak

to him now. However, as she wanted him to give her his response without being influenced by pity for her, she replied, 'Yes, I am pleased to report that the hotel is doing so very well. You wouldn't believe it, but Jessie has everything under control.' She faltered. 'But the hotel's by the by.' She stalled again. 'I know you said that you would not see me again until tomorrow, but like you I am so glad that you called in because — '

Before she could continue, he put up his hand to stop her saying anything further. 'Before you go on,' he said quite forcibly, 'I'd like you to know that I have an important reason for coming in today.' She looked at him questioningly. 'You see, I think it is only . . . ' He sat down on a chair and, rubbing his hands together, swallowed hard. 'Only fair that you should know that on Saturday the seventh of April I am getting married!'

Kirsten was so astounded that she was rendered speechless. She tried to make sense of what he had just said. She wondered, had she heard right? Did he really, in fact, say that he was getting married on April the seventh? Did he mean this year, 1973? She gave a small cry as she accepted that at last Sylvia had won him. As she tried to calm herself — to make sense of what he had just said — she thought she knew the reason for his seemingly hasty decision. She almost screamed when she reckoned that the meeting with the depute had something to do with it. Oh yes, the interfering, self-righteous (in appearance anyway) constabulary had given Eddie an ultimatum.

Her stomach lurched as she thought what a

fool she had been. Eddie, whom she truly believed was so different from Duncan, in that he cared for her, respected her, had like Duncan used her — preyed on her when she was at her most vulnerable. What was most hurtful and humiliating was that he, Eddie — her Eddie, whom she'd thought until a minute ago loved her and wished to spend the rest of his life with her — had succumbed to the pressure exerted on him by police hierarchy and had given her up.

She was trying to make sense of it all when her stomach did a triple somersault again.

Oh, please baby dear, not now. Please, please don't have me throwing up. Okay, I know you are scared because your father has just said that he is deserting us and marrying Sylvia, but don't worry. You know I had decided to be honest about your coming and not go to the clinic. Believe me, baby darling, when I say that I won't change my mind. I love you and I promise you we will manage somehow.

With a violent, quaking retch, Kirsten bolted from the living room towards the bathroom. Sinking down, her whole body heaved. Through her tremors, she believed she felt Eddie pat her on the back. So what? At the moment she was silently cursing him — wishing him to be anywhere but beside her right now. She then thought she heard him speak to her.

Exactly what he said she was unaware of. To be truthful she was feeling so wretched again that she didn't really care what he said — nothing he could say to her now would she ever wish to hear. She wished she could

250

somehow find the strength to ask him to leave her home — leave her life — leave her and her unborn child to just get on with it.

27

The third week in August saw the monthly meeting of the senior officers of B Division of Edinburgh City Police taking place in the conference room. All were present and correct and were waiting patiently for the arrival of the new commander of the division.

When the door opened, Eddie, followed by Sylvia, walked in. Immediately, all the men rose to their feet.

'Good afternoon, gentlemen, and please resume your seats,' Eddie said as he turned towards Sylvia. 'Today I am very pleased to include newly promoted Inspector Sylvia Sanderson in our meeting. I know you will all be, like myself, delighted to have her join our ranks.' Everyone present knocked on the table with their right hands to confirm their acceptance of Sylvia.

Once Sylvia was seated Eddie took a moment to assess her. She really was a handsome woman. But she was also a career woman, and having reached the dizzy heights, for a woman, of inspector, she oozed confidence today. As far as Eddie could tell, she had no feelings for marriage or motherhood at all. But then such feelings were hardly useful to a police inspector, whether male or female, and would only have got in the way as Sylvia scaled the promotion ladder.

Dismissing these thoughts from his mind, he

then said, 'Gentlemen, and of course, lady.' There was a twittering of laughter and all looked to Sylvia, who gave a mock salute. 'As you are aware, yesterday was the monthly meeting of the chief officers of the Edinburgh City Police Department. It is now my duty to disseminate the information that was given out. Naturally you will filter what I am about to say to you down to the men under your command. Now, I am aware that at the festival time we have to second men into other divisions to police the Tattoo, theatres, the Fringe, etcetera, and this leaves us short on the ground. This may be so, but we still have to police our division. Yesterday the commander of A Division pointed out that there had been an increase in pickpocketing and I know you have also reported an increase in this crime, especially in the Princes Street, Leith Street areas, so could you ask your officers to give this matter as much priority as they can. Of course, and here I would point out there is no evidence of any possibility of an attack, but given the Irish Troubles, we can see the potential for an incident here. Again, request your officers to be vigilant.'

Before Eddie could continue there was a knock at the door and the Station Sergeant came in and handed him a note. 'Telephone call, sir. Urgent.' Before the sergeant took his leave he gave a covert wink to Finlay McKenzie. Finlay, whose career had stalled at inspector, was still a tried and true friend of Eddie's.

Eddie read from the note. His face drained of colour: whatever it said, it was obviously serious.

Standing up, he looked around the gathering before saying, 'Superintendent, I have acquainted you with the information that has to be circulated to our troops, so as I have to leave, as a matter of urgency, I am asking you to take over the meeting.'

Without another word Eddie left the room, but before he could close the door on himself Finlay McKenzie followed him out. 'Is it?'

Eddie nodded. 'I just have to get to her. Be with her . . . '

Finlay placed his hand on Eddie's arm. 'My best wishes go with you. Now remember, you have been told they are as sure as they can be but if . . . you have to be strong for her.'

Eddie began to reminisce as his car left the Gayfield car park. He thought back to February and that particular Sunday — that Sunday when his life was changed forever.

★ ★ ★

Kirsten eventually stopped being sick, at which point Eddie helped her to her feet. Roughly pushing herself away from him, she then bent over the hand basin and threw some water on her face. As soon as she lifted her head, he handed her a towel. She had just finished drying her face when he asked, 'Feeling better?'

'From your kick in the teeth, I can hardly feel worse.'

'What do you mean?'

She gave a derisory laugh. 'You waltz in here and announce that you and your pal Sylvia are getting married in eight weeks and you expect me to be over the moon for you?'

Now it was his turn to laugh. 'Don't be ridiculous. I am not marrying Sylvia . . . '

'So she, like me, got a dizzy?'

'Kirsten, sweetheart, you know I'm not a man to take a woman for a fool. Don't be daft, my love.'

'Yes, I am daft. So daft that I believed you and I had something going for us and now . . . ' Try as she might she could not hold back the tears or the trembling in her legs. Before she could stop him Eddie took her into his arms and he guided her back through to the living room.

'What a goose you are. Are you really asking me to believe that you think Sylvia and I could be an item?' He laughed. 'Don't tell me that, as worldly as you would have me believe you are, you haven't worked out that Sylvia's lover is a woman.'

Kirsten's sobs stopped immediately. Her mouth and eyes widened. 'But you were always partnering each other. And she always looked so possessive.'

'It was an act. We had an agreement. I needed a partner to stop questions and to keep other women from pestering me. And, well, Sylvia — she needed a cover. She's ambitious and there are still plenty in high places who hold tight to their belief that a woman — let alone a lesbian — should not be promoted.' He chuckled. 'Or indeed even permitted to join the force.'

Kirsten was gobsmacked.

Eddie moved towards her and took her in his

arms again. 'Yes,' he emphasised, 'I am getting married on April the seventh, but it is to you, my love.'

'But how?' she gasped, genuinely taken aback. 'You never asked me . . .'

'Kirsten, have I not proposed to you, not only once, but on several occasions?' She nodded, shyly. He continued, 'But you are always saying once this is sorted, or that is sorted.'

She sniffled and wiped her eyes.

'So I felt that I had to do it this way. My love, you would never have allowed us to get married because there would always have been someone or something that got in our way.'

But instead of his words comforting Kirsten her weeping became uncontrollable. 'But . . . but . . . but you might not wish to marry me when I tell you . . . Eddie, I'm pregnant.'

'Yes, I know. I was waiting for you to tell me.'

'But you don't understand.'

'Of course I understand.' He smiled and took her trembling hands in his. 'I do hope you are not going to say that the baby is not mine.'

'Oh Eddie, who else's could this baby be?'

'I know, and I am so happy. I'm over the moon, Kirsten.' He beamed at her and then, his face more serious, he added, 'And that is why we have to get married and very quickly at that.'

'No. No,' Kirsten protested. 'Eddie, hear me out. You see, what if the baby is born underweight and I need to spend so much time with him or her. Could you cope with that?'

'Kirsten, I am confused today,' he said, drawing her closer. 'First, you seem to have

256

thought I was the kind of man who would lead Sylvia on for years and then just chuck her when I fell in love with you. Now you think that I would abandon my own flesh and blood. Don't you realise you are the most important person in my life? I promise I will love our baby and stand by you even if the wee one is no bigger than a Tunnock's tea cake? And while you are pondering what I have just said, can you let me know of any perfect human beings?'

Kirsten looked sheepish. 'You're right, we all have our foibles. But when Duncan left me because Dixie needed so much looking after . . . Look, I have been to a clinic and I could have an abortion but . . . ' She started to sob again. 'It feels so much against my nature to do that, but if that is what you want then I could, I suppose, reconsider.'

'Kirsten, your emotions are all up in the air. You are not thinking clearly. Of course you don't want an abortion, and neither do I. Kirsten, I am forty-eight years old and I have always regretted not having a child. Why would I not grab the chance to be a father to our child when he or she arrives? And it won't matter to me if they have . . . ' He seemed to hesitate to find the right words. 'Brown eyes or blue, blond hair or black, a mole on their nose or freckles on their back. I will love this baby because we created it.'

Kirsten, through her tears, said, 'Oh Eddie, we will get married in April then.' She hesitated, taking the time to think logically. 'But tell me, did the police tell you to marry me — or pack me in?'

'Yes, I admit, they pointed me in that direction.'

'So that's why you are in such a hurry to put things right?'

'No. I am my own man, and when I was advised that further promotion was dependent on me putting my house in order then I thought long and hard. I realised you were pregnant, and that eventually you would tell me. I felt sure you wouldn't abort the child — the Kirsten I fell in love with would never do that. So I knew I would provide for you and the child. Not only now but in the future. And when the grim reaper summons me up you will receive a police widow's pension! So, it all makes sense for us to get married. Besides I am too old for this part-time clandestine affair. I want you, Kirsten, in my life, in my home, as my wife and mother of my child.'

She rested her head on his shoulder and her sobs subsided.

'That is it settled,' he said, stroking her soft brown hair, 'we shall marry in the first week of April.'

'Hmm. But before you take me on you should know that I have had two proposals today.'

'Two?'

'Yes, two. And when I turned the first one down I was left with no hotel. No job. No visible means of support.'

'Not to worry, my wages will keep us all. But I am curious, tell me — who else proposed to you today and what's happened to your hotel.'

'Well, when I was too ill to get to the hotel my

ex-husband turned up and his mother put him in charge. Without as much as asking my leave she replaced me with him. You know, of course, she put up the money for our start-up, and the problem is she still is owed some of that money. If I could find the money, she suggested I could buy her out.' She grimaced. 'Jessie had reckoned I couldn't borrow that amount of money without overstretching myself. Besides,' she patted her stomach, 'by the time she gave me the ultimatum I had decided to keep our baby, no matter what.'

'So, she's made you penniless?'

'Not quite . . . ' Kirsten stopped to think. 'They are going to pay me off. I think we should keep our wedding a secret until I get the money I deserve.'

'For how long?' Eddie asked, fearful that this was another Kirsten stall. 'I have savings, so you don't need to take the pay-off!'

'Just two weeks — and, Eddie, I am due that money. Duncan left me high and dry. Now he has come back and walked into a very profitable business that was my idea. My hard work — okay, along with his mother's — is what built it up. So, my dear, I am not walking away empty-handed.' Her face now took on a hard look he had never seen before. 'Allow that sod to walk away with all the winnings,' she spat. 'I will see him roasting in hell's fires first.'

Eddie laughed. 'Oh dear,' he gasped. 'Once we are married I must be sure not to cross you!'

★   ★   ★

Kirsten did get her pay off. Three times she had Jessie adjust the payment — upwards. The cheque was in the bank and cleared when she called at the hotel again.

'If you are back to squeeze another penny out of me, you can think again,' Jessie informed her as she folded her still beefy arms across her ample bosom.

'No, no. The agreement we reached is fine by me. Wondered if Bea was going to be busy on April the seventh?'

'You would need to ask her yourself.'

'I would, but as she resides here now I never see her. Anyway, please ask her if she would like to be a bridesmaid at my wedding.'

'You're getting married!' Jessie panted as her complexion turned mottled red and blue. 'And yet you took me for far more than I was prepared to pay to see the back of you!'

'Yes. And to be honest I don't really require that money. Going to squander it, I am. I'll be taking delight in knowing that because no one else would employ him, you had to pay salt to get your spineless, useless son a job!'

★   ★   ★

Eddie had been so engrossed in recalling that Sunday when Kirsten confirmed that she — and the baby-to-be — would be his for all time that he had driven himself halfway home when he remembered he should have been going to Elsie Inglis Maternity Hospital. Of course, there were maternity facilities in East Lothian close to their

260

home in Longniddry, but Kirsten was adamant that she would give birth in Elsie's.

Reaching the junction at Fisherrow, he did a quick U-turn and then pointed his car back in the direction of Abbeyhill. He had just reached Eastfield traffic lights when his memories happily took him back to his wedding day.

Two weeks after he and Kirsten had agreed to marry they were having a quiet evening meal, when she blurted out, 'Eddie, about our wedding?'

Fearing she was getting cold feet again, he answered, 'Yes . . . '

'Would you be very upset if I — ' She faltered.

'Good heavens, you haven't changed your mind?'

'About our wedding, no. But the last time I got married it was in a registry office. This time, I am sure it will last my whole life through and I would like God's blessing on it.'

'Are you saying you have gone all religious like your mum,' he teased her, 'and would like a church wedding?'

'Yes. With all the trimmings.'

'And are you thinking of floating down the aisle in a sea of white?'

'Don't be ridiculous,' she said, though she did rather like the thought. 'But I would like to have an elegant dress and bouquet. Only there is a problem . . . '

'If it's the money . . . '

'No. The pay-off I got from Jessie is for frittering away, so I will use some of that. But the minister in my church does not marry divorcees,

261

even if, like me, they are the innocent party.'

Eddie appeared to be lost in thought for a minute or two. 'Does it matter where the church is?'

'No. Just so long as you and I are able to marry there. You see, you are right, I am turning into my mother. I honestly believe if we could be wed by a minister, then our lives together would be blessed.'

Eddie bent his head so that she could not see him smile. He was not a religious man and he would have married Kirsten in a pigsty if that was where she wished the service to be. But he loved her and the church blessing was obviously important to her, so he would do his best to find a solution.

The minister at the lovely sandstone church in the village of Aberlady just happened to be a buddy of Eddie's, as he'd known Anna's father through golf. And so Eddie approached him, and before Eddie could finish the minister had agreed to marry them. Both men agreed that it was exceptionally fortunate that it just happened that on April the seventh there was no other wedding booked for his church.

Eddie sighed as he recalled how beautiful Kirsten had looked when she had strolled into church on her father's arm.

The expensively tailored lilac dress with matching hat was exquisite. However, it was Kirsten's radiance that outshone everything that day. Naturally, Molly and Jane were resplendent as the matron of honour and bridesmaid. Bea hadn't responded to Kirsten's invite; who knew if Jessie had even passed it on. Kilted like himself, Finlay McKenzie was his best man. As the wedding party made its way over to the hotel in the main street for a leisurely lunch everyone could see that this was Kirsten's very special day. At last life was being kind to her.

For two weeks now she had felt fit and healthy. And, what was more important, she had for the past week felt her baby move within her. She was so excited that she insisted that Eddie place his hand on her stomach so that he too could feel that his baby was alive and starting to kick.

Baby, however, decided that allowing his mother to feel him move was one thing; his father was quite another. This being so, Eddie would just have to wait until the baby had another long, long sleep.

When eventually Eddie did feel the baby squirming, he was overcome with emotion. He and Anna had planned to have a family, but that was not to be. After Anna passed away, he'd given up hope of ever finding anyone to replace her — until Kirsten came along. Most men of his age were looking forward to being grandfathers, but to be a father, even at his advanced age, was to him a most welcome, incredibly precious gift.

Lost in a dream, Eddie was now at the crossing at Abbeyhill, which took you down to the maternity hospital. As he turned left to go down the brae, he breathed in deeply. He really was berating himself for having wasted twenty minutes. Home really was home now, that's probably why he'd made the mistake. Home was where he quickly headed at the end of his shift.

It was now where Kirsten would be waiting for him. He smiled when he thought how different the house was now. This was because Kirsten had put her own stamp on it. New carpets, new curtains, beds and bedding. She also had a smart new conservatory extension put on the back. In the evenings they would just sit there, sometimes saying nothing but both peacefully enjoying each other's company. Their most frequent visitor, who seemed to divide her time between Balfour Street and Longniddry, was Jane.

Jane, who Eddie had grown to love, was such a loyal, fond daughter to her mother. Eddie then thought about Bea, whom he had tried to include in his family, but she was definitely her father's girl — and, as such, a one-man woman with no space for anyone she saw as an interloper.

But now, all thoughts of the past were put on hold as Eddie drove into the car park. Getting to Kirsten was all he wished to do. Be with her, hold her hand, keep her safe when their child was born.

28

Earlier that day, at her new home in Longniddry, Kirsten awoke at five in the morning. The birds were chirping, but it was the niggling pain in her lower back that had awakened her. Before rising, she looked at Eddie, who was sleeping blissfully. *No use*, she thought, *saying to him that I think that quite shortly I may be going into labour.* Today, she knew, was the inspectors' 'greeting meeting'. A meeting that was very important to him, as it was where he found out exactly what was going on in his division. Besides, she could be wrong about the labour, and if she wasn't she could always use some of the fritter-away money to summon a taxi to take her to Elsie's.

By late morning Kirsten was on the phone demanding a taxi.

'You in labour, hen?' the taxi driver asked when Kirsten appeared at the door with her packed bag. Kirsten nodded. 'Where to?'

'Elsie Inglis.'

'Elsie Inglis in Edinburgh?' the man said as he scanned Kirsten's swollen stomach and heard her gasp with pain as she struggled into the car. Kirsten nodded. 'You are joking!'

'No, Elsie's is where I am bound.'

'Fine, but you know I have no experience of delivering babies . . . So before we set out, are you sure we have time to get there? Don't suppose you would change your mind and settle for one of the wee cottage hospitals down here?'

Kirsten laughed. 'No need to worry. I've had three pregnancies and I can assure you I am still in the early stages of labour.'

The man grunted. 'Aye well, all right then. But remember, if your baby decides to get a hurry-up on, you are on your own. Don't mind being an agony aunt and listening to people's woes, but midwifery is no' for me.' He stopped. 'Think we had better take the coast road. Always a house on hand if . . . Look, let's get a move on.'

Everything went according to plan until they were on the road to Musselburgh. It was then the pains started to come on every eight minutes. Squirming in her seat as the last contraction abated, Kirsten leaned over and whispered to the taxi driver, 'Now, please do not panic . . . ' But panic was what he did, and he gripped the steering wheel so tightly his knuckles turned white. 'I still think we have time to get to the hospital, but not with . . . how could I put it . . . with as much — 'Another intense, shooting pain gripped her. 'Time, to spare. Oh dear, oh dear.'

The gulping taxi driver responded with, 'Would it not make more sense for me to double back and get you some help at the hospital on the Musselburgh back road? You know, Eden-hall?'

'No. I will be fine. Please, please believe me, I will hang on because I just *have* to get to Elsie's. You see the nursery staff at Elsie's were so good at looking after my son when he was born. So it is really important that I have this baby delivered there.'

'Look, lady, that's okay you saying that, but what if your bairn has decided that it wants to appear right now?'

'My children are all obedient,' she joked, 'and he or she will hang on. But please do hurry.'

The cab driver was now sweating more than Kirsten, and so he put his foot down, and by jumping red lights and dodging in and out of traffic, he made it to the front door of Elsie's.

Jumping out of the cab, he hollered, 'Right, someone, there is woman here who needs you quick and I need you even quicker.'

As two kindly, starched nurses assisted Kirsten out of the car, she remembered she had not paid the taxi driver. 'How much do I owe you?' she gasped, as another pain fast on the heels of the last one gripped her.

'Look, lady, when you are back home with your wee one, give me a call and I will collect my fare then. Right now, I'm out of this!'

One of the nurses at Kirsten's side laughed. 'You know, if men were to give birth then we would be a nation of single child families.'

And so Kirsten again found herself in the warm surroundings of Elsie Inglis. Just as she had hoped, the care and professionalism of the hospital staff was excellent. Before she knew it she was in the labour suite and was being given some gas and air. Lowering the mask, Kirsten grabbed for the midwife's strong, capable hand. 'Is there any chance the baby will hold on until my husband gets here?'

The nurse took another glance between Kirsten's legs. 'Sure, if he gets here in the next fifteen, or at the most twenty, minutes.'

Kirsten flopped back against her pillows. Not knowing that Eddie, in such an apprehensive frame of mind, had been halfway home before he realised he only needed to travel five minutes down the road to the hospital, she said, 'That means he will make it.'

Eighteen minutes later a wrung-out but thankful Kirsten gave birth. 'Nurse, is it a boy or a girl?'

'A beautiful girl. Right, nurse, pop her on the scales.' The assisting midwife then put the baby on to the scales. 'Look,' the chief nurse said to Kirsten. 'She is weighing in at six pounds eight ounces. Not a heifer, but a good solid weight nevertheless.'

'Good, now please let me hold her.'

'Of course, dear, but let's just give her a wee clean up and wrap her in a blanket first.'

Kirsten sought for the nurse's hand. 'Nurse,' she pleaded, 'is she . . . what I mean is . . . is she all right? I mean, you are sure about the weight?'

Before the midwife could answer a gown-clad Eddie burst into the room. 'No need to worry, dear,' he exclaimed, all out of breath, 'I'm here now, and I will be with you when the baby arrives.'

Kirsten burst out laughing. He looked even more exhausted and stressed than her! 'Sorry, love, but your daughter could not hold on for you.'

The assisting nurse then laid the swaddled baby in Kirsten's arms. Tears welled. Running her fingers under the baby's delicate chin, she looked up into Eddie's face. 'I can't see her features because of my tears. But know something, I really don't care if she is perfect or not. I love her and will love her no matter what.'

Tenderly, Eddie took the baby into his arms. 'I don't care either, but Kirsten she looks just *perfect* . . . or she is and always will be to me.' He turned to the nurse. 'What do you say?'

Opening the blanket a little, the midwife cast a professional eye upon the baby. 'As an expert, she looks more than fine to me. In fact, quite cute and beautiful she is. But why are you asking?'

'My little boy, who I had twelve years ago, was one of triplets,' Kirsten managed to say. 'The first two babies died, poor wee souls, and my Dixie only weighed two pounds fourteen ounces. It was a struggle but, mark you, he soon became a healthy hearty boy. I just couldn't have loved him more. I miss him so. Killed in an accident he was, my precious boy. So I am wondering, being . . . how can I say this . . . '

'You being an older mother, and the risk of something going wrong being slightly increased?'

Kirsten smiled. She then indicated to Eddie to pass the baby back to her. Gazing down at her baby's face, she could see she was so like Jane. She was just so good-looking. The names they thought they would call her then jumped into her mind. 'Eddie, do you think that she looks like any of the names we picked for her?'

Eddie took the baby from Kirsten's arms again and, as he looked down at his daughter, he said, 'No. None of those names suit her.'

'Not Aileen after my mother nor Kate after yours?' Kirsten asked, before adding, 'Or even Anna. Are you saying that none of them suit her?'

'No, the more I look at her, the more I think she looks like a wee angel. She certainly has the sparkling eyes of an angel.' He lifted the baby up to press her cheek on his. 'A messenger of good hope, my darling is, so I think we should call her Angela.'

'Angela,' Kirsten repeated as she nodded. 'I like the sound of that.'

'Angela, you are,' he said as he lowered the baby away from his face so he could see her. And he then added, 'And little one, like your mum, you will be your own woman.'

Kirsten leaned back on her pillows, her whole body in bliss. She had never been happier. Eddie was such a loving and supportive husband. Jane, her dear Jane, she knew would love Angela and mother her. Kirsten's only regret was that Dixie wasn't here to meet his little sister. She stopped to smile as she thought that he wasn't so far away. Somehow, she just knew that Angela would have her own special personal guardian in heaven, a wee boy whose gift to her would be that he would always love and protect her.

We do hope that you have enjoyed reading this large print book.

Did you know that all of our titles are available for purchase?

We publish a wide range of high quality large print books including:
**Romances, Mysteries, Classics
General Fiction
Non Fiction and Westerns**

Special interest titles available in large print are:
**The Little Oxford Dictionary
Music Book
Song Book
Hymn Book
Service Book**

Also available from us courtesy of Oxford University Press:
**Young Readers' Dictionary
(large print edition)
Young Readers' Thesaurus
(large print edition)**

For further information or a free brochure, please contact us at:
**Ulverscroft Large Print Books Ltd.,
The Green, Bradgate Road, Anstey,
Leicester, LE7 7FU, England.
Tel:** (00 44) 0116 236 4325
Fax: (00 44) 0116 234 0205

Other titles published by Ulverscroft:

A CUT ABOVE

Millie Gray

It's 1962 and Freda Scott and her five schoolmates are eager to embark on their life journeys. Madly in love with the dashing but unattainable Ewan, Freda instead throws herself into a hairdressing career, and soon she and her best friend Robin have established their own flourishing business. The future looks rosy, until Freda's life is turned upside down by a brutal attack.

As Freda struggles to come to terms with what has happened to her, she relies on her old friends more than ever. However, a chance meeting with her old love Ewan, brings a potentially life-changing dilemma. Does Freda dare to finally put herself first?

MOVING ON

Millie Gray

May 1945. In post-war Leith, the Anderson family must come to terms with the reality of peacetime Britain. Johnny's hopes of a life in politics finally come true, but will his vows to remain a dutiful husband and father be kept? Peacetime is not easy for Johnny's Polish brother-in-law Hans, either. Meanwhile nurse Kitty — Johnny's daughter from his first marriage — gets caught up in a sensational trial when her friend Laura's brother is accused of murder. Kitty is fascinated by the seemingly cold but eloquent prosecuting counsel — and he is bewitched by her. When they meet again four years later, will his behaviour be a barrier to a future relationship?

SILVER LININGS

Millie Gray

1939: The unexpected death of Sandra
Anderson dramatically and ruthlessly changes
forever the lives of the family she leaves behind.
Kitty, her spoiled and pampered fifteen-year-
old daughter, has to give up her dreams of a
career, as she becomes the family drudge.
Sandra's heartbroken husband, Johnny, finds
solace for his grief by becoming the main mouth-
piece for his Trade Union in the shipyards,
leaving little time for new-born Rosebud, whose
birth caused her mother's death. And to add
to what seems insurmountable problems, Kitty
and Johnny must try to fulfil the death bed
promises they made to Sandra, which makes
a nearly impossible situation even worse.